THE
Assignment

THE
Assignment

A NOVEL

JEAN HOLBROOK MATHEWS

Covenant Communications, Inc.

Covenant

Young Woman Wrapped in Fabric © Knape. Courtesy istockphoto.com.

Cover design © 2011 by Covenant Communications, Inc.

Published by Covenant Communications, Inc.
American Fork, Utah

Printed in United States of America
First Printing: February 2011

17 16 15 14 13 12 11   10 9 8 7 6 5 4 3 2 1

ISBN 978-1-60861-081-5

To the people of the Philippines for their daily courage

Preface

AMERICA HAS WORN THE TITLE of the "melting pot of the world" for centuries, but the Philippines are the "melting pot of Asia." The Filipinos are a mixture of tribes where eight major languages and nearly one hundred dialects are still spoken: from the industrious Chinoy (Chinese-Filipinos) of northern Luzon—who descended from Chinese immigrants who arrived as early as a thousand years ago, intermarried with the native tribes, and taught them to grow rice on sculpted, mountain terraces—to the Atis tribe, whose men stand little more than three feet tall with the kinky hair, flat nose, and black skin of their African ancestors. Some of the languages reflect sounds of the South Pacific Islands, while others echo words and sounds of the Malay and Chinese. The beadwork, loom weaving, and basket weaving of some of the tribes of Luzon, such as the Bontoc tribe, reflect similarities to the beadwork and weaving of the Hopi and Navajo tribes of the Southwestern United States. An anthropologist could live his entire life in the Philippines and not begin to uncover all the roots and branches of the varied backgrounds of the people of these islands.

The culture of the Philippine Islands is an interesting combination of Spanish, American, and Asian influences. Filipinos love to dress and talk like Americans and watch American movies, but the men are saturated with the influence of Spanish machismo, which grew out of more than three hundred years of Spanish colonial rule. The family unit is fully Asian in structure, with *Lolo* (grandfather) and *Lola* (grandmother) ruling the multigenerational families with a firm hand. Filipinos, or Pinoy as they call themselves, are a beautiful people, but this mix of cultural influences often confuses the non-Filipino.

Generally speaking, Filipinos are emotionally based, usually tender-hearted, and often form deep and fast friendships, but a perceived insult can change that friendship into animosity in one heated moment. The vast majority of them genuinely like Americans. Among the elderly, a deep, residual respect is still held for the American troops who, under General Douglas MacArthur, drove the Japanese occupiers from the islands in 1945. Many Filipinos rank MacArthur with their other national heroes who include Rizal, Bonifacio, Aguinaldo, and Del Pilar.

The Philippine Islands have been caught in the midst of a serious depression for more than forty years. The official unemployment/ poverty rate is listed by the government at twelve to fifteen percent. In the metropolitan areas, it is closer to seventy-five percent. The families that comprise that seventy-five percent usually live in squatter's shanties on public land and often must be satisfied with one bowl of rice a day. Many support their families with microenterprises, such as selling roasted peanuts or boiled ears of corn on street corners.

In the rural areas, the main employment is the planting and growing of rice, but this nation of nearly one hundred million is not self-sufficient in rice growing and must import this staple from other Asian countries, such as Thailand. Many of these rice farmers live in a subsistent, barter economy, and they seldom handle Philippine pesos.

Every Filipino governmental administration since World War II has campaigned on the promise to "wipe out corruption," and each has failed. Corruption is endemic in that system where a military or law enforcement uniform is a license to take bribes, as is a government job at any level. Nothing is built without the payment of the required bribes to officials at every level.

The culture is made even more complex by the stratification within it. The lighter the skin of an individual, the higher he is ranked on the cultural scale; thus, the *mestizos* (mixed race, usually Filipino and Spanish or Filipino and American) rank the highest, and the rice farmers who feed the nation, with their darkly sunburned, weathered skin are the lowest on the social scale.

Politically, the people are caught in a whipsaw. In a political system where a vote can be bought for fifty pesos (about ninety cents), national or provincial office holders often bring less than sterling character to their positions. Winners are sometimes murdered by defeated candidates. Widespread economic discontent has made the nation a volatile incubator for a multitude of extreme political parties. The Sierra Madre Mountains of Luzon, which can be seen from Metro Manila, harbor an estimated ten thousand communists under arms (the New People's Army), which control vast areas and can count the support of as many as a million sympathizers.

Western Mindanao was home to vast numbers of Muslims for several centuries before the Spanish conquistadores brought Catholicism to the Philippines. Since the conclusion of World War II, relations between both the Muslims and communists and the Catholic-controlled government of these islands have steadily grown more rancorous as both Muslims and communists resent the working relationship that has existed between the United States and the Philippine government for a hundred years.

Not only do the people find themselves vulnerable to bribe-seeking government officials, but on western Mindanao, Islamic radicals use kidnapping, drug dealing, and blackmail to fund their revolutionary activities. At any one time, there are probably at least a dozen and often twice that many hostages held for ransom by the Jemaah Islamiyah, which was imported from Indonesia a few years ago; the Abu Sayyaf, with its links to al Qaeda; the MILF (Moro Islamic Liberation Front); and the MNLF (Moro National Liberation Front)—all of which have agitated against the Philippine government and are known to have close ties and receive some funding from al Qaeda. Some of their individual leaders have been trained by al Qaeda in Afghanistan, Pakistan, or Sudan.

Despite the attempts of the Philippine government with the assistance of the United States to eliminate terrorist activity, terrorists in the Philippines flourish for many reasons. Limited financial resources, inadequate salaries, corruption, low morale, limited cooperation between police and prosecutors, and other problems in law enforcement hinder the battle for peace in the region. Rugged terrain, weak rule of law, poverty, and local resistance among the Muslim minority have made it especially difficult to combat terrorism on Mindanao.

Despite the socioeconomic and political problems that wrack the government of the Philippines, the Filipinos deserve respect, support, and affection, and like so many people who have taken the time to grow to know them, I came to love and respect them in the time I lived with them.

The Author

Terms

ABU SAYYAF: "Father of the Swordsman"

ALIMATOK: leeches

ALLAH AKBAR: Allah is great

BANCA: a Filipino out-rigger canoe

BOLO: Filipino machete

CAFTAN: ankle-length garment with long sleeves for Muslim woman

CEBUANO: the language of much of Mindanao

CR: "Comfort Room," the Filipino abbreviation for the bathroom

HIJAB: head covering or head scarf for Muslim women

LOLO: literally "grandfather" but used as a term of respect for an older man

LOLA: literally "grandmother" but used as a term of respect for an older woman

MALONG: tube of batik material with multiple uses, such as skirt or privacy screen

NANAY: mother

TATAY: father

SABAYA: "booty of war"

SALAM ALAIKUM: "Peace to you," a greeting used among Muslims

SUNDALO: soldiers

TAGALOG: official language of the government and military of the Philippines

TOLDA: fabric or plastic used as an awning

Prologue

WHEN MELTON MALLON OFFERED JULIA Wentworth a position as the administrative director for his international foundation four years earlier, she had been excited and pleased. With her family nearly grown, this was a wonderful opportunity to make a positive difference in the lives of others. She believed it would be a privilege to be part of the work of the charity.

Mallon had founded and nurtured a candy and confectionary company from modest, early beginnings to full-blown success. When it was purchased by one of the biggest international food corporations in the world, he used the fortune he had been paid to invest in other struggling but promising companies. For the next twenty-five years, he had purchased and successfully nurtured several corporations on the verge of bankruptcy into healthy, expanding entities before he sold them. He had proven himself an extremely successful venture capitalist—one with a heart.

Though his personal fortune was in the millions, he had invested great amounts of time, energy, and money in the establishment of an international foundation meant to help the impoverished who lived hand-to-mouth in developing third-world countries. The foundation assisted small, home-based businesses through micro loans and business training. As his administrative assistant, Julia had regularly traveled to the Philippines, where three of the foundation chapters were located.

But within the last few days something had forced Mallon to set aside his normal concerns and involvements. His step had slowed; his skin was gray. He had ceased to smile, and he looked ten years older than he had a week earlier. His wife had been fighting cancer for about eighteen months, and the effects of her chemotherapy treatments were beginning to drain them both. This seemed to be a sufficient explanation for the sudden alteration in his behavior and emotional condition. So Julia had been surprised when he called her into his office and asked for her help with a vital personal matter that would require an unexpected trip for her to Manila.

The flight across the Pacific had seemed unending. She had always found sleeping on a plane nearly impossible, and the cramped seating, the heavy drone of the engines, and the fact that she had settled for a middle seat on the Delta 737 from St. Louis to Los Angeles guaranteed that she would get no rest on that leg of the trip.

The business men on either side of her were sleeping soundly and were oblivious to her discomfort. She wondered if her personal problems had prompted her to accept this assignment. She was well acquainted with the heartache caused by a lost child—lost physically or spiritually.

She had switched to Eva Air in Los Angeles, and she had been much more comfortable on the flight from LA to Taiwan and from Taiwan to Manila, but concerns about her assignment churned through her mind, knotting in her stomach. She felt as if she had eaten rocks. The flight had given her long hours to sift through the events of her life, creating a storm of despair, regret, loss, and fear in her mind—all intensified by recent events. Her heart felt like a toothache with the Novocain wearing off.

By the time the Eva Air Boeing 777 jet had touched down on the runway at the Ninoy Aquino Airport in Metro Manila, questions and fears about the task ahead of her were still tumbling through her mind like performers from the *Cirque de Soleil*. After nearly twenty-four hours en route on a flight that had taken her halfway around the world, she was still wondering if she had made a serious error in judgment. *What made me think I can carry out this kind of an assignment? What if I fail? Have I allowed respect and friendship for Mr. and Mrs. Mallon to seriously bias my feelings? My return flight is open. Maybe I had better walk to the ticket counter in the terminal and get a flight home as soon as possible. Maybe I should just call the whole thing off.* As the plane taxied toward the terminal, she knew she had to make a decision—and quickly.

1

WHEN THE STAFF AT *UMAGA* House put on the rice that would be supper for themselves and their patients, Sophie Adamson whispered to her friend Lily Corbano, "Tomorrow is Roberto's birthday. He's going to have surgery on his clubfoot, and I know he's frightened. Let's get him a birthday present. We can be back before supper is finished." Lily nodded, and without changing out of their scrubs, the two young women hurried out of the little clinic. They caught a jeepney and rode to the SM Megamall, which was located in the Ortigas Business District in the center of Metro Manila.

After they purchased a teddy bear for Roberto, they laughed and window shopped through the second and third floors of the seven-level mall. They were very different: one petite, dark haired, and caramel-skinned with a quick smile, and the other, taller, with long, auburn hair pulled back into a ponytail and touched with bright highlights from the Philippine sun, the same sun that had given her skin a generous sprinkling of gold freckles.

The two young women stopped to purchase ice cream cones on the second level from a small kiosk outside the entrance of a large department store. A dark-skinned man nearly six feet in height with a crooked nose stepped up on the left of the two women, and another shorter man with a scar that reached from his left eyebrow to his left ear stepped up on the right. After each woman had ordered a cone, the tall man turned to Lily and asked with an assumed innocence, "Are you both Americans?" Sophie's natural defenses went up.

Lily smiled and answered, "Oh, no, not me. My friend is, but we both live and work here in Manila."

The short, stocky man with the heavily lidded eyes asked with a forced casualness, "You are nurses? Do you work at St. Luke's? We have heard that it is a good hospital, as good as an American hospital." There was just a slight sneer on his face.

Sophie responded shortly, with a stiff smile, "No, we work at a charitable clinic for children." Then she turned to Lily. "We've been gone too long. We need to hurry back." Sophie handed a few coins to the ice cream seller and took both of their cones, handing one to Lily.

Sophie tried to hurry Lily away, but Lily turned to talk to the men over her shoulder. "You have maybe heard of *Umaga* House? It's a charitable clinic where children can receive surgery at no cost. An American doctor founded it a few years ago." Sophie pulled at her friend's elbow, leading her toward the escalator. As they stepped off it onto the floor below, she looked over her shoulder at the men who continued to follow them while speaking to each other in Cebuano.

Belatedly, Lily's nerves set in. "Do you think they're following us? What do you think they want?"

Sophie said nothing but hurried her friend out of the mall to the jumbled and crowded parking lot, both of them dropping their melting ice cream cones on the ground as they dodged through the parked vehicles. As they hurried their steps, the men narrowed the gap, and the tall man tried to take up the conversation again. "Tell us about *Umaga* House. I have a rich uncle who might give a generous gift to such a charity." Both men had also discarded their ice cream cones.

His manner turned the unease of the young women into alarm. Sophie glanced over her shoulder. "Please excuse us. We need to get back. We've been gone too long." Under her breath, she urged Lily, "Hurry, these men are trouble." They started to trot through the parking lot toward the bus and jeepney stop on Epifanio Delos Santos Avenue, commonly referred to as EDSA.

Unwittingly, they had been hurrying toward a black Toyota SUV. The men closed the gap, and each caught one of the women by the elbow.

"Please, let me write you a check for your charity," the taller man said. "I have my checkbook in the car right here." The men pulled both young women closer to the black vehicle.

Sophie raised her voice. "Let go, or we will scream." With a swift look around to see if he was being watched, the taller man struck Sophie on the jaw with his fist, and she went limp, dropping her purse and the bag holding the teddy bear. He grabbed her around her waist.

As Lily opened her mouth to scream, from behind her the other man put his hand over her mouth and whispered in her ear, "If you scream, I will break your neck."

While the taller man held the unconscious Sophie against him, a Filipino couple walked past, looking at him as if to ask if something were wrong.

"My wife is very ill. I am taking her to St. Luke's," he said solicitously.

After the taller man pulled the door to the rear seat open, Sophie was half lifted, half shoved onto the floor of the car. Lily was pushed down onto the seat. The tall man slammed the door, bent over and picked up the purses and the bag with the teddy bear in it, and tossed them under a nearby car. He climbed into the front seat. "If you scream, we will kill you," he reaffirmed as he looked over the seat at Lily.

2

THE ROAR IN SOPHIE'S EARS finally diminished as she regained consciousness. Eventually, she could identify the sound of the SUV's engine and the voices of the two men in the front seat. There was something else that took a minute to define—sobbing; yes, someone was sobbing.

Keeping her eyes closed, she tried to analyze the situation. Her face was pressed into a stiff carpet, and her jaw hurt badly. Then she remembered the men in the mall, and her heart beat faster, pounding in her ears. *Slow down and think!* She tried to will her heart to slow and her mind to function. She opened one eye. All she could see was the back of the driver's seat.

Carefully, she lifted her head, turning it to the other side. She could see Lily's hand where it hung over the edge of the rear seat. Lily was the one sobbing. She reached up and took her hand. The gesture startled the young woman, and rather than feeling comforted, she began to sob more uncontrollably. Sophie quickly dropped her hand and closed her eyes as the man in the passenger seat turned and yelled something at Lily. Her panicky sobs grew only a little quieter.

It was dark both inside and outside of the vehicle. That could mean it was seven o'clock or ten o'clock. Panic made Sophie's mind race like car tires on slick mud. *Have I been unconscious a few minutes or an hour—or more?* Finally, the SUV pulled into an alley and continued for a few blocks over rough and pitted roads before coming to a stop. The short man with the scar got out of the car and opened the door to the backseat. He grabbed Lily, shouted something at her that Sophie could not understand, and dragged her from the car. After he climbed back into the front seat, the driver made a wide U-turn, bumping over something.

"She would be of no use to us, too weak, too full of tears. The American woman must be more useful, more obedient," the man said in English, apparently for Sophie's benefit.

Oh, Lily. What did he do to you? Dear God, she prayed, *please protect her and bring her help. Please!* The silent prayer was urgent. *And please help me think! Help me know what to do.* Deciding that continuing to pretend that she was unconscious would get her nowhere, she turned over and sat up on the floor of the car with her knees bent and her back against the door.

"What is it you want? Why did you kidnap us?" she asked in as firm a voice as she could manage.

"Shut up, or we will put a gag in your mouth. If you try to escape, we will tie you up. Stay down on the floor. That is a suitable place for an infidel woman."

The vehicle moved in and out of traffic for another thirty minutes. Nausea threatened to overwhelm her. She laid her head on her knees. *Count and breathe; just count and breathe,* she said over and over in her mind, trying to control the fear that jammed her thinking.

The car made a gradual, ninety-degree turn, moving northward up the Cavite Peninsula that stretches like a giant lobster claw into Manila Bay. The SUV moved through the narrow, crowded streets for another twenty minutes, rattled over several deep ruts, and then finally found soft ground. The vehicle stopped, and both men sprang out. The bigger of the two yanked open the back door, grabbed Sophie's arm, and roughly pulled her out. As she stepped unexpectedly into soft beach sand, she fell to her knees. As one of the men pulled her to her feet, she looked around, noting a ship about half a mile out to sea, flying the Philippine flag. A military plane was taking off about a mile farther up the peninsula. *Sangley Point. We're near the military base at Sangley Point.* Somehow knowing where she was helped slow her racing heart a little.

The base was a mass of lights, but where they were on the unlit beach was dark enough that no one would see them unless they were within twenty feet. She looked around and noted that the shorter man had lifted two long bundles wrapped in blankets from the rear of the vehicle. She was pushed across the beach and forced into a large *banca*, a twenty-five-foot canoe with outriggers on each side. She was ordered into the small plywood cabin in the center of the boat. There, the taller man pointed to one of the thwarts next to a large, built-in ice chest. "Sit," he said. "If you give us trouble, we will shoot you." Sophie had not seen any guns but suspected that there were some in the bundles taken from the vehicle.

The smaller man then climbed aboard, making his way back to the high, squared-off stern where he kicked two sleeping men who had been resting on a heap of fish nets. Without being told what to do, both of them jumped out of the boat and into the water where they pushed the *banca* away from the beach. As it began to drift, they climbed in, and one of them started the diesel truck engine adapted for marine use. With the engine in low gear, they motored out into Manila Bay.

Sophie's emotions churned inside her: anger toward her captors, worry for Lily, and fear for her own situation, all intensified by the knowledge that she could scream herself hoarse, and no one would hear her—at least no one who would care. She doubled up her toes in her shoes to steady her shaking legs. After a while, she leaned against the plywood bulkhead of the cabin, closed her eyes, and willed her mind to think more clearly.

Her captors stood watch, one in the bow and one in the stern as the big canoe moved rapidly south for more than seven hours, much faster than most *bancas* could travel. While the quarter moon was still high, the boat driver turned the vessel east toward an island that Sophie thought might be Mindoro, the large island just fifteen miles directly southwest of the larger island of Luzon. As it came more fully into view, she thought, *No, it's too small and too low to be Mindoro. Maybe this is Lubang.* She watched out of one of the small square holes that served as a window. *Lubang,* she remembered, *where that dedicated Japanese soldier refused to surrender after World War II ended and struggled for survival for twenty-nine years.* She shuddered and thought, *I hope I get rescued sooner than that.*

One of the men cut the engine in the *banca*, and the craft drifted nearer the beach. The two men who had served as pilots leaped into the water and pulled it onto the sand. About fifty feet away, a large speed boat was moored near a crumbling stone jetty.

"Yusuf, get her on the boat. Now!" the taller man called out to his companion.

Yusuf turned to Sophie. "You come with me. Make no trouble, or Hussein will hurt you. He is one bad guy."

The thought passed through Sophie's mind, *Should I run and scream? There are people around. Perhaps someone would help me.* As she struggled over the spars connected to the bamboo outrigger, she could see two men standing on the beach. Each held an assault rifle. That answered her question. *No, there's no help for me here.*

She was forced through the water until it was almost to her chin. At that point, she was within ten feet of the larger boat, forcing her to swim the last few feet to the ladder attached to the side of the vessel.

"Up! Climb up!" Yusuf ordered.

She pulled herself up and into the boat where she saw four other people sitting on the deck with their hands tied behind their backs. Yusuf pointed at the group of captives and ordered, "Sit!" Then he tied her hands behind her with a plastic tie.

The first captive she noticed was an old Chinese gentleman. Next to him was an attractive Chinese woman of about twenty-five. *Perhaps his daughter*, Sophie thought. Additionally, there was a man of about thirty-five, dressed like a businessman in dark slacks and a white shirt and tie, and a pretty Filipina, of about twenty, in the scrubs of a student nurse. Her long, heavy hair fell straight around her shoulders like black silk, framing a frightened face. The big boat's two inboard engines were idling, and the smell of diesel fuel fouled the air.

***

The next morning, the Metro Manila police had an anonymous report of the body of a woman in a trash-filled vacant lot in Las Piñas City. It was Lily. When they arrived, they concluded from the tracks of mud that went over her legs that she had probably been pulled from a vehicle and run over, leaving her legs badly injured, but she was alive.

3

YUSUF ORDERED THE FIVE CAPTIVES into the hold. He was carrying an automatic rifle with the strap over his shoulder, looking like a cocky adolescent. "Get below," he ordered, motioning toward the hatch with the barrel of the gun.

The elderly Chinese man struggled to get to his feet as Yusuf pushed the unsteady old man with the gun barrel. Sophie's anger and indignation had been mounting ever since she had recovered consciousness in the back of the SUV, and it had finally surpassed her fear. His treatment of the old man made her normally even temperament flame into indignation. Her words tumbled out in disgust and contempt. As she struggled to her feet, she yelled, "Stop it! He needs help getting up, not a gun in his back."

Yusuf turned on her and raised the butt of the gun threateningly. "If you cause us trouble, woman, I will take pleasure in killing you."

Her adrenaline pumped wildly. "You told me one of the other men was the bad guy. Did you lie, or are you just as bad? The Qur'an teaches that you are not to make war on non-combatants like old men and women and children. Allah will be angry with you!"

By this time the old man had made it unsteadily to his feet. "I'm alright, young woman. Do not trouble yourself over me," he said respectfully, trying to smooth the emotions of the moment and avert a violent reaction from Yusuf. The others were trying to stand, the process made difficult by the rocking of the boat and lack of support from their hands that were tied behind their backs.

Yusuf put his face almost against hers. "What do you know of the Qur'an?" His words had a hard edge to them, and his breath, fouled by decayed teeth, made her step back involuntarily.

"Evidently more than you do," she answered him nearly as fiercely, despite her pounding heart. "I know that 'Allah is mindful of what you do,'" she quoted.

The man froze for a moment, and his eyes narrowed. He pushed her roughly toward the open hatchway with the gun barrel but said nothing more. When the five captives had stumbled down the narrow stairway into the fishy-smelling, cramped hold where they could not stand upright, they were ordered to sit, and the hatchway was shut, cutting off the spill of light from the deck. The other two women began to sob in fear.

Sophie's mind was working to find some way to calm the women. "My name is Sophie. What are your names?" she asked above the sound of the idling engines.

"I am Samuel Chang. The woman with me is my daughter, Emily. I am sure we have been kidnapped for ransom." The voice of the old man seemed to calm his daughter, whose sobs became sniffles.

The Filipino businessman responded in the darkness, "I am Phillip Dangwa. I work for a cell phone distributor. I am not a rich man, but I think they will ask a ransom for me too. I don't know of any other reason to kidnap me."

The sobs of the student nurse had stopped. She sniffed. "I am Carlita Martinez. I don't know why they took me. There is no one to pay a ransom for me. My mother is very poor. My boyfriend is very poor. Perhaps they will kill me when they find out."

"No, I think you and I may have been taken because we are nurses. I don't think they'll kill us if we keep our heads," Sophie said soothingly.

Soon the roar of the engines increased until it was impossible to hear each other, so each sat in the darkness with his or her own thoughts. After several hours, the roar of the engines lessened, the boat slowed, and the door to the hatchway opened. Yusuf entered, and without saying anything, he motioned for the hostages to lean forward so he could cut the bindings on their wrists. Then he called up through the open hatchway, "Abdul, bring the rice. Get Ali to bring the water."

Light splashed down the stairs from the morning sun. Two men in dirty and ragged clothing descended the stairway, one with a pot of boiled rice in one hand and a stack of banana leaves in the other. The second man carried a large plastic jug of water that he handed to Phillip Dangwa, who took a long drink before handing it to Carlita. As it was passed from person to person, the other man set the pot down and thrust a leaf at each hostage. While the captives held the leaf in hands nearly numb from the bindings, he lifted a large spoonful of rice from the pot and slopped it onto the leaf. The three men turned and climbed the stairs.

"Please leave it open so we can see to eat the rice. We are no threat to you—an old man, some women. You can't possibly be afraid of us," Sophie called out.

Yusuf turned and looked down at Sophie. "You, woman, are going to be trouble." But he left the hatchway open. The hostages used their fingers to scoop the rice into their mouths.

After she had finished, Sophie rose to her feet and started for the stairway. Carlita's frightened voice followed Sophie. "Where are you going? They will kill you if you try to escape."

Sophie tried to soothe the young woman's fears. "There's no way for me to escape, Carlita. We're somewhere in the South China Sea. I'm going to ask if they have a CR." She thought, *Right now I sure understand why it's called a "comfort room" in this country. We could all use the comfort of such a facility right now.*

"Oh, that would be such a relief," Emily Chang said gratefully.

As Sophie reached the top of the stairs, one of the crew men turned on her with an assault rifle. He yelled at her in Cebuano.

She looked at him and yelled above the sound of the engines, "We need to use the CR. Do you understand? We need a CR." The man looked around uncertainly for a moment, as if seeking approval to act. She repeated more determinedly, "CR! We need to use the CR!"

With a scowl, he waved the barrel of the gun toward the stern of the boat. Taking that as permission, she called down the hatchway, "Come up. There's a CR in the stern of the boat." Nervously, the others made their way up the stairs. The CR was just a small platform that could be pushed out over the water, with a frame and a fabric shower curtain that could be rolled down for modesty. As crude as it was, the passengers appreciated it.

They were again forced back down the hatchway to sit in the dark but were not bound. Leaning on Sophie's shoulder, Carlita quietly cried until she fell asleep.

***

For the next three days the schedule remained the same, boiled rice twice a day with a visit to the CR in the morning and in the evening. The roar of the engines made communication difficult until one of the engines began to sputter. The other one stopped too, and the boat began to rise and fall on the waves. The silence felt unnatural to the hostages, so while one or two members of the crew tinkered with the malfunctioning engine, the captives talked. Phillip Dangwa spoke of his wife and two little girls. "I hope God will let me live so I can see them again."

"I am old" Chang said. "It does not matter if I do not survive, but I want my daughter to live so she can marry and have many sons."

"Oh, *Lolo*," Emily said, using the title of respect for an old man, "you must live. You are my whole world, and I want my sons to know and love you, as I do." He patted her shoulder gently.

"You are an American. Why are you here in the Philippines?" he asked Sophie.

"I work for a charity in Manila that offers free surgeries for children with cleft palates or clubfeet. I'm afraid they will hold me only as long as they need my nursing skills—and I don't know how long that might be."

The sound of the engine of a second boat drew their attention.

4

THE HOSTAGES COULD HEAR THE sound of metal cans clanking against one another and a loud series of thumps as they were set on the deck. Phillip Dangwa said, "I think they're taking on more fuel. Maybe we're going a long way, perhaps as far as Zamboanga. If we are, it will be another two or three days, at least."

"I think you're right," Chang added. "They will make their ransom efforts from there."

"How will they do that?" Sophie asked.

"It's common knowledge that many of the officials on the Zamboangan Peninsula freely cooperate with the Islamic terrorists, perhaps out of fear or maybe out of genuine sympathy, I don't know. There is a radio station there, *Radyo Agong*, that will transmit messages to or from any of the Islamic terrorist groups," the old man explained.

"How do you know these things?"

"My nephew was kidnapped by *Abu Sayyaf* about three years ago. We paid the ransom and got him back safely."

"Why have they targeted your family?"

"We are considered rich, at least rich enough to pay three hundred thousand pesos for a ransom." Doing some simple math in her head, Sophie estimated that ransom at just under six thousand dollars. *A lot of money in the Philippines, but if they find out who my grandfather is . . .* Sophie refused to let her thoughts go any further.

***

When the engines on the boat finally stopped again, the sudden silence after so many days of engine noise seemed to press down and around the hostages. For nearly four hours, they sat in the darkness of the hold, feeling the rise and fall of the boat and speculating about what was happening.

"Why are they keeping us here? What are they going to do with us?" Carlita whispered.

"Perhaps they are waiting for the dark so no one will see us when they take us off the boat," Chang responded.

Finally, the hatchway opened. "Up, now! Hurry!" Yusuf waved the barrel of his assault rifle. Only starlight lightened the stairs. Even the boat's running lights had been turned off. As the prisoners reached the deck, they could see what looked like a flashlight blinking at them from a coastline more than a hundred yards from the bow of the boat. The low tide had exposed a wide swath of beach that lay like a white stripe between the water and the forestation. The trees and undergrowth stood out black against the midnight blue of the starlit sky.

"All of you will go down the ladder and get in the *banca*. If you try to escape, we will shoot the others." Yusuf was anticipating that some bonding had taken place between the hostages, and he was right. More than six days of captivity in the darkness and discomfort of the hold had made them a family.

After the hostages had climbed into the big *banca*, Yusuf, Hussein, and two of the men who had been part of the crew of the larger boat climbed in as well. One of the men started the outboard motor mounted on the square stern. When the boat reached the beach, they were ordered out into the shallow waves, and there in the cool, ocean breeze, they clustered together into a tight group for warmth while the four captors talked loud and long.

Sophie was fairly sure they were speaking Cebuano. She understood very little of it, but she heard the word *Basilan* repeated several times. She whispered to Samuel Chang, "Do you speak Cebuano?"

"Yes," he responded. "They have been arguing about taking us to the island of Basilan or hiding us here in the mountains."

"Where are we?" she asked in a whisper.

"This is the Zamboangan Peninsula. The terrorists are strong here but not as strong as they are on Basilan." He listened for another minute. "One man said that the son of Hamal is here and needs medical help. Perhaps Hamal is their leader. The tall man called Hussein seems to be in charge right now."

The engine on the *banca* fired up, and the boat disappeared into the darkness. While their captors sat with their weapons across their knees, the captives spent the rest of the night on the beach, linked to each other by a rope that was tied to the right wrist of each one. The ocean breeze and their wet clothing chilled them as they waited for the night to pass. As they shivered and tried to sleep, all were oblivious to the brilliance of the star-filled sky.

***

The drone of the morning prayers of their captors, who knelt on their prayer rugs with their weapons next to them, awoke the hostages from their exhausted and uncomfortable sleep. When the prayers ended, the rugs were rolled up and the weapons pointed at the hostages. Emily helped her elderly father to his feet as the others stiffly arose from their cramped positions. Chang pointed to the two men in the lead. "They are yelling at us to follow Ali and Abdul into the trees." The group moved single file into the undergrowth behind the two men who were swinging their bolo knives to clear the way. Yusuf and Hussein followed, bringing up the rear. Regardless of the heat, humidity, hunger, and thirst, the hostages were not permitted to pause to rest or drink until midday. When they heard the faint rush of water, the captors and hostages rushed to the stream to drink. Sophie hesitated only briefly, as she was pulled into the water by Dangwa and Carlita who were roped to either side of her. *I guess if I'm ever found, I'll be going home with whatever tropical parasites or diseases are in that water, but I really need a drink.* The water was cool and luxurious after the heat of the previous few hours, but after only a few minutes, the hostages were quickly motioned out of the stream by the gun barrels of their captors.

After a rest of an hour in the heat of the day, during which their captors again conducted the usual ritual washings and prayers, they began the march anew. Yusuf insisted on poking the last hostage in line in the back with the barrel of his gun, as if that were part of his job description. His victim was usually Phillip Dangwa, who the terrorists almost always tied at the back of the group.

They made their way farther inland, struggling through acres of decaying slash, the waste left behind from a major logging endeavor. They labored over the rough and uneven ground, which steadily rose toward the volcanic mountain peaks in the distance. The mountain sides were blanketed with an ancient rain forest of hardwood trees, the mahogany, teak, narra, and ebony giants that sometimes rose more than one hundred twenty feet into the sky. Only the rugged, volcanic terrain had protected the trees from being logged and the land stripped.

Abdul stopped and put out his arms to halt the others behind him. "Halt! Cobra nest! Cobra will be close." As he spoke, a large brown king cobra with crossbands of black rose from under a mass of branches near the nest, spread its hood, and made a noise like a growl.

"Cobra!" Abdul and several others yelled. "Ali, move so I can shoot it." Ali stepped aside and Abdul took aim. He emptied half a magazine of bullets on the snake. He managed to hit it three times.

The experience so frightened Carlita that she stood frozen in place and Sophie had to take her hand and pull her along to keep her moving. Eventually, the palms and rough cogon grass began to evolve into forestation. When they reached the trees that covered the steep mountainsides, the branches made a green vault overhead, a canopy that shut out the sky and shrouded everything in dark shadows. The forced march finally ended shortly before dark when the group reached a level place on a hilltop where a bamboo hut on five-foot-high stilts sat in the shade of the tall trees.

Several men sat on the notched logs that formed the stairs or dangled their legs from the porch that stretched across the front of the hut as they cleaned their assault rifles. Greetings of *Allah akbar* and *Salam alaikum* filled the air as they greeted each other with a ritual kiss on each cheek. After much back slapping and congratulating chatter, the men looked the hostages over closely. The last man to rise from the little porch stood somewhat removed from the others. He motioned toward Sophie. One of the other men stepped over to him and spoke briefly. Then he approached Sophie and pointed at the hut. He motioned for Ali to untie her from the others. He pushed her with the barrel of his gun, forcing her up the notched log that served as a stairway. The hut was lit by the faint light from a rag in a soy-sauce bottle which, from the smell, was burning kerosene. There he pointed to a boy lying on a pile of bloody rags on the split bamboo floor. He could not have been more than sixteen. He had infected and inflamed wounds high in his left shoulder and upper left arm. The perspiration of a high fever stood in beads on his forehead. The man spoke to Sophie in Tagalog. "*May sakit siyā.*"

Sophie recognized the simple Tagalog. "Yes, he's sick." She nodded and knelt to look more closely at his wounds. "Do you speak English?" she asked the man.

"A little," he responded.

"Get me some more light and clean water and clean rags so I can wash his wounds."

He looked at her blankly. Mentally pouring over her limited Tagalog vocabulary, she finally came up with the some of the words she needed. "*Liwanag!* I need light." More slowly she put together a sentence, "*Ng tubig sa paglalaba ng sugat.*" *I sure hope I'm telling him that I need water to wash the wound.*

The man hurried out of the hut and returned in a few minutes with a battered pot full of river water in one hand and another soy sauce bottle with a burning rag stuck in it. Carlita entered the hut with Yusuf behind her. He pointed toward Sophie and said, "You help her." Then he spoke to Sophie. "You make him better. He is son of Hamal."

As she examined the boy's wounds, Sophie asked, "Who is Hamal?"

"Big boss," he responded.

"Do you have any amoxicillin in the camp?" Sophie asked. Yusuf just shook his head. "You must get some. How close are we to a city or a village with a drugstore?" Then she corrected herself and said, "You can get amoxicillin at any *pharmacia*. Is there one nearby?"

Yusuf left the hut and in a moment was back with Hamal, who asked, "You need medicine? What kind? I will send a man to get some."

Sophie stood, her eyes flashing with disgust and anger. "Why haven't you taken the boy to a hospital? They can help him there. Here, he might die."

"He will not die if you want to live," Hamal said menacingly as he bent over and put his face close to hers where she knelt near the boy. He added, "There is a twenty-five-thousand-peso reward for anyone who turns in any one of us or one of our bodies. That includes my son." They looked at each other for a few seconds before he spoke again. "What do you want from the *pharmacia*?"

"Thirty tablets of amoxicillin, 500 milligrams each. I need a three-percent solution of hydrogen peroxide, bandages, tape, aspirin and a blanket . . . and soap." There were many more items Sophie wanted, but she knew she would be very lucky to get the items she had already specified.

Hamal called two men into the hut, and speaking in Cebuano, he gave them the list. They both looked overwhelmed. Sophie said, "Each one can remember some of the things. Have one remember three items, and the other one can remember the other things." After further conversation, the men hurried into the undergrowth. "When will they get back?" Sophie asked.

"Maybe tomorrow." Hamal and Yusuf left the hut, leaving the other man as guard.

The two young women began the process of washing the boy's face and arms in the hope of lowering his fever. The boy moaned as they tried to make him more comfortable. "I think maybe he will die, and they will kill us," Carlita whispered.

"Not if I can help it," Sophie said through clenched teeth.

5

For Julia, life had been complete—at times she had wondered why she had been so blessed. She had a good husband, three children who were growing into fine adults, a comfortable home, and a pleasant and stimulating job. A cheerful and sunny individual by nature, she had always loved a challenge, which she found in her position as the administrator of an international foundation.

But her oldest son, Aaron, had returned from his mission almost two years earlier to find his sweetheart married to someone else. He had emotionally unraveled right before her eyes, and as he unraveled, so did Julia's life. Within a few months, he was enticed into a relationship with a substantially older, more experienced woman whose divorce decree was not yet final. When she invited him to move in with her and he did so, his Church membership was severed. Julia thought she would die of grief.

She had wondered time and time again, *What is the pull this woman has over him? I would rather have died than see him turn his back on the principles he knows are right.* Her prayers seemed to go no higher than the ceiling of her bedroom or the roof of her car as she drove to and from work. Even Jack, her husband, who was also disappointed and hurting, didn't seem to grasp the depth of her grief. Aaron's choice seemed to whisper to her, "Failure, failure, failure. You failed as a parent."

Then one Saturday in mid-September, despite her objections, Jack, who was a busy bishop, insisted on helping a new neighbor move in next door. She was hoping he would spend some time relaxing after dinner, but, instead, he commented, "I think I've got enough daylight to get the lawn mowed."

"Jack, the lawn can wait until Paul comes home from college next weekend. He doesn't mind mowing the lawn. You need to relax," she had urged him.

Allison, a high-school senior, backed her up. "Dad, when you finished helping with that move, your face was really red. You know, you're not as young as you used to be."

He laughed and, as if to prove her wrong, went out to start the lawn mower. The St. Louis heat and humidity were high, and he came in after he had finished, dripping with perspiration. His face was flushed and his jaw set.

"Jack, what's the matter? Are you ill?" Julia was alarmed.

"Nothing serious," he answered as he headed to the bathroom to take a shower. As he got ready for bed that night, he said, "I'll take an aspirin, and I'll be fine in the morning, just like always." There was that masculine invulnerability that frustrated Julia. He laughed and added, "I've just overdone it a little." He had said that so often that Julia shook her head and tried to push her concern out of her mind.

He didn't wake up on Sunday morning. When she finally grasped the fact that her husband was gone, she felt betrayed. This loss wasn't supposed to be part of her future. At the funeral, she repeated to those who extended their condolences, "He was years away from turning fifty. He was just too young." After the services were over and those offering sympathy had left her alone, she sat on her bed and asked through angry tears, "Jack, how could you do this to me? How could you do this to *us*?" Thereafter, she buried herself in the work of the foundation, trying to take refuge from her grief.

A few months later, as if some cruel fate wanted to intensify her grief, Aaron and the woman he had been living with were involved in a crash on the loop of I-270 that circled the metro St. Louis area. The other driver had been drinking, and he was driving north in the southbound lane. The woman had walked away with little more than bruises. Aaron never regained consciousness and lay in a care center, connected to a beeping heart monitor, a stomach tube, and a respirator that breathed for him.

Several doctors evaluated Aaron's condition and each told Julia the same thing—that the damage to his brain was so severe that he would never regain consciousness. He would remain in a vegetative state permanently. As much as Paul loved his brother, he had said, "Let him go, Mom. We shouldn't keep him here." But she couldn't do it. There had to be a miracle out there somewhere for him.

As she drove to and from her office in her three-year-old Chevy Malibu, a fragmented phrase from a long forgotten song or scripture seemed stuck in her memory and played over and over like a CD with a fleck of dust on it: "Would God I had died for thee, O my son." Finally, she remembered where she had read those words: 2 Kings, eighteenth chapter. They were King David's lament for the death of his son Absalom. Suddenly, she understood David's grief and her own as she never had before. The tears streamed down her face so heavily that she had difficulty seeing the traffic as she drove.

When she reached the office, she stopped in the restroom and splashed cold water on her face in the hope of hiding her red eyes. If anyone guessed, they were too tactful to say anything.

Each day after she left the office, she went directly to the care center. In the beginning, she tried to chat with her son as if he could hear her. Somewhere she had read that sometimes that helped, that unconscious patients could hear the conversations around them. But the last few weeks, it had become more difficult to carry on the one-sided conversation with a forced cheerfulness. Her visits became quieter. Sometimes she simply sat and held his limp hand and quietly wept at the enormity of the loss that never seemed to end. Somehow the loss of Jack and the loss of Aaron had merged in her mind, like two wide streams that had joined to make a deep, fast-flowing river, and she was growing too tired emotionally to continue to tread water.

Allison took over fixing dinner for the two of them each evening before Julia got home from work. They talked a little as they ate, but Julia seldom had the inclination to share her thoughts on anything except Aaron or Jack. Just short of a year from the date of her father's death, Allison was relieved to join her brother Paul at college and escape her mother's ever-present grief.

***

Melton Mallon looked ill with emotional strain when he called Julia into his spacious carpeted and paneled office. His hand shook slightly as he motioned her to the chair across from his large mahogany desk. Close friends and associates had noticed that within the past few days he had suddenly become an old man.

As she sat across from him, he said quietly, "Julia, I don't know where to turn. I've tried to be a prayerful man for the past twenty years—ever since I discovered the Church and came to the realization that there was someone else in charge of this old world." Then he straightened in his chair and continued, "And I also believe that He expects us to do our best to work out our individual problems before we hand the load over to Him." He paused and looked at her with tired eyes. "I have finally been forced to do just that. I can't carry the load alone any longer."

That statement left her speechless for a moment. This was a man who, at seventy, had made a hobby of helicopter skiing in the Utah and Colorado mountains every winter. She could not imagine a problem that he couldn't solve in at least three different ways.

He rubbed his forehead as he talked. "He's prompted me to bring you into the matter. I can't explain why." He had her full attention. "You remember, I'm sure, that my granddaughter, Sophie, insisted on going to Manila when she completed her nurses' training last spring so she could work at *Umaga* House."

Julia nodded. She knew Sophie well. After the death of both of Sophie's parents when their plane went down on a flight to Vail, Colorado, seven years earlier, Sophie had been raised by Mr. and Mrs. Mallon. She had been baptized into the Church as a teenager about a year after her parents' death.

Julia had grown very fond of the bright girl. When she had turned eighteen, Sophie had enrolled in Julia's evening institute of religion class on the world's three great religions. Their friendship had grown as they socialized at the Christmas parties for the foundation staff that were held at the Mallons' large and impressive home in the upscale St. Louis suburb of Frontenac.

Julia had even felt a pang of envy when she learned of Sophie's plans to become part of the life-changing charity. She knew that all too often the idealism of the young was extinguished as the heart matured. The word *Umaga* meant "morning" in Tagalog, and obviously for those children and young people who received vital surgical help there at no cost, it was a bright morning in their lives.

Mallon took a deep breath as if to steel himself. Then in a tightly controlled voice, he said, "Julia, Sophie's disappeared." He paused, letting the words sink in. "We think she's been kidnapped. She disappeared from the clinic at *Umaga* House over five days ago. We've been waiting for a ransom demand, but there hasn't been any."

A chill made Julia hold her breath momentarily. *No wonder he had been looking so haggard.* "And you think I can be of help in some way?"

Nodding, he continued, "I've been impressed for the last twenty-four hours to bring you into it. I believe that you're a solid, foresighted planner who knows how to delegate, and, importantly, I think you're a good judge of people.

"I realize that you've been through a difficult time for the last couple of years. If you don't feel that you can accept this assignment, I'll understand—and I don't want you to put yourself in personal danger. Let me repeat," he emphasized the words, "I do not want you to put yourself in personal danger." He exhaled a weary sigh. "But I need someone to go to Manila and hire someone to put together a search for Sophie." He paused and looked directly at her as if to emphasize his next words. "I'm not asking you to be directly involved. All I'm asking of you is to find and hire someone who can handle this kind of an assignment. The authorities there don't seem motivated to organize this kind of a rescue effort, and, frankly, to them she's just one more kidnap victim, and they have an abundance of those." His tone of voice turned bitter.

She responded with some hesitation. "I would be willing to go, but . . . I wonder what I can do that you couldn't if you went rather than me—or one of the other staff members here."

"I can't go." He shook his head. "My wife and I haven't permitted anyone to know how ill she is, not even family members. The chemo has drained her strength and isn't making any progress against the tumor. She's declining rapidly, and I can't leave her, especially right now. I can't send Bob. His wife is due any day now and is facing a C-section. Wayne left the day before yesterday for Guatemala and a meeting with the head of their commerce department." He slowed and stressed his words, "But, importantly, as I said, I've been impressed to ask you, and it's not my intent to second guess the promptings of the Spirit."

The conversation continued, with Julia wondering if she had slipped into a dream—or a nightmare. "If you accept this assignment, I'll place ten thousand dollars in a special account in your name at the HSBC International Bank by wire transfer, which you can call upon as necessary. If you need more, it will be there." He handed her a small slip of paper. "Here is a short list of contacts you may find useful. It's a place to start. These names were given to me by Justice Ezekiel Molina, who recently retired from the Philippine Supreme Court. If none of these people can help, his number is on the bottom of that paper, and he said you could call him at any time for more assistance. He thought he might be able to come up with a few other potential names, if needed."

She glanced at it and then slipped it into the pocket of her navy blue suit. At what she thought was the conclusion of the conversation she stood, and he came around the desk. They shook hands as a signal that Julia had accepted his commission, even though her mind was still whirling and she was unsure where to begin. He added, "Be careful. Make your plans prayerfully. I don't want any harm to come to you, but . . . under the circumstances, I just don't know what else to do."

He turned and walked to the window that overlooked the affluent West St. Louis County area along the Highway Forty corridor where his office was located. From his position at the window, he looked out at the traffic and the other glass and chrome office buildings. He fixed his eyes on the spire of the St. Louis Temple that was just visible above the trees beyond the hill to the west.

He continued quietly, as if he were speaking his thoughts aloud, "Within a few hours of learning that Sophie and her friend Lily had not returned from the mall, I contacted the Philippine consulate in San Francisco for help but was told that, though their government is sympathetic, I should let the investigation proceed through the usual channels. The next day I was put in contact with a retired police detective who had been recommended to me, and I hired him to find Sophie. He had spent years on the Metro Manila police force and knew his way around." He paused. "His body was found about twenty-four hours ago in an alley in Cavite. There's no way to know if his death was related to his search for my granddaughter or not, but I feel responsible just the same."

He turned away from the window. "That was when I called Justice Molina. After ten years on the bench, he left the court very respected as an honest man. He advised me to send someone whose presence will not raise questions in anyone's mind, someone with a reason to be in the country. Additionally, he urged me to 'grease the wheels generously' and not to rush the inquiry."

Julia knew what it meant to "grease the wheels generously." On her earliest trips to the Philippines, she had been startled by the commonality in the Philippines of what many Americans considered bribe-taking, but she had come to realize that in the eyes of many Filipinos, these were simply "tips" or gifts much like the gratuities offered to restaurant servers, baggage handlers, or cab drivers in the U.S. Salaries were generally so low in the islands that those tips were a product of necessity.

"You've spent enough time there to understand the culture. You know how things are supposed to work—and how they really work."

"I'll go and do what I can. Please keep me in your prayers," she responded uncertainly.

He smiled and added as a note of caution, "Julia, be alert, be careful and keep me in the loop—and go with God." That ended the meeting. He ushered her to the door of his office.

Julia returned to her small office down the hall and sat behind her desk, pressing her hands into her lap until they quit quivering. She suddenly felt like an actor in a stage production in which she was expected to play the lead without knowing the plot or having seen the script and the audience was waiting—and Sophie was in that audience. After a few minutes, she gathered up her handbag, coat, and umbrella and made her way to the lobby. "Ruth, please just take messages if anyone calls for me," she said to the receptionist as she pushed the outside door open. She walked through the falling snow to her car and drove through a snowstorm to the temple. As she sat quietly in the celestial room intensely searching for some kind of divine guidance and direction, the words came powerfully to her mind, *"Walk to the edge of the light."* She thought about those words for a few minutes and determined that she would follow that advice one step at a time.

On her way home she stopped at the care center, making her way through the slush in the unplowed parking lot. After spending a half hour with Aaron, she drove home as if she were on automatic pilot. There, she turned on her computer and looked up several Internet cut-rate travel services. She was pleased to get a ticket for Los Angeles for the next afternoon at nearly half price. Under her breath, she whispered, "Maybe this is a sign that things are going to go well." She arranged to change planes at LAX, making a reservation for Manila that would put her on a red-eye special at one o'clock in the morning.

She pulled out both of her wheeled suitcases and the large soft-leather handbag she used on her trips. She packed summer-weight, cotton clothing, sandals, and her favorite running shoes. She was not sure what she would need so she packed casual cargo pants, two pantsuits, slacks, a skirt, and several cotton blouses. The pantsuits were dressy enough to go almost anywhere.

When she was satisfied that she was ready, she called Paul and Allison, one after another, at the university to tell them of her immediate trip to Manila. "Hi, hon," she said with as much cheerfulness as she could gather when each answered, "I'm off to Manila again. Be back in a couple of weeks or maybe sooner." She said nothing of the real reason for the trip since worrying them wouldn't accomplish anything. If something did happen, Paul knew where the small safe was in her bedroom that contained her legal papers and will.

***

So here she was, sitting in the Evergreen business section on Eva Air as the plane rolled to a stop at the gate of terminal one. During the last leg of the flight from Taiwan, as she tried to rub the knots and spasms out of her calves, Julia reviewed the list of potential contacts. Aside from the three individuals who led the three foundation chapters there and who would potentially be of little use, there was the name of the head of security at the U.S. Embassy; an investigative reporter for the *Manila Standard Bulletin,* one of the English language newspapers in Manila; a Metro Manila police detective; and Judge Molina.

She picked up the big leather handbag that she had pushed under the seat in front of her and put it in her lap as she waited for the more impatient passengers to collect their carry-on bags. As the line of businessmen, tourists, and Filipino mothers with small children in one arm and a bag in the other lined up in the aisle and waited for the outer door to open, she prayed silently for the hundredth time, *Where should I begin?*

This time an answer came as distinctly as if someone sitting in the recently vacated seat next to her had spoken. *"Since you're here, get off the plane and do whatever you can."*

Startled, she sat quietly for a moment. As the crowd in the aisle thinned, she took a deep breath and made her way to the exit. As she started down the stairs to the tarmac, the humid air enveloped her like the atmosphere in a greenhouse. It was late January, the Philippine winter, but it felt like a muggy day in St. Louis in August. Entering the air-conditioned terminal, she followed the signs in both Tagalog and English that pointed to the luggage carousel.

She picked up her other bags and started toward the exit, pulling both pieces of luggage. *Thank heaven for the guy who put wheels on suitcases.* She waited in line to pass through customs, where her bags were searched and she was asked the purpose of her visit. As the official examined her passport, she smiled and answered, "I work for a charity with three chapters here in the Philippines." The official stamped her passport and handed it back to her.

Halfway to the terminal exit, she could see the familiar figure of Mike Legaspi, the director of the foundation's Manila chapter, coming toward her. Mike was the father of six and had not yet reached forty years of age. He had a full head of thick, black hair and wore a broad and welcoming grin. He waved and called out, "*Mabuhay*," the traditional Philippine greeting.

She returned it. "It's good to see you, Mike," she said as he took her luggage. She retained the heavy handbag.

As they walked toward the exit doors, he asked, "Is anyone else coming from the office?"

She shook her head. "I've got a special assignment for Mr. Mallon, and it doesn't require more than one person."

As they made their way through the terminal and out into the sun, he asked the usual questions. "Was the flight pleasant? Was the food on the plane good? Do you want to visit clients tomorrow?"

The last question caught her off guard. She had not given that part of her visit much thought. *Of course he expects me to do the usual client visits and evaluations.* The business of the foundation had been the farthest thing from her mind throughout the flight. She responded as smoothly as she could. "I'll leave that entirely up to you, Mike. I'll be at your disposal."

"At my disposal?" he asked with raised eyebrows.

She laughed. "That's an American expression. It means that we'll go wherever you think we should go. You will make the decisions."

He grinned. "I'll remember that. I thought you wanted me to put you in a *basurahan*—a trash can." Mike's English was good, but American idioms sometimes confused him.

They both laughed. Julia realized that it felt good to laugh. She hadn't laughed for a long time. They had to walk about a quarter of a mile to where he had parked—illegally. When he saw her look at the way he was parked, he said, "It's okay. I gave the man at the gate fifty pesos. He won't complain." Julia just shook her head and grinned.

Mike had put both suitcases into the trunk of his well-worn, 1978 Chevy. It had once been painted sky blue but was now more the color of rust and exposed primer. The chrome was held on with duct tape. On her last trip, he had told Julia proudly that it had more than 300,000 miles on it. The floor was so rusted that she had to be careful where she put her feet when she climbed in. When he put it in gear and they started to move, she could feel a breeze that was not air conditioning. It was the air blowing through a hole in the floor.

"Mike, when are you going to buy another car?"

"It would just get stolen. No one wants this one," he responded cheerfully.

The engine sounded like an old washing machine. He raised his voice and said, "I received an e-mail from Mr. Mallon two days ago. When he told me what time to pick you up at the airport, he asked me to get you a reservation at the Manila Hotel. That is one expensive place, but I did what he wanted. I cancelled your reservation at the Pan Pacific. Do you know why he wants you at the Manila Hotel?"

"I wanted to stay there on this trip. I've heard so much about it, but I've never had the opportunity to do any more than drive past it. And since I was coming alone, he thought it might be a little safer there than some of the areas where other hotels are located."

"Yes, the area is as safe as any in Metro Manila—safer than most." He brightened up and added, "In the evenings at about seven, there's a light show in Rizal Park across the street. It has a narrator who tells the story of the life of José Rizal and his execution. I hear that it's really awesome."

Julia couldn't help but smile at his use of that very American word. She nodded. He continued, "While you're in the hotel, be sure to get the tour of General Douglas MacArthur's suite on the top floor. You don't want to miss that. He lived in the hotel from 1935 to 1942 until President Truman ordered him to leave before the Japanese invaded." He added enthusiastically, "And I hear that the hotel dinner buffets are really great." As he chatted, her thoughts rambled.

It was Friday—or was it Thursday? After all, she had crossed the international date line on the flight. She concluded that it was her second Thursday that week. At this point, she didn't care. She just wanted to get in a hot shower and eat a light supper before going to bed. But first they had to run the gauntlet of Metro Manila traffic.

As Mike left the airport, the real world descended upon them with life-threatening reality. From the air, Metro Manila seemed to stretch for uncounted miles, a combination of seventeen municipalities that had grown together after World War II and newer cities that had joined into one enormous population center of nearly twenty million. As usual, the roads were crowded with six lanes of cars on a road striped for four. Julia had previously learned that red lights were just teasers. No real Filipino driver was likely to stop at a light simply because it was red. He would only slow or stop if the opposing vehicle was substantially bigger than his and traveling faster.

As if the traffic did not furnish sufficient distractions, Metro Manila has been called a "city of billboards." On the top and on the exposed side of most of the taller buildings, huge faces smiled at the folks below as they advertised shampoo, cell phones, and toothpaste. Mike made a token effort not to crush any of the tricycles or their aggressive drivers who were usually clad only in ragged jeans, worn T-shirts, and flip-flops. The tricycles were lightweight Yamaha road bikes with sidecars welded on, usually loaded with three or four Filipinos. As Julia watched, one of them drove over a curb and onto the sidewalk to avoid other vehicles.

At one point, Mike stomped on the brake pedal as a bus made a left turn from the lane to the right of the old Chevy. Julia braced herself with her hand on the dashboard. She had been told that even the legally blind have been known to get driver's licenses in Metro Manila if they were willing to pay the accompanying governmental fees. She was sure that many visitors not normally inclined toward religion became very prayerful while riding in Manila traffic.

Mike continued to talk as he darted in and out of traffic, moving away from the airport. When they reached Roxas Boulevard, he slid between the heavily loaded jeepneys and delivery trucks with the gracefulness of a street surfer.

The battered Chevy finally entered the old and still gracious city of Manila proper, where the billboards disappeared and traffic thinned somewhat. Julia finally took a deep breath—not that the traffic was entirely sane, but it was noticeably improved. The various vehicles actually drove within the painted lanes.

The avenue was lined on the east with three- and four-story hotels and exclusive apartment buildings. She leaned back in the passenger seat to enjoy the view of the bay at high tide. She studied the couples holding hands in the late afternoon sun, the linear park that ran along the west side of the boulevard separating it from the water, and especially the lights that were strung like necklaces between the lampposts on the most beautiful street in Manila, where every night looked like Christmastime. There was still a whisper of the elegance that before World War II had given Manila the title of "The Pearl of the Orient."

On her first trip, Julia had learned that in these near-equatorial islands, dark comes at about six o'clock in the evening during the winter months and less than a half hour later in the summer. She had never grown accustomed to the fact that there was no lengthy dusk. Nature just pulled the shade, and folks who were able tried to be home by dark.

When Mike pulled up under the wide portico of the historic Manila Hotel, there was less than an hour of daylight remaining. The Spanish colonial architecture of the old hotel still echoed its original elegance. A doorman in a red coat watched as Mike lifted the luggage out of the trunk. Had the car been a Mercedes or even a newer Toyota, he would have made an effort to assist, but Mike's old Chevy did not speak to him of rank or wealth, so he stood without moving and watched. Mike carried both suitcases up the stairs and through the impressive doorway to the front desk in the enormous foyer.

The ceiling of the historic hotel was paneled in deep, rich mahogany, and the walls were a soft, cream-colored stucco. Each interior doorway was a Spanish arch. The large room was close to fifty feet wide by sixty feet long, and three enormous two-tiered chandeliers hung above it, which echoed the colonial theme of the building. They suffused the scene in a soft, warm light. The couches and chairs were upholstered in deep red leather or ruby-red brocade fabric, and large area rugs of the same intense color with decorative gold borders covered much of the parquet floor.

Though burned by the Japanese in their retreat from Manila in 1945, the main portion of the hotel had been restored to its original glory. At least a hundred and fifty men and women in evening dress sat in the leather couches or stood around heavy, carved tables covered with large, fresh, tropical floral arrangements. They talked and laughed as they held their wine glasses.

The scene was surreal, something out of a Technicolor movie made in 1952. For a moment, Julia wondered if the elegantly dressed members of the crowd were expecting General and Mrs. MacArthur to join them. *These people really know how to dress for a party,* she thought with admiration.

The man behind the registration desk seemed unimpressed with Mike and continued to work at his computer until Mike spoke to him in Tagalog. "*Mahal ang Amerikano babaing iyón.*" He continued to speak so rapidly that Julia couldn't catch the balance of the short statement, but she did grasp that he had told the man that she was a rich American woman. She turned to hide a smile.

Suddenly, she had the man's full attention. He stopped what he was doing and looked at her. "How may I assist you, madam?"

From there, things went smoothly. Another man in a red uniform took her suitcases. Mike grinned. "I'll pick you up at nine o'clock in the morning. Will that be okay?"

She nodded gratefully and followed the gray-haired, dignified staffer whose name tag said his name was Bert. As the elevator rose, she asked, "Is there a special event here in the hotel this evening?"

He smiled and, in slightly accented English, spoke with a bit of pride. "Mayor Lim is holding a dinner and a ball tonight especially for his supporters."

They exited at the third floor, and she followed him down the mahogany-paneled hallway on the red carpet. He showed her into a room that, though not large, was luxurious. The bellman opened the red silk, or *shantung*, draperies—they shimmered as they moved—and pushed open the French doors behind them that opened onto a small balcony overlooking a portion of the harbor that was filled with cargo ships. Some of the ships seemed deceptively close, almost near enough that someone with a long gangplank could have boarded them. She tipped the man, closed and locked the door behind him, kicked off her shoes, and lay down. The bed was a queen-sized mahogany four-poster with a red satin coverlet. She had been awake for nearly thirty-five hours. It was hard to realize that less than two days ago she had been sitting in Mr. Mallon's office. Now she was half a world away with an intimidating assignment.

After resting for an hour, her thoughts began to order themselves. She rose and removed her wrinkled cotton blouse. She was damp with perspiration where her money belt had been wrapped around her waist. Before she left St. Louis, she had tapped into the money Mr. Mallon had put in the bank. The bulky money belt carried Philippine pesos in large denominations equal to three thousand dollars and a thousand dollars in twenty and fifty dollar bills. Then she opened the large, multicompartmental shoulder bag she always used when she was traveling and began to lay out everything on the bed to make sure nothing was broken. She had brought a new iridium satellite phone with a GPS in its software that Mr. Mallon had approved. Additionally, she had her personal Blackberry, which had been converted to operate in the Philippines. It also included a GPS. Her pocket-sized digital camera had come through in good condition. She dropped her passport and wallet on the bed and took two paperbacks from the big purse.

She had grabbed them as she left the house, thinking she might need something to read to fill the time on the plane. She looked more closely at them. One was a John Grisham novel. The other was a softbound copy of the Qur'an. She had been studying the Qur'an again for background material for the world religions institute class she was scheduled to teach in a few weeks. She turned the book over in her hand and realized that it might be useful if, as she and her employer feared, Sophie had been kidnapped by Islamic extremists.

She opened her wallet and took out the piece of paper with the short list of names and telephone numbers of the contacts that might be of use to her. She picked up the satphone, stepped out onto the balcony, and dialed the number of the police detective.

She heard a strong, male voice on the other end. "Montalbon here."

She was not sure where to go from there, so she hesitated slightly before she introduced herself. "I . . . I was given your name by my employer who obtained it from a retired supreme court judge here in the Philippines. He said you were someone who might be able to help me."

Before she could continue, he answered, "Yes, I received a call from Justice Molina a couple of days ago telling me that I would likely be receiving a telephone call from you."

"Are you willing to meet with me and discuss my problem?"

"Yes, just name the time and place. Evening would be best."

His syntax was very American. Somehow that made her feel more comfortable. "I'm staying at the Manila Hotel. I could meet you here tomorrow about seven o'clock for dinner. It will be on me, whether or not you can help me. Will that work for you?"

"That's fine. Tell me what you look like so I can spot you."

"I'm five foot six inches tall with short, somewhat curly, blond hair. I'll wear a blue pantsuit and wait for you in the foyer."

"See you then."

She checked her watch. She had time to shower and change into something fresh and get something to eat before she could call St. Louis. At eight o'clock, after she came up from the dining room, she called Mallon's home. It was six o' clock in the morning there, and she was sure her employer would be up and ready to head for the office. He picked up on the second ring. She briefly reported on her flight and the planned meeting with Detective Montalban.

"I'm glad to know that things are moving forward," Mallon responded. "Oh, by the way, I don't remember if I mentioned to you that Mr. Montalbon is evidently a member of the Church. Justice Molina told me in our telephone conversation that he was a member of 'that American church that sends so many young men to the Philippines as missionaries.' That could only be us. I hope that is an asset."

Yes, I hope so, too, Julia thought.

6

MIKE PICKED JULIA UP AT nine in the morning, and they spent several hours visiting some of the clients of the Manila chapter of the foundation. They met Hilda, who, along with her two daughters, lived in a squatter's shack in a low, sometimes flooded area of Pasay. She and her daughters spent their days making leis of silk flowers. With a loan from the foundation, Hilda had been able to hire some of her neighbors, had found an outlet in several department stores in the metro area, and had tripled her family's weekly income. Julia took a photo of the little group for the foundation newsletter.

As they climbed into Mike's old car, he slapped at a mosquito. "Did you remember to bring your insect repellant?"

Julia shook her head. "I left the states in such a hurry, I forgot. I'll try to remember to get some as soon as I can."

Mike drove them to meet with Nita and Juan, a couple in Parañaque who had been selling cobs of boiled corn on the street from a big tub they pushed around on a homemade wagon. They explained to Julia how grateful they were for the small loans and training they had received from the foundation that had made it possible for them to purchase a small refrigerator and open a sari-sari shop, which they showed her with pride. The shop was just a little space of about five by five feet with a hard-packed dirt floor. It opened on an alley, where they sold a variety of snacks and candy.

For lunch, she and Mike ate pork mounted on a stick and roasted over an open flame, one of the products sold by another client. By five o'clock Mike had Julia back at the hotel. As they pulled up under the portico, she expressed her thanks for his navigation, and, more importantly, his competent driving. She breathed a sigh of relief as she opened the car door.

"You want to go out and meet more clients tomorrow?" he asked.

She shook her head. "I have another assignment tomorrow, and I will get a taxi to the airport when it's time to leave town. I won't take you away from your work anymore so you can get back to the office." As she climbed out of the tired old Chevy, she said, "I'll send back a good report of your work, Mike. Thanks again for all your help." She gave him a wave and started up the stairs to the lobby. This time the doorman opened the door graciously.

She stretched out on the large bed for a few minutes to put the tension of riding in traffic behind her. Then she rose, showered, brushed her hair, and put on a royal blue pantsuit. With her big, soft handbag over her shoulder, she made her way down to the lobby to wait for Diego Montalban, even though it was only six-thirty. She was impressed when he arrived exactly at seven o'clock, unusual in a country with a Spanish heritage where meetings seldom started on time.

The lobby had only a few people sitting or standing around, unlike the night before. As he approached her, she turned enough that he could see her face in profile. Just a whisper of a hesitation interrupted his stride. One thought filled his mind. *What a remarkably attractive woman.* Reaching back to the memory of an early university art class, he was reminded just a little of a painting of a Botticelli angel.

She turned in her chair and stood in one smooth, lithe movement. She glanced at the time as she watched his approach. *I hope that's him. He's much taller that I had expected.*

"Blue is your color." He smiled as he put out his hand. "I am Diego Montalbon, but I prefer to be called Monty." His English was completely American.

When she returned his smile, it did not include her eyes. With the eye for detail that he had cultivated throughout his professional life, he noted that her large, gray-blue eyes looked at him with a silvery depth that seemed to reflect some kind of quiet grief the way a serene lake reflects a cloudy sky.

"Unless you're very hungry, we can talk here for a few minutes," he said. She sat, and with ease he pulled over one of the heavy, carved, straight-backed chairs that were space fillers on the bright red carpeting. He sat down and faced her. His directness was more that of a long-time acquaintance than that of someone who had just entered her world.

She looked around to make sure there was no one near enough to overhear them and said, "You probably want to know why I was given your name."

"I figured it was because whatever you need, you won't be able to get it from the police or the military." His expression was neutral, alert, intelligent, but one that gave away nothing about himself or his thoughts.

She nodded. Leaning over and putting out her hand, she said, "Mr. Montalbon, let me introduce myself formally. I'm Julia Wentworth."

He took her hand, and rather than shaking it, he rose and bent slightly over it in the old Castilian fashion. Initially she wondered if there were just a little mockery in his manner but then decided he was completely sincere. He sat down again and said, "I'm sure you're wondering what my credentials are that would make Justice Molina recommend me to handle unusual problems. Ask any questions on your mind."

Julia decided to use the same frankness he had used. "You speak like an American, you have a Spanish name, and I would guess that your mother was Chinese. Am I right?"

He nodded and added, "Actually, she was Chinese-American. Her father was an American missionary. Her mother was his first Christian convert on the Chinese mainland. They fled when Mao took over in China after World War II. I'm an example of the mixed heritage common in the Philippines. I was born in Bolong on the Zamboangan Peninsula of western Mindanao. Are you familiar with that island?"

"Only to the degree that Americans are warned not to travel there because it's considered a haven for Islamic extremists."

He nodded again. "You're right. The friendliness offered to Americans and other visitors here on Luzon isn't prevalent there. Islam was the predominant religion on Mindanao well before Magellan brought Catholicism. The Zamboangan Peninsula is a mixture of both religions, but in many places, Islam is predominant." He paused, grinned, and added, "Forgive me for sounding like a geography teacher, but the geography of the area may be important if your 'problem' involves a kidnapping. Does it?"

Julia pressed her lips in a tight line and nodded.

He continued, "My childhood home of Bolong is located very near the southwest tip of the peninsula that separates the Sulu Sea on the northwest from the Celebes Sea on the southeast. The island itself is almost as large as Luzon and, on a map, looks a bit like a kneeling elephant. The Zamboangan Peninsula is the trunk of the elephant. A ridge of volcanic mountains still covered with old-growth rain forest runs the length of the peninsula. Some of the radical Islamic groups use that forest to avoid being caught by the military. Now the geography lesson is over." He leaned back and gave her another full smile. "I was only ten when my father died. My uncle insisted that I and my younger brother go to live with him in Los Angeles where he owns a string of about a dozen florist shops. He raised us like his own sons since he didn't have any and sent us both to UCLA. My mother permitted him to take us to the states because her health was poor. She only lived a few more months.

"After I had completed four years of university work, I enlisted in the U.S. Army—against my uncle's wishes. He wanted me to live a casually comfortable life like a rich man's son, simply dropping in occasionally on one or another of the flower shops."

Julia interrupted him. Quietly she asked, "Is it true that you're LDS?" Julia knew if he were not, he would not likely know what those three letters meant.

He grinned. "Yes, when I was in my teens, I joined the Church. I was tall enough to be invited to play basketball at the local ward building. Those young missionaries who rode their bicycles around LA impressed me, and I listened to their message. What do you know about the LDS Church?"

"I was raised in it." Then she smiled and added, "Not all 'Mormons' are in Utah."

"It's a small world," he said and then picked up his narration again. "I wanted to become like those missionaries in their white shirts and ties, but my uncle threatened to disown me. Out of respect for him, I selected another mission field, the army—even though he wasn't too happy about that. I received special forces training with a focus on counter-terrorism and was given several years of travel sponsored by the U.S. government to interesting places like Bosnia, Afghanistan, and Kuwait—and a couple of places I can't talk about even now."

"What did you do in Afghanistan?"

"Taught the *Mujahedeen* how to use the weapons the U.S. was funneling to them to use against the Soviets."

"Did you consider making the military a career?"

"I was proud of that green beret, but too much of that kind of work has a hardening effect on a man." After a moment, he added, "And there was pressure to become involved in black ops."

"Black ops?"

"Secret operations hidden from normal oversight or review. I had too many reservations about the ethics—the morality of some of the operations." He looked at her and said as if to explain, "I'm willing to fight the bad guys, but . . ." He left the statement hanging in the air for a moment, and then he added, "But I believe the good guys should still wear white hats. Am I making any sense?"

She nodded. "Yes, you're making sense."

"I got my U.S. citizenship, returned to UCLA, and while I was completing a master's degree in criminal justice, I met the most beautiful Filipina in the world named Alicia. I was hired into the Los Angeles Police Department, and a year later we were married in the Los Angeles Temple. After she graduated from nursing school, she worked for two years in LA at Cedars-Sinai Medical Center, but then her mother started to press her to return home to Metro Manila." He paused, and after a deep exhale, he continued. "We really preferred living in the U.S., but her mother needed her, and family ties are strong among Filipinos—so after three years on the force, I resigned, and we packed up our six-month-old daughter and came back."

He stopped abruptly and stood as a couple of Korean tourists walked past them. "Let's go into the dining room. Since the dinner hour doesn't begin until eight o'clock for those who can afford the Manila Hotel, it won't be busy for nearly an hour." He turned, looked directly at her, and added, "And we really don't know yet if we'll be doing business."

Julia put her bag over her shoulder, and he ushered her into the hotel dining room with a hand on her elbow, as if he had been there before. He spoke to the host quietly. "A table in a quiet corner, please."

The dinner hour in the Philippines is leisurely, the process sometimes taking so long that Americans grow impatient, but Julia was grateful to feel unrushed. The table was theirs for the evening, if they wanted it. When a waiter came to take their order, both chose the buffet. He pointed the way. Julia put the handbag over her shoulder, and after they had filled their plates from an expansive table filled with a colorful variety of Asian cuisine, beef, fish, pork, and tropical fruit dishes, they returned to the table. Julia dropped the big bag to the floor between her feet. The conversation began again.

Monty picked up where he had ended. "Alicia was offered a teaching position at St. Jude College of Nursing here in Manila, and I was hired onto the Metro Manila police force. I served in uniform for three years and have been a detective for the last ten years. I'm nearing retirement—not by the calendar but due to burn-out." He smiled wryly.

"Do you and your wife have any other children?"

His response was not a direct answer to her question. "My thirteen-year-old has been living with her aunt in Northridge, California, for the past three years. She and her aunt are also members of the Church." He paused so long that Julia thought he had finished speaking, but then he said quietly, "The cost of being an honest cop in an otherwise corrupt world has cost me more than I ever imagined it would." He looked at her and said, as if to close his part of the conversation, "I think it's time for you to do some talking. If you know enough about me now to think that I might be of some use in addressing your 'problem,' then I need to know something about it—and about you."

Julia nodded and put her fork down. She told him about the work she had been doing for the foundation. Then she explained the assignment that had brought her to Manila. She took a photograph of Sophie from her oversized purse and handed it to him. He studied it closely before returning it. She finished telling him what little she knew. "When Mr. Mallon called *Umaga* House, he was told that Sophie's roommate, Lily, was at St. Luke's. She was evidently left in a vacant lot, badly injured. I haven't talked to her yet."

"So, at this point, you really know nothing more than the fact that Sophie has been missing for about a week. Lily is in the hospital, badly injured, and your employer has been waiting for a ransom demand—which has not been forthcoming."

"That about sums it up."

"Do you have adequate funding for this rescue effort?"

"Yes."

"I'll need to take formal leave from the police department while we work on this assignment. That's not a problem. I haven't taken any time off since my wife and son . . ." He caught himself and then said, "For the past three years. Frankly, this assignment may prove to be extremely dangerous. What is your employer willing to pay?"

Twenty-five dollars a day was considered very good pay in the Philippines, but Julia knew he was likely to be worth much, much more than she could ever pay him. After a moment's consideration, she offered, "Two hundred dollars a day, all expenses paid, and a three-thousand dollar bonus, if you're able to get Sophie back alive. Will that be sufficient?"

"Make it five thousand if we get her back alive, and we'll shake on it. If something happens and I can't collect it, I'll give you an account number where it is to be deposited in LA." He spoke with an unexpected grimness.

Changing the subject, he said, "Now, tell me a little more about yourself."

The balance of the evening was spent with him asking questions. When Julia said that she was a widow, he said in genuine sympathy, "You're too young to be a widow. It's hard to lose a companion, but I've noticed that you still wear a wedding band."

She gave a melancholy smile and looked down at the ring on her finger. "I still think of myself as being married." She paused before continuing. "It gives me protection. Men tend to notice the ring before they approach me." She was quiet for a moment before continuing. "Perhaps I'm not as young as you think. I have three children. One of my sons will soon be graduated from the University of Missouri-Columbia, and his younger sister is attending the same university." Monty noticed that she did not make a reference to the other child. "I regret my widowhood and miss my husband—greatly at times." Her voice quivered slightly. "But I'm determined to become a whole person again." Her voice became very quiet and introspective. "It just seems to be taking much longer than I thought."

"What do you mean?"

She looked at him, startled that she had spoken this last thought aloud. But he was patiently waiting for her to continue, and it seemed so easy to talk to him. "Life is a journey that seems to get harder when you suddenly have to travel it alone, especially when you married young. Sometimes you just go through the motions, and people never guess how much you're hurting—not even family." Suddenly, she felt as if she had revealed too much.

Noting her sudden self-consciousness, Monty patted her hand. It was a spontaneously thoughtful act that made her feel as if he genuinely understood. "How did you get a commission like this?"

"I've been wondering that myself." By way of explanation, she continued, "Since I began working for Mr. Mallon and his foundation, I've traveled several times to the Philippines on foundation business, so

I'm fairly comfortable here—and he doesn't expect me to rescue Sophie, just find a qualified man to take the lead in the assignment."

She stopped and looked into his face, wanting an honest answer. "You're willing to do it? You won't have second thoughts?"

He nodded. "No second thoughts."

She was suddenly very relieved, as if someone had offered to share a heavy burden. "How long do you think it will take to find Sophie and get her back? This is such an urgent matter."

"It's important that we build bridges before we try to cross them. It's also important that you put the matter entirely in my hands and let me do the worrying."

She nodded. "I'll try." She took a deep breath and changed the subject. "You spoke of losing a companion as though you have experienced it. Have you lost your wife?"

His voice dropped. "Yes, and my son." He added, "I thought it wise to send my daughter to the U.S. after her mother died. I see her once a year."

They were both quiet while they tasted the crème brûlée dessert, and then she spoke again, "Do you have any theories about what might have happened to Sophie?"

"Several, but before forming any firm opinions, I need to speak with Lily and read the police file that was probably started when the kidnapping was reported. The file should be available through the NAKTF." Seeing her eyebrows go up at the use of that acronym, he elaborated, "The National Anti-Kidnapping Task Force. I won't take any leave until I've read all the police reports. In the morning, I'll pick you up in an unmarked car at nine o'clock, and we'll visit Lily at St. Luke's. Were you given any other names of individuals who may be of help?"

"Yes, in addition to your name, I have the name and telephone number of an investigative reporter at the *Manila Standard Bulletin* and a man by the name of Matson at the U.S. Embassy—and the telephone number of Justice Molina, if I need it."

"Set up an appointment for us to meet the reporter tomorrow after we have talked with Lily, if you can. I'll try to set up a meeting with the man at the embassy," Monty instructed.

By this time the dining room had begun to fill with well-dressed Filipinos and a few Japanese, Korean, and American tourists. Monty stood, and the waiter started toward their table with the bill. As the waiter neared the table, Monty said, "What's your room number?"

"Three fourteen."

When the waiter set the little tray with the bill on the table, Monty wrote Julia's room number on it and signed it in an almost indecipherable script. Then he dropped a one-hundred-peso bill on the table, a standard amount for a tip.

Julia decided to ask him one last question. When they reached the lobby, she turned, impulsively put a hand on his arm, and asked, "Why do you continue to live here in the Philippines instead of moving to America to be with your daughter?"

"Here, I have a better chance of finding the man or men who killed my wife and son. If I return to the U.S., they win."

7

SOPHIE KNELT BESIDE THE BOY, and in the weak light of the two kerosene lamps, she carefully examined the wound, trying to determine how deep the bullet had penetrated. "Do you have a flashlight so I can see the wound better?" The guard did not respond.

The boy moaned. "The bullet seems to have hit the rib just below his collarbone, but I don't think it penetrated his lung. He seems to be breathing okay. If these wounds had received proper care, they never would have become so seriously infected." Sophie looked at Carlita and continued quietly, "I don't know if we can keep him alive until they bring back the medical supplies. He's got a raging fever." Looking at the guard, she asked, "Has the boy eaten today?" The man who had said he spoke "a little English" looked at her blankly, so she tried her limited Tagalog again. "*Pagkain ng lalaki sa ngayón?* Has the boy been able to eat?"

He responded in his also-limited Tagalog, *"Hindi, sakít."* No, he hadn't.

Sophie shook her head and told Carlita, "I'm not surprised that he's been too sick to eat. How can I give him any antibiotics—that is, if they get any? If we can get him to take some amoxicillin, it will probably tear up his stomach and make him vomit." The women continued to wash the boy in the hope of lowering his temperature. When he began to shake with chills, they tried to find something to cover him. There was nothing. She looked at the man and said, "Blanket." He simply stood there. *"Malamig sa lalaki."* Then she raised her voice in frustration, "The boy is cold." The man did not move. She stood, and ignoring the gun barrel he pointed at her, she demanded, "Get Hamal!" Sophie's rising anger finally drove him out of the hut.

He returned a few minutes later with Hamal. "What do you want, woman?"

"I need better light. Do you have a good flashlight I can use?"

"We need the batteries for other things." His voice was firm.

Sophie dropped her head and shook it in frustration. "When was he shot?"

"Ten days ago."

"He's having chills and needs a blanket to keep him warm. Is there anything in this camp to use to keep him warm?"

Hamal left and returned with a well-worn jacket he had taken from one of the other men. He handed it to Sophie who laid it over the boy. "You will save him," he stated.

Looking at him with fire in her eyes, she said tersely, "We will try. It would be easier if you would give us a guard who can speak English."

Hamal spoke briefly to the man and then motioned for him to leave the hut. Within a minute, another man entered and Hamal left. "I am Benito. I speak English." Sophie was a little surprised at the man who looked at least ten or fifteen years older than the other men in the group, none of whom looked much more than thirty.

"Good. I need boiled water so I can wash the boy's wound. The river water is not clean." She handed him the pot of river water.

He muttered something about a crazy woman as he stepped out of the hut and handed the pot to another man. The pot was brought back to the hut when the water was hot, but Sophie was sure it had not had time to boil. "Boil the water, make it boil." As she talked, she churned her hands as if to show him what she meant. "And get us some clean rags."

The man looked at Benito and asked, *"Kumulô?"* Benito nodded and answered, "Yes, boil the water."

When the water had cooled sufficiently, Sophie and Carlita gently tried to clean the festering bullet wound with a nearly clean T-shirt they had been given. "We need to get that bullet out," Sophie said mostly to herself.

Carlita's eyes grew wide, and she asked, "How?"

"I wish I knew." Sophie gently probed around the wound and finally found a lump under the flesh. "I think I've found the bullet." Carefully squeezing the lump under the skin of the boy's shoulder, she looked up at Benito and said, "Wash your knife in the hot water. I need it."

He looked at her and shook his head. Angry with the uncooperative attitude she seemed to meet at every turn, she raised her voice. "If the boy dies, it will be your fault. Give me the knife so I can get the bullet out!" Looking at her and then out of the door of the hut as though he was not sure what to do, he finally pulled an old USMC combat knife out of his belt and handed it to her. Then he pointed the gun at her, and said, "I will shoot you if you try to escape."

Ignoring his threat, she dropped to her knees and washed the knife in the pot of warm water. As much as she wanted the knife blade boiled, she had fought one battle over the water and felt she would not win another.

"Hold him down so he can't move." Carlita carefully pinned the boy's shoulders down. Sophie took hold of the lump under the flesh, and with the point of the knife, she penetrated the skin. The boy moaned and tried to move, but Carlita held the weakened boy still. Sophie carefully made a small incision in the flesh. Then she squeezed underneath the bullet and gradually forced it out. She put pressure on the wound to stop the bleeding, making the boy moan again. After a few minutes, she ordered Carlita to cut the shirt she had used as a rag into strips, and she bound the boy's shoulder and upper arm. Then she handed the knife back to Benito, sat back against the wall of the hut, and wiped the perspiration from her forehead with the back of her hand. "Now, somehow, we have got to get some food into him."

After a minute or two of rest, she faced Benito again. "When the rice is boiled, tell them to save some of the water for the boy. We will try to get him to drink it."

Benito looked at her as if she were stupid. "When the rice is boiled, the water is gone."

"Not if they put more water in the pot than the rice will need. Do you understand? Have them put more water in the pot than they usually do."

Benito shrugged and stepped to the doorway of the hut. He spoke briefly in Cebuano to another man. Then he turned to Sophie. "We will see." While they waited for the rice to boil, the guard sat on the porch and read from a small book he carried in his shirt pocket.

In about half an hour, Yusuf brought a dirty cup half full of rice water for the boy. The two women lifted him up into a nearly sitting position, and Sophie coaxed him to sufficient consciousness to get him to swallow most of the warm water from the rice.

To keep him alert enough to drink, she asked, "What is your name?" He didn't seem to hear. "What is your name? I am Sophie." Between swallows, he whispered, "Daud." When they laid him down, he drifted off into unconsciousness again.

That night the other hostages were herded into the hut. Four of the captors slept on the porch with weapons at their sides. Chang and his daughter had to sleep back-to-back in the middle of the split bamboo floor with Dangwa on one side, between Chang and the injured boy, and Sophie and Carlita on the other side of Emily. Their captors were adamant that according to Muslim law the men and women in the hut had to be separated as they slept. The body heat in the crowded hut afforded some protection against the chill breezes that blew through the forest before sunrise.

8

WHEN THEY REACHED THE LOBBY, Monty shook Julia's hand and then moved toward the door with a stride that reflected the confidence of years of carrying authority. She was impressed with this well-spoken man with sculptured cheekbones, slightly almond eyes, and skin the color of a deep Pebble Beach tan. His broad shoulders and solid build reflected a muscular strength that she knew might be needed on the assignment he had just accepted.

She watched him until he disappeared into the darkness outside. She intensely hoped that he would prove as competent as her first impression of him suggested he would be—so much would depend on it.

She returned to her room and called the reporter. After Estilita Roque answered, Julia explained how she had come by her name as someone who might be able to be of assistance. They agreed to meet at her office about eleven the next morning.

That night Julia paced in the hotel room until nearly midnight, pausing to step out onto the little balcony on more than one occasion, unable to sleep, troubled by what might lie ahead, especially for Sophie. The moon was just a sliver in the east, and she noted that through the haze of polluted air that perpetually hung over the Metro Manila area during the dry months, the stars were like scattered pinpricks in black construction paper, the light shining through weakly from the other side.

***

When Monty arrived in the morning at about nine, Julia was pleased to see that he was driving a department car, a Hyundai Sonata that was only two years old. He was wearing the impeccably fitted gray suit he had worn the previous evening. The French cuffs of his pale blue dress shirt were fitted with pearl cuff links.

As she got into the car, she said, "We have an appointment with the reporter at eleven."

"Tell me about this reporter."

"Her name is Estilita Roque. I don't know anything else, except that she was recommended to my employer by Justice Molina as someone with useful connections."

After hearing her name, he smiled with a grim satisfaction. "I've known her by reputation for the last several years. She will get herself killed eventually. She plays hardball with powerful people, some of whom may not hesitate to put out a contract on her some day."

He continued, "She used to be a lower-level official in the Agriculture Department but left governmental service disgusted by the abuse of power and bribe-taking. She approached the editor at the *Philippine Standard Bulletin* and asked if she could get a job working as an investigative reporter to expose corruption in government." Monty laughed quietly and added, "No editor was going to refuse that kind of an offer, so she was hired on the spot. Her stories are usually exposés of governmental corruption, but despite the evidence she accumulates, the cases seldom move into the courts. Where large amounts of money are involved, judges and juries can sometimes be purchased wholesale."

Saturday traffic was a little lighter than usual, so the trip to St. Luke's Medical Center on East Rodriguez Avenue in Quezon City went more quickly than might have been expected. When Monty halted the car at a stoplight, a thin beggar woman of indefinable age, wrinkled and sunburned almost black, hurried off the curb with a stiff-legged, limping walk. She knocked on the window of the passenger-side door and put out a dirty paper cup, hoping for a few coins. Julia reached into the big handbag and pulled out a small coin purse. She pressed the button that rolled down the window with a quiet whir and emptied her coin purse into the woman's cup. The old woman nodded at her and offered a nearly toothless smile of thanks.

As the window closed, Monty grinned and shook his head. "I didn't see that. If anyone asks, I was looking out of the driver's-side window."

"She was in such desperate need. I couldn't turn her down."

"I appreciate your compassion, but begging is illegal in Metro Manila. But as I pointed out, I didn't see it." He grinned again.

In the entrance foyer of the five-story hospital, beautifully designed with green marble floors and wainscoting, Monty asked for the room number of Lily Corbano. The staffers only looked at one another. After he showed his badge, they quickly gave him the number and directions on how to find the room in the large hospital. He was moving across the marble floor before they had finished the directions. A uniformed police officer stood outside her door. To access the room, Monty showed his badge again.

The young woman's right leg was suspended above the bed in a cast, her tibia held together with screws. The bruises on her cheekbone and upper arms were turning green. After they had introduced themselves and explained their mission, she cried and apologized repeatedly. "This is my fault. I know it's my fault. I should not have answered the man when he spoke to us. When Sophie tried to hurry me away, I was too slow. I'm afraid she is dead, and it's my fault."

Monty patted her hand, and his manner calmed her. "There was nothing you could have done. Don't blame yourself. Just tell us everything you can."

Lily smiled tentatively through her tears, and she recounted what little she could remember. She described the two men, including the crooked nose of the one and the scar on the face of the other. "They were Pakistani or Malay, I think. They spoke Cebuano to each other. They spoke English with an accent. Do you think they kidnapped Sophie for a ransom?"

"Possibly."

"You will get her back?" she asked hopefully.

"We'll do everything we can to get her back," Monty answered.

She was tiring quickly, so they thanked her and excused themselves. As they started down the hall toward the elevator, Julia asked, "Do you think Lily's life is in danger?"

"Apparently someone does, or there wouldn't be a uniformed officer outside her door. But when she goes home, she'll be on her own." There were two other people in the elevator, so they rode in silence down to the street level. As they left the elevator, he said, "I doubt that Lily is a threat to them—they probably think she's dead. If they thought she was alive and a threat, they would have killed her by now. That uniform outside of her room would be very little deterrent."

They drove to the address given by Estilita Roque, which was the office of the *Standard Bulletin* located in Makati City, the heart of the business community. She met them at the front door of the two-story building, above which was inscribed, "Balanced, News, Fearless Views." She was a diminutive Filipina, no more than five feet tall with a short, spiky hairstyle and blue eye shadow that glittered. She wore a short, tight skirt and spiked heels.

When Monty introduced himself and Julia, Estilita put out her hand. "I've heard of you. I'm very glad to meet a man whose honesty is so well known that I have heard it ridiculed."

"And I've heard the same about you," he responded with a very charming smile.

She led them to a lounge–lunch room on the second floor, where—because it was early in the day for a newspaper with an evening deadline—they could talk without being overheard. She walked very quickly, as if she were wound with tight springs.

She pointed at two chairs for her visitors. She sat down on the couch that faced her two visitors and folded her legs on the couch cushions. After hearing what Julia had told Monty the evening before, she responded, "Sounds like *Abu Sayyaf.* The kidnapping went too smoothly for it to have been the MNLF. Right now they are too disorganized to have pulled off something like this."

Julia looked at Monty. He explained the acronym. "The MNLF is the Moro National Liberation Front. It's a small, fiercely independent Islamic organization in the western peninsula of Mindanao. Sometimes they work with *Abu Sayyaf,* and sometimes they compete with them."

Julia's heart had sunk at the mention of *Abu Sayyaf.* She had read enough in the English language newspapers of Manila on previous visits to know of *Abu Sayyaf* and its ties to al-Qaida. A group such as this might be willing to kill the granddaughter of an American businessman and forgo any ransom just to make a point.

The conversation ended with a promise from Estilita that she would contact some of her sources in Mindinao and see if any of them had heard about the young kidnapped American woman. "My sources will be more forthcoming if I can offer them a monetary inducement."

Julia swung the big bag from off her shoulder and reached into the wallet. "What do you need?"

Estilita thought for a moment and then said, "Two hundred dollars should be enough."

"You prefer American money?"

"Always."

Julia took out four fifties and handed them to her, adding, "Thank you for any help you can give us."

"You will hear from me when I have anything to report. If there is a story in this, you will consider it mine?"

"Of course," they both responded.

As they returned to the car, which was parked illegally in front of the building, Julia said, "Two hundred dollars doesn't seem like much to get vital information."

He answered, "Even fifty dollars goes a long way in this part of the world. If it requires more, she'll let us know."

Julia asked, "When are we going to meet with the man at the U.S. Embassy?"

Monty looked at his watch. "Right now. We may be a bit early, but I think he'll forgive us."

9

As Monty comfortably navigated the busy streets, finally turning onto Roxas Boulevard not far from the Manila Hotel, Julia was surprised to discover that the U.S. Embassy sat inconspicuously back off the boulevard to the west between the street and Manila Bay. She had unknowingly passed it on many occasions on previous visits. It overlooked the water, protected by a wall with a large wrought-iron gate across the driveway.

Monty spoke to the marine at the gate. "We have an appointment with your security chief, Captain Gary Matson." They were requested to show their identification, and then the gate swung open to neatly manicured grounds filled with a profusion of color: patches of red, pink, and white bougainvillea; red hibiscus; and creamy gardenias in bloom. From the top of the flagpole, the Stars and Stripes lifted and rolled in the breeze. Julia was caught off guard by the sudden tightening in her throat.

"Sir, if you will report to the sergeant in the foyer, he will lead you to Captain Matson's office."

Monty put the car in the small parking lot at one end of the building.

The foyer of the embassy was quietly elegant, with a marble floor, potted palms, and a few heavy mahogany tables with brocade table runners and fresh flowers, but Matson's office was plain and utilitarian, suitable for a marine. Olive green, three-drawer file cabinets lined one wall. The military-issued desk and two chairs for guests took up most of the floor space. The captain rose from where he sat behind the desk as the sergeant showed Julia and Monty into the office. Even if he had been in civilian clothes, his military haircut would have given away his profession. "Close the door, Sergeant," he said as the man exited the office.

Offering his hand, he said, "Well, Detective Montalbon, I haven't seen you since President Arroyo's Christmas reception last year, where I believe you were part of the security detail." He turned to Julia and put his hand out.

As she shook it, she introduced herself.

"What brings you here to the embassy?" He took in both of them with his gaze.

Monty spoke. "I've been asked to assist in locating a young American nurse, Sophie Adamson, who was kidnapped nine or ten days ago. Do you know the case?"

"Yes, I'm familiar with it." He motioned for them to be seated and then sat behind the desk once more. "From your presence here, it's apparent that Miss Adamson's family or friends have chosen not to use traditional methods to locate her." Looking at Monty, he asked, "Has there been a ransom demand? We haven't heard of any."

Monty shook his head. "Not to our knowledge. Do you have someone at the CIA monitoring *Radyo Agong* and any satellite phone usage in that area?" Matson nodded. Monty continued, "We're hoping that the kidnappers don't know who she is. We think they may have taken her because they need a nurse. She was wearing scrubs at the time of the kidnapping. What we need from you is information. Do you know who might be behind the kidnapping and where she might be?"

Matson rubbed his chin and looked out the window at the water of the bay before answering. "We think we've discovered her location. The satellite phone chatter among the al-Qaida groups on the peninsula and Basilan increased about the time she was taken, and our interpreter said there was talk of 'an American infidel woman who would lick the wounds of the martyrs.' We have concluded that they were referring to a nurse to treat their wounded."

"Seems likely," Monty agreed.

"What wounded are they referring to?" Julia asked.

"The recent increase in the 'round-trip' kidnappings on the Zamboangan Peninsula has caused an outcry by the families of the victims, and some of the local officials are demanding government action to end the problem, so at the present, the AFP—Armed Forces of the Philippines—have been putting on a hard press against the Islamic terrorists on Mindanao. There have been casualties on both sides."

Julia interrupted by asking, "Round-trip kidnappings?"

Matson laughed. "Monty, maybe you need to tell her about them."

Monty smiled cynically. "Kidnappings in the Zamboangan Peninsula have become so common the last few years that riders on crowded jeepneys simply trying to get to work are sometimes taken captive in the morning and are ransomed by late afternoon by friends and family. They are often back home by evening, thus the title 'round-trip' kidnappings. The ransoms are usually not more than a few thousand pesos as these are not wealthy people. We know this is one way the MNLF funds its activities when its members are not running drugs to support their activities. The *Abu Sayyaf* groups are more demanding, seeking much larger ransoms in addition to running drugs."

"So you believe that Sophie was kidnapped to give medical care to wounded members of *Abu Sayyaf*." Julia's words were more a statement than a question.

"Yes, that's our guess," Matson responded.

"Then, in all likelihood, they don't know that she's the granddaughter of a wealthy American businessman?" Julia did not know whether to be relieved or to be more concerned. The request for a straight-forward ransom would be more easily dealt with.

Matson nodded. "That's right."

She continued, "And you think you know where she is?"

"If we're right and she's in the hands of the *Abu Sayyaf*, then we can track the signal of the satphone used by the leader of that group, at least part of the time. The only problem is that there are several *Abu Sayyaf* groups, at least two on the peninsula and one on Basilan and another on the island of Jolo. If we're wrong and she's in the hands of the MNLF, then we will have more difficulty locating her as they usually use prepaid cell phones that we can't track."

Julia looked up at him, her eyes flashing. "If you've been able to track these groups and you think you know where she is, why haven't you gone in to get her? She's an American citizen."

"Mrs. Wentworth, the 1946 Philippine Constitution has a clause in it that prevents foreign troops from fighting on Philippine soil. We must honor that restriction. If we don't, we will rupture our relations with this government, and they are a good ally in this part of the world."

"But I understand there are hundreds of American troops in Mindanao. What are they doing there?"

"They're military advisors teaching strategy and techniques, but when it comes to the actual conflict with the *Abu Sayyaf*, the AFP is in charge.

If it were different, then that terrible fiasco with the Burnhams back in 2002 would never have happened." Matson looked from Monty to Julia and asked, "Do you remember that situation?" Monty nodded.

While Julia searched her memory, Matson explained, "The Burnhams were Christian missionaries who had spent several years in the Philippines, raising their kids here while Martin Burnham worked as a bush pilot, flying medicine and food to remote areas and bringing out sick or injured natives for medical treatment. They took a break from their work to celebrate a wedding anniversary on Palawan in 2001. The *Abu Sayyaf* took them and about a dozen other hostages from the Dos Palmas resort. Though two of the male hostages were beheaded and another badly wounded, eventually each of the other hostages were ransomed by family and friends with the exception of Martin, his wife, Gracia, and Ediborah Yap, a Filipino nurse whom one of the kidnappers had claimed as a wife. The ransom for the Burnhams was paid twice, but the kidnappers still refused to let them go, insisting that they could still get more money for them."

At that point, Monty took up the narration. "After a year of captivity, in a botched rescue attempt, the AFP mistakenly shot all three of the hostages as well as some of the Abu men, killing Martin and Ediborah. I'm not going to let anything like that happen again—if I can help it. "

Julia asked, "What happened to Gracia?"

Matson continued, "Gracia's leg wound wasn't life threatening, and she went home to Kansas and her family. In addition to the satphone the leader had been using, the CIA had tracked the movements of that group of *Abu Sayyaf* with a UAV." He paused and explained for Julia's benefit, "Unmanned aerial vehicle—a remote-controlled drone."

"Our government has drones over here?" Julia asked.

Matson glanced at her and then continued as if she had not interrupted his thoughts. "If the Philippine government had given the okay, we could have had them out of there before the *Abu Sayyaf* knew what hit, but we never received a green light from the Presidential Palace. Martin Burnham and the nurse paid the price." He rubbed his forehead for a moment before he looked up and said, "I suspect that if Monty has his way, the AFP won't be part of this rescue effort."

Monty simply gave one short, quick nod. "Can you tell me where the most likely group of *Abu Sayyaf* is located, and do you have any information on the number of men in the group?"

"Give me a few minutes." Matson rose and exited the office. When he returned, he handed a copy of a document on U.S. State Department letterhead to Monty, who read it quickly and then handed it back. "Keep your source confidential," Matson said.

"No problem."

Monty stood, and Julia followed suit. As they turned to leave the office, Matson stopped them. "Keep me in the loop, if you can. Maybe I can be of use to you."

"We will if you'll give me your cell number."

Matson wrote the number down and handed the paper to Monty. He slipped it into his pocket.

Julia thanked the officer. "Thank you for your time, Captain. Your help is deeply appreciated."

As they pulled into traffic on Roxas Boulevard, Julia asked, "Where do we go from here?"

Monty was deep in thought and did not seem to hear her. After a few minutes, he said, "Let's get something to eat. Do you have a cell phone with you?"

"Yes, I have my Blackberry. I keep it for local calls. Do you prefer it to the satphone?"

"It'll be better for some purposes. Each has its own uses."

"You don't have a cell of your own?"

"It's property of the Metro Police Department. When I take leave, I'll have to turn both the cell and the car over to my temporary replacement."

Monty found a parking place near a small Chinese restaurant on Taft Avenue. They were shown to a table on a quiet patio where palm fronds, split-leaf philodendrons, and ficuses nodded in the garden that surrounded the tables. Monty ordered sweet-and-sour chicken, calamari, and fried rice for both of them, looking at Julia to see if it met with her approval. He smiled. "You'll like the food here. The owner is my cousin on my mother's side. But it would be a good place to eat even if he weren't a relative."

While they waited for their food, Monty took Julia's cell phone and made a call. "Hey, Rick, it's Monty, a voice from your past. Give me a return call ASAP."

"Is that someone who can help us?" Julia asked as he disconnected the call.

"I think so. He's an old friend from my special forces days. His name is Ricardo Calvin. His father was a U.S. Army grunt who stayed in the islands after the end of the Vietnam conflict, married a Filipina, and had nine kids. Rick was the oldest and married the only daughter of a wealthy Chinoy businessman who owns a string of computer shops here in the islands. Now that he has married into money, Rick only does what he chooses to do—and just enough of that to stave off boredom. If we're lucky, he'll find what we're up to interesting enough to join us."

While they ate, Mr. Wu, Monty's cousin, appeared quietly at the table like a well-dressed wraith. Monty pushed back his chair, and the two men bowed and then embraced. They spoke briefly in what Julia thought sounded like Cantonese. Mr. Wu bowed deeply to Julia and then hurried away.

"Does your cousin speak English?" Julia asked with a raised eyebrow.

"Of course, but he thinks the less he speaks it, the more atmosphere it lends his establishment—you know, the inscrutable Asian thing." They both chuckled. Julia thought, *I've laughed again. I'm glad I haven't forgotten how.*

As they ate, she asked, "Why did Captain Matson avoid my question about the drones?"

"I'm sure that any information about the use of predator drones is classified, even though it's widely known that the U.S. uses them here in the Philippines for tracking Islamic extremists and in hostage situations. They've been predominantly used in Afghanistan and Pakistan, but they're often flown into other hot spots in Asia."

"Does the U.S. have air bases here for them?"

"I don't know where they're hangered, but they're controlled out of Nellis Air Base in Nevada, near Las Vegas."

"They're controlled from Nevada? I know it is a cliché, but I've got to say it, 'Will wonders never cease?'" Julia said in amazement.

Monty grinned. "I sure hope not."

Rick returned the phone call before they had finished their dessert of glazed bananas, a gift their host insisted they try. When Monty ended the call, he offered the Blackberry to Julia, but she said, "Why don't you keep it for now. I've got the satphone."

He nodded and dropped it into his shirt pocket. "Rick will join us tomorrow morning at seven o'clock in the foyer of the hotel. We'll talk over breakfast."

As he pulled the car underneath the hotel portico, she opened the door. "What's your phone number?" he asked.

Julia reached into her bag to get a pen and paper to write it down, but he said, "Just tell me the number. You don't need to write it down. I'll remember it."

She repeated the twelve-digit number of her satphone, which she had made the effort to memorize, and he repeated it back to her with ease. She closed the door, and he drove away. Little did he realize that her hope followed him.

As she rose to the third floor of the hotel in the elevator, she realized that she had been more relaxed in Monty's presence than she had been since she had been widowed. *He's easy to be around*, she thought with pleasure.

That evening she called her employer and reported on what had taken place to that point in time. "I'm impressed with Mr. Montalbon. He seems to be a capable man."

"Good. I have to trust your judgment in this matter."

10

AT SEVEN O'CLOCK THE NEXT morning, Julia recognized Monty coming toward her across the lobby. He was talking to the man at his side, whose light complexion was testimony to his American-Filipino parentage. When they reached Julia, Monty motioned toward his companion. "This is an old friend, Julia. Meet Ricardo Calvin, better known as Rick." The man was dressed in a pale cream-colored barong made of pineapple fiber and dark slacks, the most formal dress in the islands. "As you can see, he dressed up for this meeting. I have told him enough about you that he wanted to wear his best." There was a gentle, slightly mocking tone in Monty's voice.

Rick smiled and bowed slightly. "He's not exaggerating, Mrs. Wentworth."

Julia was not sure how she fit into this subtle, verbal teasing between the two men, so she said simply, "I'm flattered, Mr. Calvin. Thank you for joining us."

"Please call me Rick."

"And call me Julia."

Monty motioned toward the dining room that was crowded with Sunday morning visitors. During a breakfast of omelets as fine as any made in a European restaurant, Rick reconfirmed that he had served with Monty, though neither got very specific as to where or how. With very little encouragement, she told him of the task she had been given and her need for expert help.

Rick said nothing for a few minutes while he ate. Then he put down his fork and grinned at his old army buddy. "I think this sounds like an adventure worth my time. Count me in."

"Will your wife object? This may be a dangerous 'adventure,' as you call it," Julia asked.

"No, she's in San Francisco waiting for the delivery of her youngest niece's baby. She won't be home for a few weeks." He laughed wholeheartedly. "My father-in-law has been threatening to put me to work managing one of his computer stores if I didn't find something to keep me busy." Looking at Monty, he added, "Where do we go from here?" Julia noted that he did not ask about payment.

During the meal, Rick had kept one leg or the other bouncing slightly under the table in an unconscious drumbeat. Julia noted that where Monty seemed to be a controlled, focused personality, Rick appeared to be restless, filled with an electric energy. *An interesting combination*, Julia thought as she looked from one man to the other.

Monty put down his fork. "I need at least one more good man, or preferably two, if we can find them. The prerequisites are American military training, Filipino citizenship, dependability, and," he added with a smile, "not a whit of common sense, as things may get tough. Do you have any suggestions?"

Rick thought for a moment. "Filipino citizenship?"

Monty nodded. "If things get hot, we don't want to initiate an international incident by using non-Filipinos."

Rick grinned broadly. "This is sounding more and more interesting." He paused and thought for another moment. "Did you ever meet Bill Jackson? He was a cook in the U.S. Navy during the Vietnam conflict. He's from Iowa, but he married a Filipina after his time was up and settled up near the old Clark Air Base at Angles with a bunch of other American military expats. His retirement goes a lot farther there than it would in the U.S."

Monty shook his head. "Don't know him."

"He had a flock of kids, but the ones who might be useful are his two youngest sons, twins who enlisted in the U.S. Navy up at Subic in 1991 when they were just barely seventeen, about a week before Mt. Pinatubo blew its top. The eruption closed the base, so they were shipped to Norfolk, Virginia, and trained as SEALS." He looked at Julia and smiled as if at a private joke. "After they finished their four years and obtained their U.S. citizenship, they each thought they wanted to find an American girl to marry and settle in California, but once they saw the cost of living there, they hurried home and each married a pretty Filipina. They both live in Cagayan de Oro on Mindanao."

"How did they make it into the SEALS? Most Filipinos are just too short to pass the entrance tests," Monty said.

"You've got to know Bill Jackson, their dad. He's six-foot-five and two hundred and sixty pounds, so his kids are tall by anyone's standards. He raised those kids like they were in the military. It was up every day at six in the morning and twenty pushups for the boys and ten for the girls and then thirty minutes of reading the Bible. They marched in line to mass every Sunday. They said, 'Yes, sir' and 'No, sir.' Now the kids are all married and even the grandkids know to answer him respectfully."

"Sounds like they may be of use, especially if they speak Cebuano. What are the chances they'd be willing to join us?"

"Who knows? Let's see if I can raise one or the other of them."

"What're their names?" Monty asked.

"Don't know their given names. They've always been called Bing and Bolly." Rick pulled out a cell phone and, after making several calls, finally had the number of Bing Jackson on Mindanao. Looking at Monty, he said, "What do you want me to ask him?"

"Ask him to meet us for dinner tomorrow evening. If he can get his brother to join us, that would be better yet. He can pick a restaurant in Cagayan de Oro."

He dialed the number and talked for a few minutes with Bing. When he finished, he looked from Monty to Julia. "It's all set up. He's sure he can get his brother to join us as his most recent business venture just folded. They'll expect to be paid." He looked at Julia.

She nodded. "Of course." She turned to Monty. "Then we're flying down to Mindanao right away?"

"Yes. I've looked into chartering a plane. We can leave tomorrow afternoon. I'll give you a phone call when the time is firm. That works for both of you, I hope?"

With a nod all around, the three stood, and the waiter hurried to the table with the bill. After Rick had left, Monty turned to Julia while they stood in the lobby. "I'll need enough money to cover the cost of the charter flight and other expenses; let's start with twenty-five hundred dollars. If you have it in pesos, just make it fifty thousand pesos. That's close enough."

Stepping into an alcove just off the lobby for more privacy, Julia fished around in her large bag. Knowing that he would need money to move the rescue effort forward, she had taken the time that morning to band the bills into bundles of ten thousand pesos each. She pulled the money out of the oversized purse and handed the requested amount to him in five bundles. "Let me know if you need more."

He nodded and took his leave. As he moved through the hotel lobby and out the door, his mind was already moving from the first challenge of finding the men for the task to locating the equipment that would be needed.

Monty spent much of the balance of that Sunday on the telephone firming the arrangements for the charter flight and for a special package Matson was willing to arrange to have delivered to Camp Evangelista, the largest military base on Mindanao.

***

As it was only eight-thirty, Julia had the concierge at the desk call a cab so she could attend church services in Makati at the little white chapel, the first built by the Church in the Philippines several decades earlier. It sat nestled among tall, high-rise buildings in the Makati business district on property that had steadily increased in value and was now probably worth millions. The louvered windows were tipped open to a slight breeze, and the temperature in the building was almost pleasant. The meeting was conducted in what was smilingly referred to as "Tagalish," a mixture of Tagalog and English, with a little Spanish thrown in. She was able to translate enough to understand that the subject of the talk was the payment of tithing, a very difficult concept in a country where many of the people only get one meal a day, and some have to choose between eating on Sunday or paying a tricycle driver to take them to church. Her attention began to wander, and her thoughts turned to Sophie and her situation. She bowed her head and fervently prayed that a way would be opened to rescue her. She ended her mental prayer by adding, *Heavenly Father, please rescue Aaron, as well.* She suddenly felt very guilty that she hadn't thought of him for the last couple of days.

After the meeting, several members of the congregation crowded around her and welcomed her back, remembering her from previous visits. *How I love these sweet and gentle people—despite the occasional dangers and difficulties in these islands.*

As she rode back to the hotel in another cab, her thoughts were taken up with the contrasts that are part of the Philippine culture and economy. While international businesses were housed in the skyscrapers that were built as the economy of the islands and the world rebounded after World War II, the vast majority of the people saw very few of the benefits.

As the cab drove into the temporary darkness of an underpass and the driver stopped at a red light on the other side, the street vendors flowed around the halted vehicles like a surging river, offering everything from fresh vegetables to printed T-shirts. Julia's heart was touched when she saw a little girl about eight years old knocking on the windows of the cabs and other vehicles, offering sweet-smelling, white Sampaguita blooms in the hope of receiving a coin. As she neared the cab, Julia rolled down the window and offered her a twenty-five peso coin and took one of the wilted blooms. The child's charming smile was sufficient thanks. Its fragrance quickly filled the cab. *How hard these people work to provide for themselves and their families. If only the foundation could assist more of them.*

While the cab threaded its way through the traffic, Julia's thoughts continued to dwell on the contrasts in the culture—contrasts as pronounced as day and night, wealth and poverty, a culture like a two-sided coin: one side bright and the other dark and tarnished.

After she returned to the hotel, she spent much of the rest of the day reading the Qur'an. As she read, she thought, *I wonder how much Sophie remembers of what we learned about Islam in my institute class on world religions.*

Both she and Rick received a call that evening to tell them that the charter flight was arranged for one o'clock the next afternoon and would leave from the Cebu Pacific Airlines terminal at Aquino Airport. Monty stated that he would pick Julia up by taxi at noon after she had checked out of the hotel. Rick would meet them at the terminal.

11

THE TWO MEN SENT TO obtain medical supplies arrived just before dark the next day. Sophie and Carlita carefully washed the infected wound with the hydrogen peroxide and wrapped the boy's shoulder and upper arm in clean bandages. The men had not brought any medical tape, so Sophie looked at Benito and asked, "Is there anything in the camp to use to hold the bandages in place . . . some kind of tape?"

"Duck tape. Duck tape good for many things."

"Please get me some duct tape then." He stepped to the doorway and spoke to one of the men sitting on the porch. The man returned in a few minutes with a battered roll of the shiny gray tape. After she taped the bandages in place, Sophie encouraged Daud to drink some rice water, and after he had eaten a little rice, she insisted that he take one of the amoxicillin tablets the men had brought back. As Julia adjusted the blanket the men had brought back with them, the boy whispered weakly, "*Salamat po.*" She knew the thank you that included the respectful *"po"* was the first and likely the only sign of respect that she was going to receive in her present situation, and it made tears come suddenly to her eyes.

***

The next morning, after the prayers, Hamal announced that they would be "mobiling." Sophie looked at Benito. "Mobiling? Does he mean we're going to move?"

Benito answered belligerently, "Yes, the men saw some soldiers when they came back yesterday. We will go higher into the forest in the mountains."

"But Daud is not ready to be moved. He is too weak."

"Hamal has said we will move, so we will move. We will carry the boy."

"How?" Sophie asked incredulously.

Benito stepped out of the hut and gave orders to one of the men sitting there. In a few minutes, the man came back to the hut with two six-foot-long bamboo poles. Behind him were three other men. Benito pulled two *malongs* from a pack of supplies in the corner of the hut. The poles were put into the *malongs*, which were simply forty-inch tubes of coarse cotton material about a yard wide with the ends sewn together, making a simple stretcher.

By midday the heat, humidity, and hard climbing without anything to eat left the hostages weak and exhausted. Sophie stopped, pulled the rope off her wrist that was little more than a symbol of the subservience of the captives, and stepped out of line to wait until Hamal reached her. "We can't go on without some rest, and Daud must have something to eat or I can't give him his medicine."

Hamal looked at her with narrowed eyes. "Woman, you are trouble."

"Am I trouble because I speak the truth?" she responded, trying not to show any intimidation.

He looked around at the group and said loud enough for all to hear, "We will stop at the top of the next hill." Then he looked at her. "What is your name, woman? I need to know the name of any woman who is so much trouble."

"My name is Sophie . . . actually, Sophia." Then she added, "Is it trouble to save your son?"

Hamal gave one great contemptuous "ha" on a burst of air. "Do you know that your name means 'wisdom'?"

"So I've been told."

"Then be more wise and speak with the humility of a wise woman."

"If I speak with humility, will you still listen to me?"

"Maybe." He pushed her back into the line with the barrel of his gun.

When camp was made that evening, several of the men located trees suitable for tying up their sleeping hammocks. The exhausted and hungry hostages sat on the ground to rest. When Yusuf walked by, Sophie asked, "Are you going to let us starve? Hostages dead from starvation will bring a poor ransom." Yusuf looked at her with angry eyes. She continued, "Mr. Chang is too old and weak to live long enough to bring you a ransom if he is not fed."

His eyes flashed. "Shut up, woman. You are only *sabaya*." He looked at her for a moment and then pointed to her wristwatch. "Give it to me."

"What? You want my watch?" She was startled by the pettiness of the request. She had only paid 500 pesos to a street vendor for it.

He said, "Let me see it. I give you my OPM."

"What is your OPM?"

"'Oh promise me,' like what you call IOU in America."

Curiously and without emotion, she pulled the expansion band off her wrist and dropped it into his hand. "How long will you keep it before you give it back?"

"Maybe always," he said with a sneer.

"The Qur'an says it is a sin to steal."

"You are only *sabaya*. It is not a sin to take from *sabaya*." He pocketed the watch and walked on.

Sophie looked at Chang. "Do you know what he meant by *sabaya*?"

The frail Chang nodded. "*Sabaya* is a word that means the 'spoils of war.' They feel they can do anything with *sabaya*. It is only because we will be a source of money when our ransoms are paid that we are kept alive."

Late in the afternoon as they ate a handful of rice, Sophie asked the guard, "Benito, how long have you been hiding in the forests as a part of *Abu Sayyaf*?"

"Three years."

"Is this what you want to do with your life?"

He thought for a moment before he answered. "Maybe I will go back to Afghanistan some day and die in the holy war there." He paused for another moment before he added, as a new idea struck him, "Or maybe I will go to America and get a good job there."

Sophie was startled at the answer. "Why would you want to go to America? You call America the great Satan."

"I would find a good mosque, marry an American Muslim woman, and fight the jihad there, like the men that flew the planes into your Trade Towers and your Pentagon on Nine-Eleven." His words made Sophie grow cold.

As she thought about his words, she watched a large black spider, as big as a man's thumb, which had woven a web between two tree branches. It waited at the edge of the web, which was nearly a yard across. A large fly became entangled in the web, and its struggles made the web vibrate. The spider quickly skittled over the web filaments toward it. Feeling a sudden sympathy for the fly, Sophie picked up a stick near her and rose to her knees. She reached up and poked at the web, tearing it, trying to free the fly. It was too late. The sticky filaments held the insect tightly. She sat back down on the ground and watched the spider as it carefully and systematically rebuilt the web and located the fly within a few short minutes. It proceeded to wrap the fly in the filaments its body exuded, storing it for a hungrier time.

Poor fly, caught in a web . . . just like us, Sophie thought to herself. *I hope we meet with a better fate.*

That night as some of their captors began to snore, Carlita whispered to Sophie, "Can it get worse here? Can anything get worse?"

"Oh, yes. Things can always get worse. We're very lucky that it isn't the rainy season. Sleeping in mud would be much worse."

Carlita whispered again, "Why don't they ask for a ransom for Mr. Chang or Mr. Dangwa? Do they have a plan?"

"They don't seem to have any real plan. They just seem to make it up as they go along."

Carlita was quiet for a minute and then responded, "I don't think that is good for us."

Sophie did not respond, but she thoroughly agreed with Carlita. For the next hour, both women listened to the night breezes that rustled the shaggy fronds on the palm trees with a sound like rats running through the undergrowth. The cool breeze chilled them thoroughly before morning.

12

THE WEARY HOSTAGES AND THEIR captors were awakened by the crowing of a rooster, a sign that they were within walking distance of a village. Hamal sent two men to find the village and obtain rice. They hurried back to the camp, each with a twenty pound bag of rice on their shoulders and pockets stuffed with candy. When they reached camp, they called out, *"Sundalo, sundalo."*

"What are they saying, Mr. Chang?" Sophie asked.

The weakened old man responded wearily from where he lay with his head in his daughter's lap. "They have seen AFP troops somewhere between the village and here. That means we will be moving camp again."

As the Abu men talked excitedly, they passed out candy to everyone but the hostages. Chang translated, "They are saying that when they reached the village, all the villagers were watching cockfights, so they were able to steal the rice and the candy. On the way back, they were forced to hide from the soldiers."

Hamal began to call out, "Mobiling! Mobiling. *Sundalo!*"

Despite her weariness, Sophie rose to her feet and shook her head. "They have seen soldiers in the area, so Hamal stands there and yells at us to relocate. If he yells loud enough, they can follow the sound of his voice."

"I wish they would," Carlita said angrily.

"I don't think we want to be caught in the crossfire between the AFP soldiers and the *Abu Sayyaf*," Dangwa said quietly.

The group of ten captors and five hostages rose to their feet and started through the forest. Ali led the way, swinging his bolo knife where necessary to clear a path. Benito followed the hostages with his weapon pointed at them, looking as though he really believed the five weary, hungry men and women might try to run away. Instead, they perspired as they labored up the hillside, trying to sweep cobwebs, insects, and vines out of their faces. The four men carrying Daud in the makeshift stretcher slowed the group. Dark hovered over them when Hamal called a halt to the trek.

As the men hung their hammocks between the trees, they pointed below them, signaling that the hostages were to sleep there again. Instead of dutifully crawling beneath one of the hammocks, Sophie pulled off the rope on her wrist and sought out Hamal. "Mr. Chang will not live much longer if he is not fed more. He is almost too weak to walk."

"That is no concern of yours, woman."

"It is my concern," she responded with intensity. "If he has been kidnapped for ransom, why don't you ask for one?" Her moral outrage at the treatment of Mr. Chang radiated from her so powerfully that he felt it almost as a physical force.

He turned on her. "He is not your concern, woman!"

"I have made him my concern."

Hamal swiftly backhanded her hard across the face. The momentum of the blow carried her backward, knocking her off her feet. After a few seconds, she sat up and rubbed her cheek, fighting the tears that both anger and the stinging blow threatened. She got up slowly and moved over to Benito's hammock where she crawled under it, but she did not sleep for a long time. Hamal went down to the nearby stream to wash because he had touched an unbeliever.

***

To that point in time, Hamal's orders had appeared to Sophie to be entirely arbitrary, but as the camp was packed the next morning, Sophie watched him as he talked on the satphone and remembered that the orders to move camp often followed his telephone conversations. She made a mental note to watch for the connection in the future.

At midday they heard the engine of an old jeepney, and with hand signs, the men leading the group signaled for everyone to hide. They watched from positions behind the large trees as an old jeepney with a dozen twenty-pound bags of rice tied on the roof struggled toward them on the rutted, dirt road. Leaving a scowling Benito to watch the hostages, the other men dashed out and halted the old bus. They commanded the passengers and the driver to get out while Abdul and Hussein climbed on top and tossed the bags of rice down.

The women watched the situation from where they were crouched in the trees. A frightened Carlita asked Sophie, "Do you think they will kill the passengers?"

Sophie just shook her head as she had no way of guessing, but Benito, who was standing with them, answered, "Maybe not. Maybe they take some to get ransom if they look rich—or maybe they let them go."

The two women in the jeepney wore burqas, and each held a small child. The four men in ragged clothing looked like poor rice farmers. None of these people had money to pay a ransom. A boy who looked about fifteen stood near a woman who was probably his mother. All looked terrified. After each one of the Abu, with the exception of Hamal, had picked up a bag of rice and put it over his shoulder, Hamal spoke to the boy. The boy did not move. Instead, he turned and looked at his mother with frightened eyes. Hamal waved the barrel of his AK-47 and raised his voice to a command. Finally, the boy took a few steps away from his mother, who put out a hand toward Hamal and wept pleadingly.

Sophie spoke to Benito, "Is Hamal taking the boy from his mother? Why would he do that?"

Benito looked at her in contempt. "He will make a good *Abu Sayyaf*. He is young and strong. It is his destiny."

Sophie's heart went out to the begging mother. *So this is how they recruit!*

They watched Hamal order the other passengers back into the jeepney, including the weeping mother. As it rattled away, Hamal motioned for the boy to fall in line behind the hostages. The Abu men watched him closely. Sophie noted that he wiped away an occasional tear.

When they paused that evening to make camp, Carlita cried out in disgust, *"Alimatok, alimatok."* She bent over and tried to pull something off her leg.

"Leeches, look for leeches on your skin. Carlita has found leeches on her legs," Chang said to the other hostages.

Sophie looked down at her own legs and arms and saw three, inch-long worms that had attached themselves near her ankles. They were enlarging with blood as she watched. She pulled them off and threw them on the ground. "Where did they come from?" she asked, her voice filled with revulsion.

Dangwa answered as he pulled one off his neck, "They live in the leaves of some of the trees, waiting for someone to pass by close enough to drop onto them."

The sores the leeches created where they attached themselves were slow to clot and itched badly for many days. Even though the bites often became infected, Hamal would not permit anyone to use the remaining hydrogen peroxide. He was saving it in case Daud needed it.

The boy kidnapped from the jeepney said little but watched the activities of the camp with frightened eyes. Sophie tried to draw him out, but finally concluded that he spoke only Cebuano. When Chang spoke to the boy, he responded with wide, frightened eyes and words that tumbled over each other.

The next day the Abu and their hostages moved through a small, empty village. Rather than halting that night as everyone had expected, the hiking continued well into the night. The men who carried the heavy bags of rice grumbled.

"Why can't we stop and rest? I'm so tired," Carlita asked Benito.

"The village is empty because they know we are in the area. The villagers hide from us. The empty village tells the AFP that we are near so we must keep going."

Before midnight the group had found an old, deserted hut, and for several hours, the weary men and women rested, the Abu men using the bags of rice as pillows. The hostages were put in the hut, which made them easier to watch, but more importantly for them, it offered some protection from the chill of the early morning hours. After the morning washing and prayers, the men stretched out again to rest. Even Benito was dozing where he lay against a bag of rice.

Sophie surreptitiously pulled the rope from her wrist and very quietly made her way to where the kidnapped boy sat. He was no longer roped to the other hostages as the Abu considered themselves to be too far from his village for him to try to run away.

She knelt and signed to him by putting her hands together and laying her head on them that the Abu men were all asleep. She then motioned that he should run away. He looked at her with wide eyes. Struggling to remember a few words of Tagalog in the hope that he might understand them, she whispered, *"Tumakbó,"* the word for "run." Then she made a pushing motion with her hands and whispered, *"Tumakbó.* Go find *nanay.* Go find *tatay."*

Suddenly, a light went on in the boy's eyes. *"Nanay, tatay,"* he whispered and nodded. He smiled and added a respectful, *"Opo."* He rose to his feet and moved quietly toward the forest that began about ten feet behind the spot where they were sitting. She waved her hand at him, motioning him to hurry. When he had moved into the trees, she cautiously returned to lie near Carlita and closed her eyes.

Hamal's angry voice roused the camp. He was yelling and pointing to where the boy had been sitting when they had lay down to rest. Timidly, Carlita asked Mr. Chang what he was saying.

"The boy is gone. He has run away."

Benito had heard the question and answered angrily, "He is a coward—and cowards never enter heaven," he said with venom.

"But he was just a boy," Carlita responded.

To demonstrate his contempt for the boy, the guard spat. Sophie just turned her head and pretended to be asleep as she hid her smile in the crook of her arm.

Later that evening Sophie spoke to Dangwa. "You have been very quiet today, Mr. Dangwa. What are you thinking?"

"I wish that I could see my wife and hold my two little daughters again before I die."

"We'll get through this. You'll see. We'll be rescued."

"Perhaps you will, but, somehow, I feel that I will not see my family again. Will you tell them for me that I love them?"

"Of course, but don't give up. I'm sure that you will be able to tell them yourself."

"My wife must be brokenhearted with worry, and my little girls will think I have left them." Sophie knew he was right and sensed that she had nothing to say that would offer any real comfort to him.

***

The next morning, Hussein came over to Chang and commanded, "Come with me." Emily and Sophie helped the old man to his feet, and he shuffled in a stooped fashion behind Hussein to the other side of the camp. He had been frail when he was kidnapped, but now Sophie could see he was hardly more than a shadow. The neat, tailored suit he had been wearing was soiled and torn. His thin hair was dirty and unkempt.

As the other captives watched, Hamal took a portable, cassette tape recorder from a pack. He told Chang to sit and then commanded the old man to speak into the built-in microphone. Sophie looked at Benito, the everpresent guard, and asked, "What is Hamal doing, Benito?"

"He is making the old man record a tape that one of the men will carry to Zamboanga City for *Radyo Agong* to broadcast. Hamal will tell him how much ransom to ask for."

"Why didn't he do this sooner? Why wait until Mr. Chang is so weak he can hardly speak?"

"So his family will hear he is weak and be quick to pay the ransom," Benito answered matter-of-factly.

After he was finished with Chang, Hamal ordered Hussein to bring Emily over to him, and she was ordered to add a statement to the tape. Abdul was given the tape to carry to the radio station. When the father and daughter were allowed to rejoin the other three, Carlita asked curiously, "What did he make you say, Mr. Chang? Did he make you ask for ransom?"

The old man nodded. "He told me to ask my family to pay two million pesos ransom. He made Emily tell them I was weak and might die if they do not pay it quickly."

The next day, several banana trees, the remnant of a long-deserted plantation, were located. Each plant supported a large bunch of green bananas. Before dark the hard green bananas had been turned into *bianbons*. First, they were roasted, and then they were mashed and rolled into banana leaves and roasted again in hot coals. For the first time in many days of hunger, most of the hostages ate until they were full. Only Mr. Chang seemed too weak to eat very much.

Sophie could see that Benito's expression had been mellowed by a full stomach, so she asked, "How will Hamal know the tape has been broadcast?"

"He has a contact in Zamboanga City that will call him on the satphone to tell him."

"How will the ransom be exchanged for Mr. Chang and Emily?"

"We have done this before. Hamal's contact will call him and tell him when it is arranged."

Since Benito was talking so freely, Sophie continued her questions. "Do you know who the contact person is?"

"Probably somebody at the radio station or maybe someone in the army."

Sophie grew very quiet after he said that. After a few minutes, she whispered to Carlita, "So the army, which is supposed to rescue hostages, is riddled with officers who help *Abu Sayyaf.* May heaven help us all." She wiped away a tear of sudden, overwhelming discouragement.

Yusuf had heard her and responded from where he was lying in his hammock, "Yes, you will need the help of your heaven because Allah does not help unbelievers."

With a little of her old fire, Sophie responded, "My God loves all men—even you. He only hates their sins."

Neither Yusuf nor Benito would rise to the bait. Yusuf responded as he made himself more comfortable in the hammock, "Your god is not Allah. Allah only loves believers, not Jews, not Christians, not bad Muslims. He loves only those who bow down to him."

Sophie put her head in the crook of her arm on the hard, damp ground. She pictured her grandfather. *Grandpa, surely you know I've been kidnapped. Is anyone going to come to rescue me?* She let the tears of anger, fear, and frustration flow.

13

THE NEXT DAY MONTY AND Julia met Rick at the Cebu Airlines terminal where Rick quietly and unobserved passed his .45-caliber Smith and Wesson to Monty who slipped it into his duffle bag with his handgun. Then they preceded through the inspection lanes inside the airport where Monty's police I.D. got his bag and the weapons past the inspector. The stairs were rolled to the plane hatchway, and the three of them climbed into the cabin of the Asian Spirit charter that could have seated eight.

A mechanic closed the door from the outside, cutting off the splash of sun that had allowed some light to flood the cabin. Monty sat behind Julia where he looked unseeingly out of one of the windows for nearly the entire hour and three-quarters it took to fly directly to Cagayan de Oro. He had deliberately chosen to sit behind her, rather than next to her, to minimize the distraction her presence might cause him. Though he had made no sign of it, he had discovered that her nearness sometimes made it hard to give over his entire concentration to the assignment he had been given. His thoughts kept him quiet. *I'm leading this "adventure" on a wing and a prayer and a whole load of faith. My concentration will improve when I can leave Julia in Bolong and put some distance between us.* He smiled as he remembered that there had been times when being close to Alicia had made him feel this way.

Julia watched the green islands that passed under them as they flew south at about ten thousand feet. Some were still covered with the extensive blanket of hardwood forests; others were a patchwork of wet rice paddies or green fields and forests skewered by volcanic mountain peaks. She wished that Monty had chosen to sit by her. There were so many questions she would have asked, but he apparently had much on his mind.

When the island of Mindanao came into sight, Monty roused from his thoughts. *I'm being a poor host.* He moved over to sit by Julia and spoke to her in a voice raised enough to be heard above the engines. "You can see Macajalar Bay and the city coming into view. Have you been here before?"

"No, I've never visited Cagayan de Oro." As she leaned forward to see the city through the small window, she asked, "How large is it?"

"Maybe half a million. The folks that live here refer to their city as the City of Golden Friendship. Despite that homespun title, it's a sophisticated city. Cebuano is the language here."

"Will that cause a problem—the Cebuano, I mean?" Julia asked with a raised voice.

"Not likely. Cebuano is my first language," Monty answered with a smile. "Rick may have to work at it a bit, but his English and Bamboo Tagalog will get him by." When she looked at him with a question in her eyes, he explained, "That's what we call the mix of Tagalog and Spanish that's used in most village marketplaces throughout the islands."

As they talked, the plane descended and landed hard with two rebounds on the runway at Lumbia Airport, where it eventually shuddered to a stop. A mechanic pushed the stairs to the plane and then opened the door to the fuselage from the outside, letting in a splash of warm, humid air and sunlight. With luggage in tow, they started toward the terminal. Realizing once more just how dependent on Monty she had to be in this assignment, she asked, "Where will we be staying?"

"I have three rooms at the Hotel Koresco in the Lumbia area. It's a good neighborhood," he added as if to soothe any fears she had.

"You don't need to be concerned on my account," she responded confidently. "The foundation's clients don't live in the 'good neighborhoods.' I can handle just about anything that might get thrown at me in these islands."

Though it had been an inter-island flight, they were still required to show their passports and have their luggage searched. Again, Monty's police I.D. got the two weapons through the inspection.

With his hand on her elbow, Monty guided Julia toward the cab sporting the least body damage in the line outside the main terminal door. As he opened the door and assisted her into the front passenger seat, he told the driver to take them to the Hotel Koresco. The two men climbed into the rear.

The cab ride to the hotel stifled any real conversation, as the driver dodged in and out of traffic with a speed and recklessness that would have stood him well in Metro Manila. Upon reaching the hotel, they were shown to three rooms on the third floor of the clean and modern building. As Julia's bags were removed from the brass luggage cart and placed inside the room, Monty said, "We'll meet in the lobby at six. Dinner with the Jackson brothers will be at the Grand Caprice Restaurant. See you then." He lifted his bag from the cart, stepped across the hallway, and entered his room. Rick followed his example, entering a room two doors down from Monty's.

Julia offered the bellman a tip and thanked him, cutting off his prepared statement about the air con, as the Filipinos called air conditioning; the automatic coffeemaker, which Julia would not be using; and the hair dryer located in the bathroom. He looked a little disappointed. He had worked hard to learn the little talk in English.

After a short rest and a long shower, Julia dressed in a rose-colored pantsuit with embroidered lapels made for her on her last trip to the islands and brushed her short, curly hair.

Monty smiled with approval when she arrived in the lobby at ten minutes to six. He liked the fact that she consistently dressed in a refined manner, as though she respected the culture she was visiting, rather than in the worn and ragged jeans that so many American tourists wore like a universal uniform.

Rick arrived immediately after her. Without comment, they set out at a brisk walk toward Robinsons Mall. Next to the mall, Julia could see the Grand Caprice Restaurant.

During introductions, Julia studied any differences she could find in the appearance of the Jackson twins, hoping to be able to learn to tell them apart. She noted a small mole on Bing's cheek near his nose. Bolly wore his hair longer. He regularly brushed it out of his eyes with his left hand. Both differences would be useful in recognizing which man she was talking to at any time. They were tall, slender, and had laugh lines around their eyes and mouths. Julia spontaneously liked them both.

The five of them were seated in a secluded corner of the dining room that was elegantly decorated in a Filipino-influenced Chinese motif. As the meal progressed, the conversation covered many personal matters as the five became better acquainted. Julia answered all the usual questions, including her marital status, how many children she had, how much education she had, what she did for a living and, most importantly, did she like the Philippines. Like any good visitor, she spoke glowingly of the country's beauties, which she genuinely loved.

No business was discussed until the dessert arrived, a pineapple cheesecake with a mango sauce. Then Monty changed the direction of the conversation. "Julia, it's time for you to tell Bing and Bolly what we're up to."

Julia explained the task they faced and finished by saying, "Monty is leading our efforts, and I trust his expertise. Will you join him?" With a glance, she handed the conversation back to Monty.

Bing looked at his brother and then at Monty. "What will this involve—at least what do you *think* it will involve?"

"It looks like we'll be going into the forest on the Zamboangan Peninsula, and it's likely that we may need to go up into the mountains. The kidnappers are probably hiding up there in the old-growth rain forest. It will be up to us to locate the *Abu Sayyaf* group that we think has kidnapped Sophie, and then we have to get her away from them."

"This will pay?" Filipinos were very seldom so direct, even those raised in the United States, but in this case, it was an appropriate question.

Julia turned the question on them. "How much will it take to get you to join us?"

Reaching for the sky, Bing answered, "One hundred dollars a day and a thousand dollars if we get Sophie back alive—each." He held his breath as he anticipated a counteroffer.

Julia simply said, "Done." Both the men seemed somewhat stunned. They looked at each other simultaneously and then back to Julia as if they had misunderstood her. She added, "All expenses will be covered, and you'll be paid when the task is finished."

Forgetting the dignity they had been trying to maintain, they slapped each other on the back and each yelled, "Ooooeeee," drawing frowns from other diners.

Monty looked at Julia with a smile. "I think that means they're pleased to become part of our team."

As the brothers tried to reclaim their former dignity, Monty cleared his throat and asked as tactfully as he could, as he looked from one to another of the three men, "Before the deal is set in concrete, I do need to make sure that none of you are smokers."

Rick grinned and said, speaking directly to Julia, "Monty cured me of that habit. While we were in Afghanistan with the special forces, he caught me absentmindedly lighting up while we were on sentry duty. He knocked me flat."

Julia simply looked at Monty for an explanation. "The smell of American tobacco can travel a long way if the wind is right, so smoking in hostile territory isn't very smart." He gave a half grin to Rick. "Isn't that so, Rick?"

His friend laughed heartily. "I haven't lit up since."

"While we trained as SEALS, we had a lieutenant who would have had us hung from the yardarm if we had taken up smoking. That cuts lung capacity too much," Bing said.

"And I have a wife who would do more than that if I took up that habit," Bolly added.

Monty nodded. "That being made clear, when can you get away from your present responsibilities?"

"When do you need us?" Bing asked.

"ASAP."

Bolly responded, "Then you've got us as of right now. My wife is so mad at me that she isn't speaking. I think she'll be glad to have me gone from home for a while."

"Is it about your recent business failure?" Bing asked.

"Yes, and I think it will take her a while to get over this one." He grinned sheepishly. "This is the third in a row."

Julia's concern showed in her voice. "How are you getting along?"

"My brother here sees that we don't starve," he responded.

The seriousness in Monty's face brought everyone back to the task at hand. "In the morning, Rick and I will be going out to Camp Evangelista, where we'll be picking up some items Matson told me he would have shipped here for our use, courtesy of the U.S. military. We'll meet in the lobby of the hotel at two o'clock tomorrow afternoon. Dress casually and pack one small bag of clothing you won't miss if it doesn't go home with you—no more than one change—and wear sturdy shoes." Looking directly at Bing and Bolly, he added, "Bring your cell phones and a second battery, binoculars, a compass, a canteen, and a military knife, if you have them." Looking directly at the brothers, Monty asked, "Do you have a personal weapon—a hand gun?"

Bing and Bolly both shook their heads. "If I kept a gun in the house, my wife would probably use it on me," Bolly said.

"Same here."

Monty nodded. "Okay. I just needed to know how many weapons we will have. Rick and I have each brought a .45. If you have military-style khaki pants and shirts, wear them. We're going into the forest—not you, Julia, but the rest of us."

"And what will I be doing?" she asked, with both eyebrows elevated.

"You'll be staying with my aunt and uncle in Bolong, keeping your cell phone handy." He stood, and the men shook hands all around. "See you all tomorrow."

***

In the morning, Monty and Rick checked out of their rooms and caught a cab that took them down to the Hertz rental lot in the middle of the city. Monty rented a two-year-old, black Toyota Tundra. He paid the attendant for two weeks and added, "If we need the truck longer than two weeks, we will cover the cost when we return the vehicle." To make the attendant behind the desk more comfortable with the rental, Monty allowed him to photocopy his Manila police I.D.

They arrived at the AFP camp at ten and asked the guard at the gate for Captain Villoso. They were shown into his office, and after shaking hands, the captain said, "A large box arrived early this morning by air freight special delivery. It's marked to the attention of Captain Diego Montalbon, U.S. Army. I was told in a telephone conversation from the American Embassy that I was to turn it over to no one else."

"Thanks for your help. We'll be glad to take it off your hands. I have a vehicle that will carry it." After another twenty minutes of talk that Filipino courtesy required, Monty and Rick stood. He thanked Villoso again and carefully palmed the expected five-hundred-peso bill as a thank you for keeping the box secure. Monty transferred it to the officer's hand as the men shook hands once more. The very large box was loaded into the bed of the rented truck, and Villoso tossed off a salute as the men climbed into the cab and drove away. As the truck exited the base, Monty commented, "I hope Matson didn't forget anything."

Monty parked in a corner on the empty third level of the hotel parking terrace, a fairly private location as few guests had personal vehicles with them. The men climbed into the truck bed. Using a key, Monty split the packing tape and opened the box.

After another few seconds of examining the contents, Rick whistled under his breath. "Whew! Look at this stuff. What kind of pull do you have, Monty?"

14

As the two men carefully examined the items in the box, they kept an eye out for any other vehicles that might enter the third level of the garage. "I'll say it again, Monty. Where do you get your pull?"

Monty grinned. "I'm sure you've heard the old saying about 'it's all in who you know'?"

Rick lifted out a set of ITT night-vision goggles and a headset adapter. As he examined them, he said, "How many of these do we have? Do you have any idea what these are worth on the black market?"

"There should be four in there. I gave Matson my word that none of this stuff will end up in the hands of *Abu Sayyaf*."

"What else do you have in there?" Rick lifted out a military map of the Zamboangan Peninsula. He opened it up and noted the latitude and longitudinal markings. He nodded with satisfaction and handed it to Monty, who looked it over, refolded it, and put it into his hip pocket.

Monty lifted out an M16. Looking it over closely, he commented under his breath, "Fully automatic. This is what I ordered." Reaching back into the box, he lifted out a second similar weapon and handed it to Rick.

As Rick examined the one in his hands, he said, "I can still smell the packing grease. These are great. Couldn't ask for more." In the box, there were two flash suppressors for the weapons and a box of thirty-round magazines for the guns.

By this time Rick had the grin of a ten-year-old kid on Christmas morning. "Anything else of use in there?"

Looking back into the box, he answered, "It looks like there are a bunch of MREs." As he talked, he lifted some of the military meals-ready-to-eat out of the box and examined them. "I suspect Bing and Bolly will like these. There's spaghetti, lasagna, mac and cheese, and several others."

He dropped them back in and picked up a six-inch black, round sphere that looked like a cannonball. On a paper label around its circumference, it read Zambelli Fireworks. "Is this what I think it is?"

"It'd better be. Let's see if the launching tubes are included." At the bottom of the box there were three more black spheres and four tubes for launching the shells.

Rick examined the launching tubes. "These look too short to be effective."

"That's because we don't want these fireworks to go too high—no more than a hundred and twenty feet, preferably less. Any higher would defeat their purpose. Whatever we do, let's not forget the matches on this 'adventure.'" Looking through the packing straw in the box, Monty found two 9mm Beretta automatics with holsters still in their shipping boxes. In the bottom of the box, wrapped in newspaper, were four bolo knives and a couple dozen batteries for the night-vision goggles. Additionally, there were four small grenade-like items.

Rick's forehead wrinkled as he examined them. "These aren't standard military grenades."

"No, they're law enforcement flash-bang grenades. Actually, they were Matson's idea. I have no idea where he got them. We're just about ready for this little party we're planning."

"What more do we need?" Rick asked in surprise.

"We need four backpacks to carry this stuff. Frankly, I forgot to put them on the list when I called Matson. It took a few phone calls, but I've arranged to pick them up in Zamboanga City. My cousin, Reynaldo, is stationed there at the AFP Southern Command Headquarters." Monty jumped down from the tailgate. "You know someone has to stay with this stuff. I'm going to see if Julia has checked out. It's about one-thirty. While I do that, be sure to repack everything. The Jackson brothers should be here soon. We'll stop at a Jollibee and get some burgers for lunch on the way out of town."

When Monty strolled into the lobby of the hotel, Julia was sitting with her luggage and the ever-present leather handbag over her shoulder. The doubts she had felt the night before quietly melted when she saw him. *This is going to work. Whatever he is planning will surely work.*

She was wearing tan cargo pants, a light blue cotton blouse, and a pair of Addidas walking shoes. As he approached, she said, "I've checked out, and I'm ready to go."

"Both Rick and I are checked out, and they're holding our bags behind the registration desk. As soon as the twins get here, we can leave."

As Monty spoke, Bing and Bolly came through the front door, each carrying a leather duffle bag over his shoulder. They were wearing black T-shirts, khaki pants, and soft, crushable hats made of camouflage fabric. They both looked a little sheepish. Bing spoke. "Sorry to be so early, but we're both in trouble."

Bolly added with a grin, "We decided to get an early start. Hope our wives cool down before we get back. When I told my wife, Girlie, that we were headed out on a paying adventure, she threatened to throw a frying pan at me. I don't think she believes that there's any money in anything I try."

"My wife told me that if I was going off with Bolly not to come back until I had some money in my pocket," Bing added.

Julia smiled and tried to reassure them, "When you come home with the money for rescuing Sophie, you will both be heroes."

"Hope you're right." Bing's grin matched his brother's.

Monty took the time to pick up both his bag and Rick's from where they were checked at the desk and asked the clerk for a black permanent marker. Then he nodded his head toward the back entrance to the lobby that led to the elevator and the parking terrace. When they reached the third level, they found Rick sitting in the truck bed with his back against the box, nearly asleep in the humid heat.

Monty called out, "Toss your bags into the back."

Rick rose, leaned out of the truck bed, and took Julia's bags. Monty leaped into the back of the truck and began to write on the box in large letters, "Salted Pork Products." As he straightened up to look at his handiwork, he said, "The further west we get, the safer our box is likely to be." Then he and Rick jumped down from the tailgate, and Monty instructed, "Julia, you'll ride in front with me. You three will have to make do with the backseat." He leaned the front seat forward so the other men could climb into the cramped second seat.

Rick and Bing climbed into the backseat, but Bolly said, "I'll ride in the back with the box. There's more room back there, and since we'll be going west, I'll be in the shade of the cab." He leaped into the truck bed and arranged the bags to make a spot to lie down with the softest bag as a pillow and his hat over his face.

After picking up burgers, sodas, and rice cakes at the first Jollibee they found on their way out of the city, they headed west. After eating, the two men in the backseat drifted off to sleep, despite—or maybe because of—the cramped seating and the sun that filled the cab, almost overwhelming the air conditioning.

"How long will it take to get to Bolong?" Julia asked quietly to avoid disturbing the sleeping men.

"We'll follow the costal highway along the north coast. In a few hours, it will drop south to Pagadian, where we'll stop tonight. I've made reservations for what I hope will be good hotel rooms there. That will be about the halfway point. Then tomorrow, we'll have five or six more hours on the road, if we don't run into major construction or any landslides."

"How will you guard the things in the big box?"

"Hopefully we can get it up to my room tonight. If not, then Bing and Bolly will be sleeping in the truck bed to guard it."

The afternoon passed quickly for Julia as she watched the changing scenery. The road ran west near the coast where the Sulu Sea could often be seen to the north. She said little but was conscious of Monty's nearness.

Sometimes the coconut palms obscured the view of the sea, but much of the time Julia could see the sun glint off the swells and waves of aqua silk as they broke like ragged, cream-colored lace against the beach or against the occasional lava cliffs that lifted the highway above the ocean.

On the south side of the road, where the hardwoods had been cleared a hundred years earlier, rice fields in different stages of ripeness reflected varying shades of green. The wind off the ocean made the fields pulse in slow waves, as if greeting them as they passed.

The rice fields gave way to areas of rough cogon grass and thorny bushes where an occasional resting carabao, the great water buffalo of Asia, lay in a muddy spot or in the long, rough grass and chewed its cud.

The truck moved down the two-lane road, described on some maps as the Pan Philippine Highway because it had once been paved in asphalt and striped down the middle. Julia couldn't help but smile at the occasional jeepney that had to move fully into one lane or the other to permit the big truck to pass. Each one was driven by men who seemed to have formed an unofficial union whose first and foremost rule was that each vehicle must straddle the faded white line and so utilize half of each lane.

As the motion of the truck sedated Julia's thinking, she thought, *I could love this country if it weren't for the heat, and the insects, and the traffic* . . . At that point, she drifted off to sleep.

After another hour, the road turned away from the northern coast, making a ninety-degree turn to the south. The change in direction awakened Julia. The road had been cut through the weathered remnants of the ancient volcanoes that had formed the island millions of years earlier. In several places Monty had to guide the truck around large chunks of weathered volcanic debris that had lost its grip on the mountainside and thundered down to explode apart on the road. The rubble would lie on the road until the next rainy season washed it away.

Julia broke the silence. "Monty, I think I understand why you labeled the box 'pork products.' That will make it unappealing to the Muslims on the western part of the peninsula, but may I ask what's really in it?"

"Some very vital items courtesy of Captain Matson, including weapons, night-vision goggles, and some fireworks."

Julia smiled and raised her eyebrows. "Fireworks?"

Monty just nodded.

After another short silence, broken only by the soft snoring of the men in the backseat, Julia asked quietly, "How did your wife die?" Then she hurriedly added, "If it's too personal, you can tell me to mind my own business."

After several seconds of silence, Monty responded, "No, it's not too personal. It was on the front page of every newspaper in Manila when it happened." As he drove, he rubbed his forehead with his left hand as if it ached. "I was working on a big drug bust in Navotas, up in the reclamation area. I had followed the money trail all the way to a provincial council member, and it looked like it went even higher, maybe even to one of the governor's aids. We scheduled a raid on the lab—the date is easy to remember as it was two days before my birthday." His voice was suddenly cynical. "Someone leaked the plan, and when we got there, we ran into a hail of gunfire. I took a hit in my left thigh, and by the time two of my buddies had dragged me back to the cover of the police vehicles, it was total chaos. The warehouse was being used to cut methamphetamine and cocaine, and in the gunfire, it erupted like Mt. Pinatubo. When the fire had burned itself out the next day, they found five bodies in the ashes, but they were unidentifiable. The councilman I

suspected insisted that he was in Cebu with his sick mother. I thought
the entire investigation was just another dead end, but evidently I hit a
nerve with someone.

"While I was still in the hospital waiting for my femur to mend, my
wife received a midnight phone call telling her that I had taken a turn for
the worse and that she needed to get to the hospital if she wanted to see
me before I passed away. She called my daughter, who was at a sleepover
at the home of a friend, to tell her where she was going. My son, Richard,
was seven and couldn't be left home alone so he went with her."

He paused for nearly a full minute, the muscles in his jaw hardening.
"No witnesses were found, but the car had been sideswiped and forced
off an overpass on C-5. That isn't the highway they would have normally
taken to get to St. Luke's, so I feel sure that they were trying to get away
from someone. I don't know if I'll ever know the whole story."

"I'm so sorry," Julia whispered, suddenly remembering the overwhelming
sense of loss she had experienced when her husband had died so
unexpectedly. She had unwittingly ripped open an old wound. She tried to
divert the conversation. "Considering how seriously wounded you were, you
show no sign of it in your walk."

"Not usually. I'm lucky."

In the hope of finding something less painful to talk about, she asked
him to tell her about his daughter.

His tone brightened, as if he had pulled the shade on the unhappy
memories she had advertently brought up. "She's thirteen now. Her name is
Anna Lou. She's very close to her Aunt Isabel, my wife's sister, and she gets
along well with Belle's husband. She's studying the piano and doing great. She
recently won a statewide piano competition for kids her age. When I sent her
to live with Belle, I arranged to send support money each month, and I asked
Belle to see that she got to church every week. After taking her to church each
Sunday for a year, Belle was baptized, though her husband has shown no
interest yet." He glanced at her and asked. "Tell me about your family."

Julia started slowly, as if she were carefully making her way through
memories as sharp as broken glass. But she had done it to him, so now it
was her turn. "My husband died unexpectedly about sixteen months ago.
Heart attack. He was only forty-six."

Monty responded while she regained her composure, "Just a little
older than I am. Indeed, much too young to die." Though he smiled as
he said it, he meant it.

After a few seconds, she continued, "He never learned how to relax. He was always pushing himself beyond his limits." She paused for a moment, trying to regain her composure before she could continue. "I don't get angry with him anymore the way I did at first."

"Angry with him?"

"Angry with him for dying. Why didn't he take better care of himself? The first year was hard. I have a friend who's a grief counselor, and she tells me that I'm finally progressing through the steps of grief—you know, denial, anger, finally acceptance. I'm working on the acceptance part of it." They rode for a few minutes in silence.

"Tell me about your children. When we were talking in the dining room of the Manila Hotel you said you had three children, but you only mentioned the two that are in college. Is there a reason for that?"

Julia was silent for nearly a full minute. Monty had concluded that she was not going to answer when she finally responded, "I'm very proud of Paul. After he came home from his mission, he went back to the university and has been carrying a double load of credits. He'll soon be graduated from Mizzou—University of Missouri at Columbia. He's done it with only three years of classes, just a year behind the class he started with. My daughter, Allison, is a freshman there." She paused and then quietly added, "My other son, Aaron, is lying in a care center in what the doctors call a vegetative state. He's connected to a respirator. I was told that there's no hope—no hope that he will ever regain consciousnesses." She added with intensity, "But I have to hope. I can't give up."

"Tell me what put him there." Monty's voice was gentle, probing. It reminded her of her friend, the grief counselor.

"He was in a terrible crash. The passenger in the car was the woman he was living with, the woman who led him away from the Church. She wasn't injured, but he was almost killed." A sob slipped past her self-control, and she hurriedly picked up the big handbag that had been sitting at her feet and searched for a handkerchief. Wiping her eyes and dabbing at her nose, she took a deep breath to still her quivering chin. She bit her lip for a few seconds. He was willing to let her continue at her own pace.

"When he got home from his mission to Mexico, his girlfriend had married another young man, and Aaron just slowly came apart. He simply unraveled. Then Jack died, and a few months later, Aaron was in that terrible auto accident. I felt like I was watching my life turn into a slow-motion train wreck, and I couldn't get out of the wreckage." She was silent for a minute. "Allison was so glad to go off to college. I think living with me was like living in a funeral home. Since then, I've thrown myself into my work for the foundation. I'm so grateful to have that to keep me busy—and sane."

They each remained lost in their own thoughts until they reached Pagadian at about seven-thirty. They stopped at another Jollibee for a quick supper, and Monty located the hotel. He parked the truck at the front entrance of the small, gray four-story building. He climbed out of the truck. "I'll register us and bring you your keys."

When he returned, he explained, as he passed out the plastic, computer-programmed door keys, "To avoid any questions, Julia, if anyone asks while we are here, you're Rick's wife. Needless to say, you'll be in the room registered to Mr. and Mrs. Calvin, and Rick will be sharing my room. Bing and Bolly will also share a room." He started the engine and moved the truck around to the small parking lot at the rear of the hotel. "There's an elevator just inside this door where we can get the box up to my room."

The light on the lock of the back door turned green when Julia put her key into it. She held it open as Bing and Bolly carried the box in and put in the elevator. When they reached the second floor, they carried it down the hall to Monty's room and set it down inside.

"Hey, is there someplace to get something to eat in this town? That Jollibee burger just didn't cut it. I'm still hungry," Rick said.

Monty laughed. "I saw a Chinese restaurant down the street when we pulled up in front."

Having slept for most of the ride, the Jackson brothers and Rick made plans to eat again. As they started to walk toward the elevator, Monty said, "There's a little restaurant off the lobby that'll be open in the morning where we can get breakfast. We will be leaving at eight o'clock tomorrow. Be in the lobby then or be left behind." As Rick nodded his agreement, Monty added, "You might as well put some gas in the truck while you are out and about. I saw a Shell station back a couple of blocks." He tossed the keys to his friend. "Just save the receipt and give it to me in the morning."

Julia bid Monty good night. As she lay in bed, her thoughts turned to Sophie. She couldn't help but wonder what the young woman was going through. As she drifted off, she prayed, *Please protect her, and help Monty find her. Just keep her alive and well. Please, God, please . . .*

15

DURING THE NEXT DAY'S TRAVEL, while the others slept, Monty and Julia talked. He explained that he had been released as a bishop a few months after the death of his wife and son. "Right now I'm serving as a Sunday School teacher for the youth in the ward. Unofficially, I try to help the new bishop as much as I can. He's a young man with only three years in the Church."

"How did you keep going after you lost your wife and son?" Julia asked. "How did you survive the grief and depression that comes with that kind of loss?"

He took a deep breath and answered slowly, "It took a long time. After I sent my daughter to California, I almost quit eating and sleeping. I could only see one reason to keep going and that was the hope that I could find the men who were responsible for their deaths. So I worked eighteen hours a day, and after about two years, the depression began to lift. If I hadn't believed that the Lord was still there no matter how alone I felt, I don't know what I would have done." He glanced at Julia on the other side of the truck cab. "How did you handle it?"

She simply whispered, "I haven't 'handled it'—at least not yet." Her voice was tight. "Like you, I've been throwing myself into my work and waiting for the grief to pass." She was looking out the window. "There were two reasons that prompted me to take this assignment. One, I care about Sophie very much, and the other—I felt that it would help get my mind off my own problems and focused on someone else's." She turned and looked at him and added with a crooked little smile, "And I think it's helping."

They said little more as Monty drove southwest through several small villages where nearly naked children paused in their play to watch the big black truck with the big box in it pass. They drove through some old-growth forest and could occasionally glimpse the Celebes Sea to the southeast.

Julia broke the silence. "Yesterday, you mentioned that the raid on the drug lab took place a couple of days before your birthday. Does that mean your wife and son were killed on your birthday?"

"The day after."

"You must dread seeing your birthday come around each year."

"Yes. It's a tough few days." He took a deep breath and slowly exhaled. "I still haven't opened the birthday present from Alicia I found when I was released from the hospital to make the funeral arrangements. Keeping it sitting on my dresser keeps her alive somehow." His voice had dwindled to a near whisper.

About one o'clock they arrived in Bolong. A full view of the ocean finally opened before them, spreading to the south and east like a liquid sheet of opal over the pastel coral clumps beneath its surface. The calm surf advanced toward the shore in long, smooth undulations, caressing the sand.

The community was comprised of several barrios, Christian, Chinese-Filipino, and Muslim. It almost literally rose out of the water from its position on the shore. The fishermen's *bancas* were pulled up on the shore where they rested under coconut palms. In the late afternoon, they would go back out into the water to pull in their nets. Monty drove through the narrow, potholed lanes near the beach where almost every shop was open to the street and had a variety of fish, mollusks, and small squid laid out for potential buyers. Julia saw a few ancient, battered jeepneys and several pedicabs peddled by young men made old by hard physical labor.

Monty stopped the truck in front of a small shop with a hand-painted sign that read *Agbulos*. It looked much like the other shops, but as he stepped down out of the cab of the truck, a short, rotund woman of Chinese descent who was probably in her seventies came hurrying out of the shop. "Diego, Diego!" she screamed in pleasure as she threw her arms around him. Turning, she called out an unintelligible stream of Cebuano to someone still hidden in the shadows inside the little dirt-floored hut. Almost immediately, a stooped Filipino with thinning white hair hobbled out to join his wife. He put his arms around Monty while tears streamed freely down his face. While Monty returned the greetings of his aunt and uncle, Julia watched with a smile, noting the aunt's dark, almond eyes that were so similar to Monty's.

Finally, he stepped back from his relatives and said to them in English, "Can you speak English with our guests?"

Their heads bobbed up and down, and they responded, "Yes, yes, English."

In a country where the average life span is only fifty years, Monty's aunt and uncle were truly venerable for their age. Monty introduced them as Luz and Enrique Agbulos. "They were like a second set of parents to me until I went to the states. Aunt Luz and my mother were sisters." Turning to his aunt, who was holding his arm tightly, he said, "My friends and I have come to taste some of your wonderful fish for lunch. Do you have time to feed us? We had only a small breakfast and are very hungry."

Luz nodded vigorously. "Yes, yes, come. I fix tilapia. Very good fish." Her kitchen was the hard-packed dirt yard behind the shop, and the chairs were wooden crates used for shipping fish. While her guests sat in the shade of an enormous Philippine banyan tree, Luz cooked the tilapia in coconut oil in an old frying pan over an inverted five-gallon metal bucket. It had a four-inch square hole cut in it where the fire inside could be stoked. The smoke flowed out of another hole cut higher in the back side of the bucket.

The fish was tender and savory and served with *pancit* noodles that had been cooked with bits of fish and vegetables the day before. While they ate, Monty explained, "I offered to buy Aunt Luz a microwave oven many years ago, but she told me that no microwave could cook fish properly. I think she's right."

After the meal was finished, Monty explained to his relatives the reason for the arrival of the five of them and the need for secrecy. "I need to ask you to take Julia into your home until we get back. Will you do that for me?"

Again the two aged heads bobbed up and down. "Yes, yes. She will stay here." His aunt's hospitality was generous and sincere.

"Perhaps I can help in the shop," Julia responded.

Monty shook his head. "We can't have you working in the shop. It's important that as few people as possible know about you." Then he spoke rapidly in Cebuano to his relatives. He handed his aunt a thousand peso bill, and she hurried away. "I have asked her to purchase a caftan and a head scarf or a burqa for you. She will have to go into the Muslim side of town to find a shop, but she will be back in an hour or two. You will not appear outside without covering yourself like a Muslim woman. You've got to cover your light skin and blond hair to avoid drawing unnecessary attention."

Julia nodded but smiled as she asked wistfully, "No walks on that beautiful beach?"

"That's right." Monty's voice was firm. "You're to stay inside and be prepared to respond to my phone calls." He looked around and asked, "Does everyone's cell have a GPS like Julia's Blackberry?"

Each man nodded. Bolly laughed a little ruefully as he pulled his from his pocket and demonstrated the GPS. "Selling cell phone contracts for these was my last business endeavor. But these are so fancy, nobody could afford them."

Monty continued, "At some point, we may have to separate into two teams. If that becomes necessary, Rick and Bolly will be one team. Bing and I will be the other. I'll use Julia's satphone." He pulled Julia's Blackberry from his pocket and handed it to her. "I want everyone to have access to a GPS, even you, Julia. Should anything happen to one or more of us, it's vital that we keep a cell phone with us so we can be located."

She looked at Monty with concern but simply nodded.

Luz returned with a black, full-length caftan embroidered in white and a white hijab, a headscarf that would cover Julia's head, neck, and shoulders. Monty insisted that Julia put them on over her western clothing.

Leaving Enrique to run the shop, Luz wrapped some fish in brown paper, and Monty helped her into the front seat of the truck. He assisted Julia into the second seat, and the other three men sat in the truck bed with the box. Monty drove about two miles out of town, through the thick undergrowth and down a wide path he remembered from his childhood to the Agbulos home. The nearest neighbor's hut was about four hundred feet to the west, nearer the beach. The few huts they saw were built on five-foot, bamboo stilts so the water driven onto the island by the seasonal typhoons would not wash them away.

Luz and Enrique's little hut had two rooms, and a single light bulb hung from the ceiling in each room. It had a porch across the front and several pigs, chickens, and a dog that lived in the shade beneath it. Two futons were rolled up in one corner, and in the second room was an old, battered table with a small wash tub on it. A makeshift shelf held a box with kitchen utensils and a few well-worn tools. That was the extent of the furnishings.

For dinner, Luz cooked fish and rice over another five-gallon, metal bucket under the hut, shooing the animals away as she did so. In addition to the fish and rice, she sliced a papaya and a guava for her guests to enjoy. That evening when her watch read nine o'clock, Julia called Mallon's office and discovered he wasn't in. She simply told his secretary, "Please tell him I called and everything is moving forward."

The precious box was removed from the truck bed and placed in the hut. That night Bing slept in the front seat and Bolly in the back. Both simply hung their feet out of the open windows. The women slept in the hut, and Rick and Monty slept on the porch alongside Monty's uncle. Julia was grateful for the warmth of the caftan in the cool ocean breeze that swept through the hut.

***

In the morning as the men prepared to leave, Monty took Julia by the arm and pulled her aside. He reminded her to wear the caftan and hijab whenever she appeared outside of the hut. "Don't forget, there are more Muslims in this area than Christians. I'll keep in touch by cell phone to let you know what's happening. Please be careful. I'm responsible for your safety, and I don't want anything to happen to you." His eyes were dark with intensity. It was only after Julia nodded her assent that he let go of her arm.

The men climbed into the truck, and in a cloud of dust, they headed for Zamboanga City.

Her host and hostess left to work at the fish stall, and Julia spent the morning in the long robe, sitting on the porch. She divided her reading between the Grisham novel and the English translation of the Qur'an. When she put them down, she thought, *I'm going to need more reading material if this rescue mission takes more than a couple of days.*

16

MONTY TURNED THE TRUCK ONTO the narrow, costal road that connected Bolong and Zamboanga City. As the men rode, he talked. "I've arranged to meet my cousin Reynaldo at the Jollibee near the base around eleven o'clock. He's got the backpacks and has a place where we can store the truck. He also says he has a man who'll take us in his *banca* up the coast, near the location of the most recent satphone signal of the *Abu Sayyaf*."

"Can we trust this guy?" Rick asked.

"Rey can be trusted. I grew up with him. He has no sympathy with the *Abu Sayyaf*, and I'm sure he found a boatman who feels the same. When we've finished, if we need the boat to get out, I'll call him, and he'll then call the boatman and tell him where to pick us up—if all goes well."

"Do we know where to start looking?" Bing asked the question, but it had been on everyone's mind.

"I called Matson at the U.S. Embassy before breakfast this morning. He told me that the CIA will continue to track the satphone the leader of the group is using. The last time the CIA got a fix on it, it was on the north slope of the mountains about ten miles inland from Patalon at about six hundred feet elevation. As the crow flies, it's about twenty-five miles northeast of there. For that reason, we'll go by boat up the northwest coast and get as close as we can." He paused and grinned. "Rey had to do some fast talking to get the boatman to take us there. That old fisherman is afraid the *Abu Sayyaf* will hijack his boat if they get the chance. We'll pack in from the beach to those coordinates."

When they finally reached Zamboanga City, the highway took them through the eastern part of the sprawling city to where it joined Governor Camins Road. Rick spoke, "What d'you know about this place, Monty?"

"It's a good-sized city—over half a million and has its own modern airport, which the AFP uses. It has one of the biggest ports in the islands. It supports the AFP Southern Command Headquarters for all security forces, including several hundred U.S. soldiers and marines stationed here as military advisors. Despite that fact, or maybe because of it, the city averages at least two kidnappings a week by the *Abu Sayyaf* or MNLF. It doesn't seem to matter whether the victims are men, women, or children. Ransom demands are seldom made. The bodies are found a few days later in alleys or nearby villages. The kidnappings evidently have no more purpose than to maintain a fear of the Islamic terrorists."

Monty made a right turn, and the truck moved past the Zamboanga International Airport. Just a short way beyond, Monty finally found the Jollibee. After he and Rey exchanged a hug, Rey climbed into the truck and directed Monty to drive down a narrow road to a warehouse on the north edge of the base where it met the extensive property of the Zamboanga Golf Club and Beach Resort. There, he stopped before a warehouse. Rick jumped out and raised the large door so Monty could drive the truck inside. They put the backpacks Rey had obtained into the truck bed, and the men helped Monty get the items from the box into the packs. He handed the 9mm Beretta handguns and their holsters to Bing and Bolly and one of the M16s to Rick and kept the other one for himself.

When the big box was empty and each backpack full, he straightened up. "Does everyone have some matches or a lighter?" All nodded. "If you want a change of clothing, now's the time to put some things in your backpack." Each man pulled a shirt and a pair of socks out of his bag and stuffed them in the packs, making the zippers hard to close.

Turning to his cousin, Monty shook his hand. "Is it still okay for me to leave the truck here in the warehouse?"

"Yeah, I'll put an AFP officer's decal on it, and it ought to be okay. Lock anything in the cab that you aren't taking with you." As he jumped out of the truck bed, he added, "Follow me, and we'll find the boat."

The four men swung the backpacks onto their shoulders and followed Rey out of the warehouse and through the undergrowth in single file as they headed for the beach they hoped would be deserted. After about ten minutes, they reached the beach where they could see a large *banca* pulled up on the sand and a man sitting near it, a small fire of driftwood glowing next to him.

Monty turned and shook his cousin's hand again and slipped him two thousand-peso bills. "Thanks. See that the backpacks are paid for." Giving the others a hand signal, he led the men to the large canoe where they loaded their packs.

They pushed the boat into the water and leaped in. The fisherman pointed the big canoe to the northeast. Above the sound of the engine, Monty yelled to him, "How long to Patalon?" The boatman held up five fingers, meaning five hours. After the first fifteen minutes, the boatman shifted the engine into a higher gear, and the roar increased as they sped across the water.

Darkness had wrapped the peninsula by the time the sound of the engine grew quieter, and the dark shape of the coast rose into sight, extinguishing the stars on the eastern horizon.

The boatman pointed the *banca* toward the beach and cut the engine. It slid with a scraping sound onto the sand. After they pulled the boat higher onto the beach, Monty asked the man if he had been paid by Reynaldo. The leather-skinned fisherman shook his head. Without asking how much, Monty offered the man five thousand pesos, nearly a hundred U.S. dollars. The man was quiet a minute as though not entirely satisfied but then took the money. He returned to his boat, started the engine, and headed out to sea.

Monty and his team started into the darkness of the palms and undergrowth. He simply said, "Put on your goggles. We'll hike tonight and rest in the morning." The forest around them came into focus in shades of luminescent green. Using the bolo knives, they moved through the undergrowth in single file. When the moon rose, they turned off the goggles. The ground rose gradually for the first three hours but then swiftly became steeper.

They were soaked with perspiration by the time the dawn began to dilute the darkness. Monty raised his hand. "I hear water. When we find that stream, we'll rest and get something to eat." While they rested, Monty called Matson and asked if the GPS coordinates for the *Abu Sayyaf* satphone had changed.

"The signal is moving to the north, as though the group may be headed toward Malayal. It's a small village on the coast north of Patalon, but the GPS signal says they are still at about five hundred feet elevation." Monty pulled out the map and checked their relationship to the coordinates Matson had given him. *Not far as the crow flies, but if they know every old foot trail in these mountains, we might conceivably never catch up with them,* he thought grimly.

They spent the afternoon and the early hours of the night hiking to the northeast, eventually reaching the old-growth forest on the steep hillsides at the base of the mountains. About ten o'clock, Monty again called Matson. Without identifying himself, he simply asked, "Anything new?"

"*Radyo Agong* broadcast a recording today of a man named Samuel Chang and his daughter, Emily, asking for a large ransom of two million pesos. The family is to call the radio station for instructions on the exchange. I've talked the CIA into sending a UAV over the area where we most recently located the satphone signal to see if we can determine just how many Abu there are and how many hostages they have. If we're lucky, maybe we can confirm whether or not Sophie's with them. Call me tomorrow night to see what we've found out."

"Will do."

Monty immediately called Estilita Roque at the newspaper. She answered the phone simply, "Roque."

"Montalbon here. What info have you got for me?"

"We monitor all *Radyo Agong* broadcasts here in the office, and I made some telephone calls to my contact there after we heard the broadcast for Mr. Chang and his daughter. He said that after the exchange for the Changs is made, he thinks there's going to be another ransom request within a few days."

"Did he know who it would involve?"

"No."

"Did he know where the exchange for Chang is to take place?"

"He said that one of the former mayors of Sibuco will oversee the exchange, which means that he will take a sizable cut of the money. He's known to sympathize with *Abu Sayyaf.*"

After the call ended, Monty and Rick located the GPS coordinates for Sibuco on the map. Wanting to reach the town before the exchange took place, each man pulled on his night-vision goggles, and they started through the rain forest again.

17

THE SOUND OF THE ENGINE of a small plane awakened the guards. They rolled out of their hammocks and began to kick the hostages to get them to their feet, yelling, "Hide! Hide in the trees."

When they reached the heavier forestation at the edge of the camp, Yusuf yelled, "Do not move!"

The hostages were fascinated by the sight of the small plane, watching it through the gaps in the treetops. Its wingspan was about twenty-five feet, with the propeller on the tail. It circled around and above the opening in the treetops and after two or three minutes, disappeared. Dangwa asked Benito as he watched the small aircraft, "What kind of plane was that?"

"A drone—the CIA uses them. No pilot, just a camera."

Hearing that, Sophie's heart leaped. "They know where we are," she whispered to Chang and Emily. "They know where we are." Suddenly, the slack sails on her little boat of life were briefly filled with the winds of hope.

They immediately moved camp. Chang was stumbling with weakness. When the group found a stream, everyone waded into it to cool down. After sitting down under a tree to wait for her clothing to dry, Sophie watched as Hamal and Hussein carried on a long conversation. She quietly asked Chang, "What are they saying?"

"Last night Hamal called the man who took the tape recording to *Radyo Agong*. He said that the arrangements for payment of the ransom have been made, and the exchange will take place the day after tomorrow."

"For your sakes, I hope nothing happens that might stop the exchange."

"When I get home, Sophie, I will do all in my power to get you and the others freed." He feebly patted her hand.

"May God bless you, Mr. Chang."

In the morning, a man entered the camp and greeted several members of the Abu group as if they were acquainted. When he saw Hamal, he hurried to him and offered a deferential greeting and the customary kiss on each cheek. The two men sat on the trunk of a fallen palm and talked animatedly for some time, the conversation growing heated.

"Do you understand what they're talking about?" Sophie asked Chang.

"The man who just came into camp is inviting this group of Abu to combine with him and his men. He says that combined they will be stronger. The debate seems to center upon who would lead the combined group. The other man says that his group can bring money and many guns so he should become the leader, but Hamal has told him to leave as there will be no discussion about changing leaders."

Chang paused for a couple of minutes as he listened to the continuing discussion. "The other man is changing his position. Apparently, he is willing to take a lesser position, perhaps second in command."

The man stood and offered a bow to Hamal before turning and hurrying back into the forest. Three hours later he returned with four other men. The man who had talked with Hamal carried what looked like a laundry bag of currency and two SACO M60 machine guns on his shoulders. Another carried a bag of rice over one shoulder and several ammunition belts for the machine guns on the other. The third man carried two large heavy oblong objects in a bag draped over his shoulders. The last two men carried the grand prize: a shoulder-mounted, surface-to-air missile launcher. As it was laid at Hamal's feet, all the men chattered excitedly and pointed at it.

Sophie watched the new arrivals with creases of worry in her forehead. "More weapons, more Abu men." She shook her head in discouragement. Looking at Benito, she asked, "Is that a missile launcher?"

He nodded and proudly answered, "It is a Stinger. The other man is carrying two of the missiles it uses." He folded his arms across his chest and bounced on the balls of his feet as he explained, "The leader is telling Hamal that it was smuggled to them from Pakistan. It will be of great use when the CIA sends another drone to spy on us." His tone was full of venom.

The members of the two groups sat down to share a meal of boiled rice and buko juice to seal the new association. To celebrate the new arrangements, even the hostages were offered a handful of rice. As they finished eating, Hamal pulled two of his men aside and spoke with them at length. Then he motioned for Chang and Emily to come to him. Benito untied the ropes from their wrists.

After speaking with them for a few minutes, he motioned for them to go with the men. The four of them disappeared into the forest with Chang leaning on his daughter.

Sophie asked Benito, "Where are they going?"

"To make the exchange."

"I didn't get a chance to tell them good-bye." She suddenly felt that someone she loved like a grandfather had been taken from her. She tried to wipe away a tear without the guard seeing it.

***

Julia received one phone call from Monty. The sound of his voice meant more to her than she had realized it would. "We're in contact with Matson and hope to get to the exchange site before it takes place."

"Exchange for whom?"

"Two of the hostages that *Abu Sayyaf* took the day before Sophie disappeared. We're trying to verify that she's with the same group. *Radyo Agong* broadcast the demand for the ransom yesterday, so we're headed to Sibuco. I'll let you know what we find out." He paused and then added, "Are you okay?"

"Yes, I'm okay. Just facing a nearly fatal case of boredom." He laughed as he ended the call. *It's good to hear her voice.* She held the phone and just looked at it for a moment, regretting the brevity of the call.

After dark that evening Julia decided she had to have a bath before Luz and Enrique came home from the fish shop. Though the evenings were cool, the days had been sultry. She took a hotel-sized bar of soap from her bag and, by moonlight, made her way across the sand to the water's edge. In the quiet darkness, the languid evening breeze made the palm trees whisper to each other. The moon was just above the horizon and had turned the world into a scene of silver and shadow.

She pulled off the caftan and scarf, laid them on the sand and unbuttoned her blouse, dropping it beside the caftan. She made her way into the ocean still wearing her undergarments and slacks. The water caressed her like the jets in a lukewarm hot tub. As she floated on the rise and fall of the gentle surf, she studied the stars spangled by the millions across the sky. Suddenly overcome with a sense of guilt, she thought,

Here I am floating in the ocean while Sophie is in the hands of terrorists. Her pleasure dissipated. She swam back to the shore where she used the caftan as a towel and then dropped it over her head. She shivered under the damp fabric. Upon reaching the hut, she took off her wet clothes that dried before Luz and Enrique arrived home.

***

The next evening she could hardly wait until dark to hurry to the beach again to wash and cool off. As she walked out of the water and picked up the caftan to dry herself off, she thought she saw movement—something or someone watching her from the edge of the undergrowth. Nervously, she threw the caftan over her head, grabbed her blouse, and hurried down the path to the dark hut. Without turning on a light, she quickly dried off and put her blouse on over her wet underwear. Then she put on a dry pair of cargo pants. On an impulse, she put the money belt on under her blouse.

As she changed, she watched the moonlit area outside the doorway as far as she could see. *Maybe it's only the palms stirred by the breeze.* But as she pulled the caftan down over her clean cargo pants, she was sure that she saw someone or something moving through the shadows in the undergrowth. She picked up her Blackberry, put it on vibrate, and slipped it into one of the pockets in her pants.

Hearing a soft footfall on one of the stairs to the porch, she dropped to her knees and crawled underneath the small table where she hoped the black caftan would help her hide in the shadows. She held her breath so her panicked breathing wouldn't give her away. As she pulled her caftan over her knees, she saw two brown feet in flip-flops standing in the patch of moonlight that fell on the split bamboo floor. Suddenly, a hand reached down and roughly pulled her out from under the table and into a standing position facing two dark-skinned men.

One of them shouted at her in Cebuano. In the moonlight, he had the face of a beetle, with a flat nose pressed across his face. He picked up the hijab and held it out to her. He wanted her to put it on. As she did so, he pulled an assault rifle off his shoulder and pointed it at her. He motioned toward the doorway of the hut. They marched her along the beach about three hundred feet to a *banca* that had been pulled onto the sand. Pushing her into it, the men shoved the long canoe into the water.

When she tried to sit up, one of the men yelled at her, motioning for her to stay in the bottom of the boat.

***

When Luz and Enrique arrived home, they were startled to find the hut dark and Julia nowhere to be found. "Maybe she took a walk on the beach," Enrique said. His wife began to cry with worry. He patted her on the shoulder. "She will be back soon. Her big purse and her suitcases with all her clothes are still here."

***

Monty repeatedly tried to call Julia that evening but received no answer. *Something's wrong!* He left the same message twice. "Julia, it's Monty. Call me." His hands were slick with nervous perspiration by the time he made a third call. He steeled himself against the alarming thoughts that filtered into his mind and called Matson. As soon as Matson answered, Monty pulled a small tablet from his pants pocket and said urgently, "You've got to help me. Julia's not answering her cell phone. I need you to contact the CIA and get them to track her. Here's the ESM number of her phone. Hopefully, she has it with her and it's turned on."

"Will do. I'll get back to you as soon as possible. No change in the coordinates for the Abu group. Our source says the exchange for Chang and his daughter is going down in or near Sibuco."

Monty interjected, "According to my contact at the *Standard Bulletin* that's the plan."

"When you get back to Manila, I want to meet your contact. About an hour ago, I got a report back on the UAV flight. On the video, we could see about eight, maybe ten *Abu Sayyaf* as they scrambled to hide in the trees and at least five hostages. One of them is an auburn-haired woman in flowered hospital scrubs. We figure that must be Sophie."

Monty took a deep breath. "Good to know. Thanks." The call ended and he dropped his head and pinched the bridge of his nose while he thought. *That accounts for Sophie. Now what has happened to Julia?* Worry for her safety hit him like a sudden illness. *I should have insisted that she stay at the Manila Hotel. I should never have brought her to Bolong. What has happened?*

He decided not to say anything to the other three until he had a better idea of what had happened to Julia. They had enough on their minds for the moment.

***

As the *banca* moved out into the Sulu Sea, its throttle wide open, Julia lay on her side in the bottom of the boat with her knees doubled up so she could fit between the thwarts. She turned her head so she could look at the sky. *How stupid—how stupid of me to think I could take a bath in the ocean after dark without being seen. Anyone who saw me take off the caftan would have guessed that I'm not a Muslim,* she thought disgustedly. Another thought struck her with force. *Anyone who saw me sitting on the steps of a hut with pigs living underneath would know I'm not a Muslim. It isn't Monty's fault. I should have kept out of sight the way he told me.*

Her mouth felt like cotton, her palms were sweaty with fear, and her heart was beating so fast and hard that she could feel it making her body shudder with each beat. *Where are they taking me?*

Her legs were stiff, and her back hurt where it was pressed against the side of the canoe. After the first hour, the man in the bow signaled that she could sit up. The boat moved westward for another three hours. Gradually, it swung to a northerly direction, always just barely in sight of the shore. Julia felt the cell phone in the leg pocket of her cargo pants vibrate repeatedly, but the sound of the engines covered it. There was no way she could answer it. She yearned to scream, "Monty, I'm in trouble. Please help me."

Calculating the speed and direction of the boat and noting the brightness of the sky that had obscured the stars for about an hour, Julia concluded that they were probably passing Zamboanga City. After the sky darkened again, the big canoe was pointed toward the beach, the engine cut, and in the darkness it slid onto the sand. Julia was ordered out of the boat with hand motions and pointed toward a dilapidated and deserted hut that sat back in the trees and undergrowth about thirty feet from the beach. After she was pushed down into a corner of the weather-beaten hut, the two men began an argument, which finally ended with one of them making a cell phone call.

The man spoke for several minutes, and then in quick succession, he made two more calls. While he talked, the other man brought a rope from the *banca* and tied Julia's hands in front of her. Then he tied the rope around her ankles. When the two men settled themselves for the night, he tied the rope to his left foot so each time she moved it would wake him. Where she lay on the floor, she clasped her hands between her knees to stop their shaking. Eventually, she drifted off to sleep.

The next morning her captor untied her from his ankle and gave her a dipper of two-day-old boiled rice for breakfast. She was left in the hut while her captors talked on the beach. She removed her cell phone from her pocket and tried to call Monty. The call wouldn't go through. The screen read "battery low," and the disappointment hit her like a punch in the stomach. She sat down and fought tears of fear and frustration. *I can't let them see me cry!*

She stood and watched through the hole in the wall of the hut that served as a window as a battered pickup truck drove through the trees on a path so narrow that the branches and vines caught on the antenna and scratched the sides. It stopped at the edge of the undergrowth. Two men jumped out of the cab and lifted five-gallon gasoline cans from the truck bed. They proceeded to fill the gas tank of the big canoe and stowed two additional gas cans in the bow of the *banca*.

One of the men from the truck lifted a package about twelve inches square out of the truck bed where it had been hidden by a load of coconuts. The package was wrapped in green plastic sheeting and tied with heavy twine. He carried the bundle to the *banca* and stowed it in the stern. Then the two men climbed back into the truck and drove away. Julia's kidnappers stood on the beach and talked for an hour, making intermittent cell phone calls.

She guessed it was about noon from the location of the sun in the sky when they forced her into the boat again. To avoid the intense sun, she folded the hijab so it shaded part of her face and pulled her hands inside the sleeves of the caftan. As the time passed and the sun slipped behind her, she concluded that they were moving in a northeasterly direction. The sky darkened, and she glanced over her shoulder to see the sun leave only a sliver of red-orange fire along the horizon before it was extinguished in the western sea.

What do they plan on doing with me . . . or to me? What's in the bundle? She was feeling ill with apprehension and concern that Monty might not be able to trace her cell phone signal once the battery died. It had been a long ride without anything to eat or drink. At about ten o'clock, they beached the boat, and she ended up sitting in another hut under guard for the rest of the night.

***

Using one of the age-old paths that had been hardened by two or three hundred years of foot traffic and ran like a maze through the forest, the four men were able to move more quickly than when cutting their way through the undergrowth. They remained alert so as not to come upon any of the natives of the area without warning. At one point, when they heard laughter, they melted into the trees and watched as two native men leading a boney mule made their way past them, heading toward the coast.

After dark, they again put on the night-vision goggles and continued through the trees, avoiding huts or recently cultivated fields. Stumbling across a deserted Del Monte plantation, they each put a ripe pineapple in their backpacks.

While they rested for a few minutes, Bing said, "Monty, what are we going to do when we get to Sibuco? Are we going to try to grab the Abu as they make the exchange of money for Chang and his daughter?"

"I'm hoping to follow the Abu back to their camp and grab the hostages out from under their noses. If Chang and his daughter have been exchanged for the money by that time, so much the better. Then we have fewer hostages to rescue."

"So we're going to get all of them out, no matter how many there are?" Rich interjected.

"I can't see leaving any of them in the hands of the Abu."

The other men nodded and pulled their night-vision goggles on again. By the time daylight came, they were soaked with perspiration and tired but had located the village that appeared to be made up of one east-west road that snaked out of the forest, two short north-south roads, and perhaps fifty huts clustered unevenly near the roads. Surrounding the village was a vast coconut-palm plantation that furnished much of the income for the villagers. The village sat on the coast where a silt-filled river drained from the mountains into the Sulu Sea.

Finding a gully on the edge of the plantation, Monty motioned for the four men to squat and listen. "Keep your cell phones on vibrate. If you're seen, do your best to pass for local natives. Bing and Bolly, take off your holsters and keep your hand guns in your belts under your shirts. Rick, keep your M16 with you, but try to keep out of sight. If you are spotted, let's hope the villagers take you for Abu. Considering how you speak Cebuano, you'll have to keep your mouth shut. We're going to split up. I'm going to stay here on the road that leads into the village. Rick will move to the beach on the south side of the village in case the hostages are brought by boat. Bolly, you find a place to watch what's going on from the north near the beach. Bing will find a spot on the river where it enters the town in case they bring the hostages in a *banca* on the river. When you find a spot where you can see what's going on, stash your backpacks where you can get at them fast."

While the others cut up the pineapples for breakfast, Monty called Estilita again. "Have you got anything new on the exchange arrangements?"

"My contact at the radio station said that the former mayor will put the suitcase with the money in it into the back of a jeepney that will be parked near the fish market. When the money is in the hands of the kidnappers, Chang and his daughter will be released in the village."

When Monty repeated the information, Bing asked, "Shouldn't a couple of us be in the fish market?"

"No. We're not going to interfere with the exchange. We want to identify the Abu men that bring Chang and his daughter into town and follow them back to their camp. We don't know how long it'll be until the exchange is made. It might not even take place today.

"Rick, you'll call me on the hour and the half hour to report in. Bing, you'll call me five minutes after the hour and the half hour. Bolly, you'll call ten minutes after the hour and the half hour. To save your batteries just report in unless you see something worth mentioning."

The men each moved in a different direction and were quickly out of sight of one another. Monty moved toward the road that led into the village. It was made of crushed coral and was just barely wide enough for two jeepneys to carefully pass each other. Finding a berm about thirty feet from the road that was meant to keep excessive rainwater from flooding the road in the rainy season, he settled into place with his back against a coconut palm. If he raised his head, he could see over the small rise between himself and the road.

The next several hours passed with only the occasional buzz of the satphone as the other three men briefly checked in. At a little after five-thirty, Bing reported in to say that he had moved in close to the market. "From where I'm hidden, I can see a jeepney. There's only a driver in it right now. Do you think they've planned the exchange so late in the day so they can get away in the dark?"

"Probably. Keep me posted if you see any boats coming up onto the beach that might be big enough to be used for an escape."

Within a few minutes, Monty heard voices. He stretched out on his stomach on the hidden side of the berm and lifted his head enough to see two men with rifles prodding an elderly man and a younger woman along the road. *There they are.* Despite the gun barrel in his back, it was obvious that the old man couldn't move any faster. He staggered, and his daughter caught him, trying to prevent him from falling. His face was contorted with pain and exhaustion. His daughter tried to hold him upright, but he staggered once more and fell forward, clutching his chest as he hit the ground. One of the gunmen poked the old man with the barrel of the gun and then kicked him. The old man did not move.

His daughter knelt by the body and wailed, "*Lolo, Lolo,* wake up. Don't die. Don't leave me!" Then she looked up at the two armed men and cried out, "You killed him. You killed my father."

One of the men jabbed her with the barrel of the gun. "Get up. Keep moving. It is the will of Allah."

The men pushed her ahead of them, leaving the old man's body in the road, the woman looking at the ground as she sobbed.

As they neared the village in the growing dusk, Monty carefully made his way to Chang's body. He rolled the old man onto his back. He could see that the old man's eyes were open, but he wasn't there any more.

He closed his eyes and then patted his shoulder. In a tender whisper he said, "Go home, *Lolo.* Go home to God. It's a better place to be."

Returning to his position in the palm grove, he made a call to each of the other men. "One of the hostages is dead, the old man. The woman is being escorted into the village on the main road. They should reach the village within the next few minutes. Have any boats come into the harbor that they could use to get away?"

Rick answered, "A small fishing *banca,* but there was only a couple of men and a woman in a caftan in it. One of the men and the woman got out, but the other man left them on the beach and put the boat back out into the water. I don't expect any boats of any size to be coming in for the next several hours since the tide's going out now."

Monty ordered Rick and Bolly to join him. Ten minutes later, Bing called and reported, "The two Abu men have reached the fish market with the woman. They left her standing in the road and climbed into the jeepney. They're just sitting there." After another few seconds, he added, "Hey, here's a twist. The man and the woman from the fishing *banca* have climbed into the jeepney."

"What does she look like?"

"Hard to tell. I'm a bit too far away to get a good look. She's wearing a black caftan and a white hijab that nearly covers her face. Wait a minute. It looks like she's trying to straighten the scarf. She's pulled it off. She has short, curly blond hair. The man that came in the *banca* with her just threatened to hit her with his rifle if she didn't put it back on. She sure looks a lot like Julia . . . but we left her at your uncle's hut. How would she get here?" His voice was low but filled with excitement. "It looks like they plan to take the jeepney as well as the money."

The line was silent for a moment. *Could it be Julia?* Monty dropped his head and took a deep breath. *And if it is, is that good or bad?*

"They didn't let the driver get out. He's turned the jeepney around, and now it's heading east, toward you. Chang's daughter has been taken in by three of the village women. It looks like she'll be okay."

"Get back here ASAP. We don't want to lose sight of the jeepney in the dark." Within five minutes, the jeepney, which was being erratically driven, rambled past Monty's hiding place.

A few minutes later, when Rick and Bolly rejoined him, panting from the distance and speed they had run, he was on the satphone to Matson. "The old man is dead. It looked like he had a coronary. His daughter's in the village, and his body is on the main road into the village, about a half mile to the east. Is there any change in the GPS signal location of Hamal's satphone?"

"Yes. Here's the new coordinates." Monty pulled out a pencil stub and wrote the numbers on the margin of the map. Matson continued, "We'll see that the old man's body is brought back to his family."

"Have you been able to get a fix on the GPS in Julia's Blackberry?" Matson could hear the tension in Monty's voice.

"Yes, she was located early today, the signal moving northeast up the coast. The most recent location was near Malayal."

"How long ago?"

"About six hours, but the signal became so weak that we're not likely to locate it again."

"The Abu that just left Sibuco had another female hostage with them. Bing said the woman looked like Julia. Considering what you've just told me, I think it must be, and it looks like she's being taken to join the other hostages."

"That's a possibility. In fact, I think it's very likely," Matson added.

Monty exhaled slowly. "I don't know if I should hope it's her in the bus with the ransom money or hope that it isn't her. There's just no way to tell if the situation is good or bad."

"Should I try to notify her employer that we think we know where she is?"

"Not until we have something more solid to tell him." With a brief thanks, he pressed the off button. Then he called Estilita Roque and told her about the death of Chang and the exchange of the money. He said nothing about Julia's kidnapping.

"I'll run the story tomorrow. By the way, you need to know that the AFP is aware of the exchange. It wasn't very secret since the ransom demand was made over *Radyo Agong*. I have no way of knowing if they know the exact location of the exchange, but it's likely that someone leaked the information. The word is that the Scout Rangers are coming in to try to locate Hamal and his men when the exchange is made."

Monty's jaw tightened. He was silent so long that Estilita said, "Hey, are you still there?"

"Yes." He let out a great breath of frustration. "Thanks for the information."

"Ditto."

Monty called Bing again. "We're starting after the jeepney. They won't drive it very far on this road because it turns north just a few miles east of here, and they'll probably head into the forest at that point. We're going to stay on the road to make the best time. I recommend that you do the same. If you put on some steam, you can catch us before we find the jeepney. Hurry, but keep your eyes open for any military you might see in the area."

The three men started east toward the mountains at a steady lope. By the time they had gone two miles, Bolly begged for a rest. "Hey, you guys, I'm not in fighting condition. Give me a few minutes to rest."

While they rested, Monty put on the night goggles and looked up and down the road. "I see someone coming this way. It looks like Bing."

While they gave both Bolly and Bing ten minutes to rest, Monty explained what Estilita had told him. "The AFP is going to mess up this whole rescue effort if they get the chance. To them, the Abu is a bunch of thugs to be squashed, and if hostages get in the way, that's no great loss. Our only advantage is that they don't normally do much at night. Bing told me on the phone that two more people climbed into the jeepney before it left with the money, another man who is probably Abu and a woman in a caftan. Matson and I think the woman is Julia and that she's being taken to join the other hostages. We're going to go on that assumption."

Rick let out a low whistle. "It just gets more complicated, doesn't it?"

They started down the road in the dark at a brisk trot, and within a half hour they spotted the jeepney off the side of the road, its nose angled into a shallow ditch. Monty put his hand on the hood. It was still warm.

Bing and Bolly climbed into the back to see if anything or anyone was left in the jeepney. Rick called out from the other side of the battered vehicle, "Monty, they killed the driver. His body's over here."

18

AFTER TWO HOURS OF HIKING through the forest the next day, Sophie called to Yusuf as he pushed past the hostages, "Daud is exhausted. He isn't strong enough to travel so long without rest."

His expression made it clear that her concerns meant nothing to him. By late afternoon, they had located another deserted hut, and the hostages and Daud were ordered into it. The boy lay in a high fever, occasionally muttering incoherently. Sophie and Carlita washed his face with wet rags, and when the rice was boiled, Sophie held him in a half-upright position and encouraged him to eat while Carlita tried to feed him. Shortly thereafter, Carlita lay down, feeling weaker than usual. By that evening, both she and Philip Dangwa were racked with chills and fever.

Irritably, Benito asked Sophie, "Why are they sick? Will we get sick?"

"No, I think it's malaria."

"You give them amoxicillin." He was sure he had a solution.

Sophie shook her head. "They need quinine. Amoxicillin won't help."

Benito's look of contempt said that as a woman she knew nothing.

As Sophie supported the boy's head and helped him drink a cup of rice water, she asked Benito as he stood over them, "How will the men who exchange Mr. Chang and Emily for the money find us now that we have moved camp?"

"They know where we are. They will find us."

"How will they know where we are?"

"We have been here before. Now be silent, woman. This is not your business."

"If Hamal can call them on a cell phone, he could tell them to get some quinine drugs for Carlita and Dangwa," she insisted.

Benito seemed to lose his patience. "You are only *sabaya*. You are not worth special medicine. Be silent!"

***

Later that afternoon, Ali came to Sophie with a message that Hamal wanted to see her. She approached him with trepidation. He was speaking with Abdul and ignored her for several minutes. She sat down and folded her legs into the lotus position and waited.

Finally, he turned to her. "Abdul wants to marry you." Sophie's head lifted as if she had received a blow to her chin. For the first time in her life, she was totally speechless. Condescendingly, he continued, "I do not know how much longer I can protect you."

Hah—as if you've ever given us any protection, she thought.

"There is talk among some of the men of forcing themselves on you, but if you belong to only one of them, the others will leave you alone."

Sophie found her voice. "Why would any of your men want to marry an infidel?" Her voice was high and tight. "They have refused to even touch me—you went to the stream to wash after you struck me."

Speaking in a tone that suggested he believed the request reasonable, he stated firmly, "You will, of course, convert and become a good Muslim as will the other woman when she is well. Ali desires to marry her."

Sophie was still struggling to order the confusion churning through her mind: fear, anger, disgust, amazement. Not forgetting that these men had the power of life and death over her and the other hostages, she tried to choose her words carefully, which was a challenge for the outspoken young woman. She was striving to keep her tone even and hide her rising emotions. *Hamal seems to think this offer is a kindness.* Her thoughts were still racing—*after all they have put us through, now they think they can force a marriage upon us and we will be happy to comply?* She responded in a tight and high voice, "I can't speak for Carlita, but I will speak for myself. I am flattered that any man would desire me for a wife, and I hope you will tell Abdul that I am honored by his offer, but I am not willing to change my religion."

"Woman, you are foolish!" Hamal spat out the words with contempt. "You know that with one word I can have you beheaded?"

Sophie stated quietly but as firmly as she could manage, "Threats won't change my mind." She was quiet for a moment and then added as the thought struck her, "Doesn't the Qur'an say that 'you are forbidden to inherit women against their will? Nor should you treat them with harshness'? The Qur'an also says that slaves should be treated with kindness."

"The Qur'an does not apply to you. You and the others are only *sabaya*, not even equal to slaves." His voice was hard.

She had no recourse but to come back to the original argument. "I will not convert, and no good Muslim man would take a wife who is not of your religion."

"Will you not convert, woman, even to save your life?" Hamal's voice was rising, drawing the attention of the others in the camp.

She dropped her head but answered in a whisper, "No, I will not convert. I worship Jesus Christ, 'and him only will I serve.'" Unwittingly, she had quoted the familiar words of the Apostle Paul.

Hamal put his face close to hers and said in a low hiss, which was more frightening than his raised voice, "You will change your mind, or I will remove my protection from you and the other woman. You will give the matter much thought." He stood and walked away from her.

Her face was suddenly flushed with anger. *It seems that I'm going to trek through this miserable forest at the point of a gun for the rest of my days. Perhaps a swift beheading is the best that I can hope for.* But in her heart, she knew that wasn't true. *Surely someone will be sent to find me—and please, God, make it soon,* she pleaded in her mind.

She made her way across the camp with an angry and stiff-legged stride toward the hut, wondering if she had sealed her fate when she heard shouting. Four figures entered the camp. Two were the men sent with Chang and Emily, and one of them carried a suitcase. The third man was unfamiliar to Sophie. He carried a bundle wrapped in green plastic and heavy twine. The fourth figure was a woman in a tattered caftan and a torn hijab over her hair, who, from her stumbling walk, was exhausted.

The men of the camp, with the exception of their leader, began to call out, *"Allah akbar"* and *"Salam alaikum"* as they hurried to greet the arrivals and give each of them a ceremonial kiss on both cheeks. Hamal stood aside until they turned to him with increased respect, and the one with the bundle presented it to him with great ceremony. Hamal then stepped forward and offered the same ceremonial greetings and perfunctory kisses on the cheeks to the newly arrived men. The man with the suitcase laid it at his feet, and a loud and excited conversation began, filled with gestures. Hamal simply pointed to the woman they had brought and motioned for her to make her way over to join the other hostages.

When she had crossed the camp, Sophie put her arm around her and started to usher her toward the hut. As she looked into the eyes that peered out from under the hijab, she caught her breath. "Julia?" she said in a strangled whisper. Julia simply nodded and put her finger to her lips.

Looking around to see if they were being watched, Sophie noted that Hamal had opened the suitcase and the men had rushed to look and feel the money in it. Even Benito had slung the ever-present AK-47 over his shoulder and had joined the group.

"Come with me into the hut where we can talk. Can you make it up the stairs?"

Julia simply nodded and unsteadily made her way up the notched log. As they sat in the darkness of the hut, Sophie asked breathlessly, "What are you doing here? Tell me everything before Benito comes back."

Julia looked at Daud where he lay sleeping and at Carlita and Dangwa where they sat against the split bamboo wall, shaking with chills, too ill to care what was going on around them. She whispered, "Is it all right to talk here?"

"Yes, you can talk," Sophie whispered back. "Tell me what you're doing here."

"After you disappeared, your grandfather asked me to fly to Manila and hire someone to organize a search for you. The man that was hired to lead the effort is determined to keep the AFP out of the matter. He and his team are out there in the rain forest somewhere searching for you. He left me with his aunt and uncle in Bolong, but about four days ago, two men kidnapped me. All I could do was keep my cell phone on vibrate until the battery ran out and hope that someone could trace me."

As Julia talked, Sophie's heart began to lift with hope. *Someone is coming to help us.*

Julia changed the subject. "Do they know who you are? Are they going to ask for a ransom?" she whispered.

Sophie shook her head to both questions. "They wanted medical help for the boy," she said as she motioned toward Daud. "And now they want wives for two of the men." She drew her knees up and buried her face in her arms. After a few moments of weeping, she raised her head. "Oh, Julia, it's been awful. I've tried to be strong, but I don't know how much longer I can pretend."

Julia rubbed her back and shoulders as she wept, trying to comfort the young woman. "Have you tried to escape?"

"They told us they would kill the hostages that remain if any one of us tried to escape . . . and Julia, we're too weak and sick to escape. They keep us so hungry . . ." Her voice trailed off.

She wiped her eyes with her sleeve and gave her nose a wipe with the back of one hand. She laughed halfheartedly. "I never fully appreciated simple things in life—like tissues—until now." Her look turned from nervous humor to fear. "We only have a few minutes to talk before they're done celebrating and Benito comes back to watch us. Tell me what else happened."

"After I was kidnapped, I was put into a *banca* and guarded by two men who only spoke Cebuano. We spent two days traveling in the *banca* and sleeping in deserted *nipa* huts. The second day another two men delivered gas for the boat engine and some kind of a package. You probably saw it when we got here. It's wrapped in green plastic."

"What's in it?"

"I don't know—probably drugs. They made some cell phone calls while the other men delivered the gas cans. Then they forced me back into the *banca* for another long ride to a little village where they beached the boat. One of them made me get into a jeepney with him, two other men, and the driver. They made the driver take us out of town where we drove past the body of an old man lying on the road—just lying there with no one to care."

Sophie's eyes widened, and her hand went to her mouth. "Oh, no! I wonder if that was Mr. Chang!"

"After they forced me to get out of the jeepney, they beheaded the driver." For a moment, she held her arms and hands close to her chest and shook with revulsion. "Oh, Sophie, it was so unnecessary—and so heartless. He was a nice young man, and he pleaded with them to spare him for the sake of his wife and children." After a few seconds, she continued, "For the last two days, the three of them have prodded and pushed me through the forest while we've been living on rice and buko juice. Since no one would speak to me in English, I don't know why they've brought me here. I suppose they'll want a ransom." She dropped her voice even lower and added, "I'm so glad they're unwilling to touch an infidel. If they had searched me, they would have found the money belt around my waist. I'm sure that if I offered to pay my own ransom, they would take the money and still demand more."

"Why are you wearing a caftan and scarf?"

"Monty said they would keep me from standing out with my light skin and blond hair, but the men who kidnapped me weren't fooled."

"Monty? Who's Monty?"

"He's the man your grandfather is paying to find you. He and three other men are hunting for you—and hopefully for me." Julia was silent for a moment and wiped away a tear with the sleeve of the caftan. "Oh, Sophie, I'm so sorry. I've ruined everything. I was supposed to arrange your rescue. I was supposed to get you home to your grandparents, safe from harm. Instead, I've just managed to get myself into the same fix you're in. I've made everything worse." After a quiet minute, Julia took a deep breath and regained her composure. "Tell me what you meant when you said they want wives for two of the men."

"Hamal told me a few minutes before you got here that Abdul has asked to marry me, and Ali wants to marry Carlita when she's better."

"What's she sick with?"

"She and Mr. Dangwa apparently have malaria." She nodded toward the two who were huddled against one wall of the hut. Returning to the subject of the marriage proposal, she whispered, "I'm sure they both have wives wherever they call home, but that won't stop them from trying to force us to marry them. Hamal informed me that I'd simply convert to Islam and then I would become Abdul's wife. I told him that I won't convert."

Her words slowed with emphasis. "That made him *very* angry. A good Muslim man won't marry an infidel woman, so to scare me into obeying him, he threatened to allow the men to," she paused and then quoted him, "'to have their way with me.'"

"To have their way with you?" Julia's voice rose. "You mean rape?"

"That's what you and I would call it, but I remember that you taught us in that world religion class that rape isn't a crime in a strict Muslim society. It's simply what a man does when he's tempted by a woman, and it's always considered the woman's fault."

Julia finished the thought for her, speaking more to herself than to Sophie, "So the women are forced to wear a burqa, or a caftan and a head scarf, so they won't tempt the men." Julia rubbed her eyes with the heel of her hands, as if she might wake up and the bad dream would be over. "Sophie, this is an awful situation."

"I told him that his threats won't make me change my mind." Looking into Julia's face, she added, "But Julia, I'm scared. This has all been like a bad dream, a nightmare that never ends—and I'm so sorry that you're caught up in it." She paused and tried to smile. "But I'm so glad to have someone to talk to—and to lean on, even though I know that you're scared too."

Both women leaned back against the wall of the hut and closed their eyes, as if to try to absorb the ramifications of what they had been talking about. After a few minutes, Julia asked, "Do the men pray each day?"

Without opening her eyes, Sophie responded, "Yes, at dawn, at midday, and in the evening."

"Then while they pray, so will we. They surely can't stop us and 'the fervent prayer of a righteous man—or a righteous woman—availeth much,'" Julia paraphrased the well-known scripture from the fifth chapter of James.

"I'm ashamed to admit that I've done no more than offer silent prayers in my heart since this nightmare began, and I've wondered if any of them have done any good."

Benito returned to the hut to guard the hostages. "Benito," Sophie said, "if one of the men here in this camp wanted to take a wife, who would perform the marriage ceremony?"

"Hussein is an imam. He would say the words of the *shahadah* that would make you a Muslim and a wife." Sophie said nothing but looked at Julia with wide, worried eyes.

19

IN THE MORNING, SOPHIE EXPLAINED the call of "mobiling" to Julia as she was roped to the other hostages. By midafternoon, they had come upon a mountain village of about twenty-five bamboo huts where women sat in the doorways weaving baskets. A little stream with a log for a bridge ran down the hillside and through the village. On the far side of the stream on the sloping hillside, a little government school had been built several decades earlier. The building was about forty-five feet long and twenty feet wide. The siding was made of milled wood that had once been painted white, but too much rain and humidity left only small patches of paint still adhering. It had louvered windows along the side that faced the village that were open to the breeze. About fifty barefoot children played on the hard-packed dirt around it.

As the group entered the village, many of the women called to their children. More than half of them left the school yard and hurried to their mothers, looking at the strangers with wide eyes as they ran past them. The other children simply stood still and watched these people who had entered their village and frightened the women.

Hamal motioned toward the school with his head, and Hussein led the group over the log and into the little building. Inside the doorway, in the first classroom lined with nearly empty bookshelves, three teachers were tutoring four students. They looked at the men and their captives with frightened eyes.

Hamal gave orders, waving the barrel of his assault rifle, telling them to move into the adjoining room. The hostages were ordered to follow them.

The Abu men separated into three groups of five, and each group made themselves comfortable in one of the three classrooms. Benito, Ali,

Hussein, Yusuf, and Hamal settled themselves on the floor in the middle classroom with the hostages, whose number had grown by seven.

Hussein said to the frightened teachers and children, "Sit, sit. We will not hurt you." When they did not respond, he repeated himself in Cebuano. Cautiously, they gathered together into a group in one corner where they sat on the floor. The little girl began to cry. Yusuf attempted to speak to her in a softer tone of voice and with a smile as if to comfort her. She buried her face in her teacher's shoulder and continued to cry. Then he yelled something at her to intimidate her into silence. She cried harder.

Julia spoke quietly to Benito who was sitting near her under the windows that ran along the one wall. "Why have we come here?"

"Hamal called one of his contacts last night, and they said that the AFP had many men in the area, looking for us. We come here so they won't find us."

"But what if they find out where we are?"

"They will not shoot at us in a school. They cannot. It is against the Geneva Convention to shoot into a school or a hospital."

Julia looked at him in amazement. "You think you're covered by the Geneva Convention?"

"Why not? We are an army, and we are fighting a war." Julia and Sophie exchanged looks of amazement but said nothing more.

They sat for an hour in the hot classrooms. Some of their captors stretched out on the floor to sleep. Others prowled around the little building, picking up and examining the meager teaching supplies, pocketing any they wanted, and looking at the pictures in the little storybooks.

One man stuck his head in the door of the classroom where the hostages sat on the floor and announced, "CR." He was smiling and pointing behind him, genuinely pleased to make such an important announcement.

Wanting water for washing and prayers as well as for drinking, Hamal ordered two men out to the stream to fill the canteens and the two big plastic jugs they carried with them. As they waited for the jugs to fill, they noticed the villagers had quietly fled up the mountainside into the rain forest, leaving half-finished baskets lying in the doorways and in the dirt under the huts. As the two men carried their jugs and canteens back toward the school building, a shot rang out. Then another and another, and one of the men fell, wounded. He struggled to his feet, and the other man helped him reach the doorway of the building. Both men yelled, "AFP."

Every Abu man grabbed his gun, poked the barrel through the louvers of the jalousie windows, and began to fire. The glass from the louvers shattered and fell like a cloudburst as bullets poured into the little building, making the children and teachers scream and put their hands over their ears.

Julia and Sophie called out together, "Get down. Lie down on the floor." Sophie pulled Carlita down with her. The teachers and children did not understand the words, but they followed their example. The noise of gunfire and the crying of the women and children was almost deafening. *Thank heaven this little building is built of more solid stuff than most of the buildings in these islands,* Julia thought as she lay on the floor with her hands over her ears.

Hamal stopped firing and looked at Julia. "Come here, woman. You will make a phone call and tell the AFP to stop shooting. You will tell someone you know to call the president and tell her to make them stop shooting into a school. You will tell her that there are children and teachers here."

Julia shouted above the noise of the gunfire, "I don't know anyone in your government. Who would I call?"

"You will call the U.S. Embassy!"

"I don't know how to call the embassy." Her voice was strident with nerves.

Remaining stooped below the level of the windows, Hamal reached out and grabbed Julia by the wrist and pulled her through the broken glass on the floor. He yelled in her face, "You will call someone and tell them to make the AFP stop shooting, or I will shoot one of the teachers." He thrust his satphone at her.

She took it in one hand and, with the other, unconsciously tried to brush some of the broken glass off her upper arm and leg.

"You will call now!" Hamal put his face against hers. She didn't doubt that he meant what he had said.

She closed her eyes for a moment, *Dear God, who can I call?* Monty's face appeared before her eyes, and she pressed the numbers of the satphone he was carrying, the only number she could think of. As she waited for the connection, she silently prayed that it would be turned on.

***

Monty had been trying to reach Matson for several minutes. Finally, he dug around in his backpack until he found another battery for the satphone. When the call with Matson connected, he asked, "Isn't it a little late for you to be at the office."

"I've been keeping my satphone with me since you started this rescue effort. I even keep it on the nightstand at night. My wife is wondering what's up. What d'you need?"

"Is there any likelihood that you could get the CIA to send in another UAV to try to verify whether or not Julia is with the group we're trying to locate?"

"I'll try. Call me about noon tomorrow, and I'll try to get you more information." After he had disconnected the call, Monty was about to turn the satphone off to save the battery when it vibrated in his hand.

He pressed the talk button and heard Julia's voice, screaming above the sound of gunfire, "Monty, call the U.S. Embassy. Tell them to call the president. The AFP is shooting at us in a school in a village in the mountains. There are teachers and children here. Get them to stop, please."

"Julia, Julia, where are you? Is Sophie there? Can you tell me where you are?"

"Yes, Monty, Sophie's with me. Please make the call. Get them to stop!" Then the phone went dead.

Monty immediately placed a call to Matson. As he waited for Matson to pick up the phone, the knot in his stomach tightened. He put the phone in his left hand and wiped his sweaty right hand on his pants. *Julia's caught in a firefight. We've got to get her and Sophie out of there!*

"Who was that? I could hear someone yelling," Rick said.

Without taking the time to respond to Rick, Monty yelled at Matson when he picked up, "Matson, you've got to call the palace. Tell the president to contact the AFP headquarters down here and call off the firefight. The Abu are holed up in a school in a village up in the mountains, and the soldiers are firing into the school!"

"How do you know?"

"Julia just called. I'm sure the Abu made her do it, but she said that there are teachers and children in the school as well as the Abu and the hostages. Get the president to call off the AFP."

"I'll do what I can."

"Get back to me when you know what's happening," Monty added.

"Will do."

***

The firefight continued for another thirty minutes, but, suddenly, the AFP gunfire ceased. The Abu jumped up and cheered until Hamal yelled for them to get back to their positions at the windows.

The rooms in the schoolhouse were quickly growing darker as the shadows brought by the dusk began to creep up the mountainside.

After about ten minutes of silence, Julia took a deep breath and asked Hamal, "Will you let us take the children and the women to the CR? The children are so frightened they might wet their pants."

He was unresponsive for a moment and then motioned toward the CR over his shoulder with his thumb. "Do not take too long." He returned to watching out of the window again.

Julia waved at Sophie, and in a bent position to avoid being seen through the windows, they both made their way to the huddled group of teachers and students in the corner. Sophie said, "CR? Come to the CR with us."

Neither the children nor the teachers understood anything but "CR." Julia and Sophie hurried them through the third classroom, and when one of the men turned from the window, Julia said simply, "CR." He turned back to the window.

When they opened the door to the little restroom, Julia and Sophie stepped inside. Without turning on the single bulb that hung from the ceiling, Julia motioned to the smallest child and pointed to the commode. The child took advantage of the opportunity and sat on it. As was the case in most villages in the islands, there was no toilet tank, just a pump above a well in one corner and a bucket to use to flush the toilet.

Julia pointed at the old casement window that was stuck in the open position about four inches above the sill. "Help me get it open," she whispered. While Julia lifted, Sophie got down on her knees and pushed. It slowly began to move. Julia whispered, "Sophie, cry, cry loudly."

Without asking why, Sophie began to sob as if she were frightened. Her sobs covered the sound of the window sash as it rubbed against the frame. When it was fully open, Julia opened the door to the CR and pulled one of the terrified teachers into the room. She pointed to the open window and made a pushing motion, to urge the woman to climb out.

The woman was obviously frightened, but Julia and Sophie pulled her over to the window and pointed out. The woman shook her head, so Julia made a cutting motion with her hand across her throat and pointed toward the Abu men in the classroom.

The teacher timidly put her leg out of the window and then bent and put her head under the raised sash. Lifting her other leg out of the opening, she dropped the five feet to the ground. As she turned to run away, Julia leaned out and whispered, "Sssst, sssst, sssst," the universal Filipino hiss that meant anything from "stop it" to "shut up" and caught her attention. Sophie handed the smallest child to Julia, and Julia helped the child out of the open window. Seeing what they were doing, the teacher reached up and caught the child. Quickly, Sophie opened the door of the small restroom and grabbed the arm of the next child. She pulled the child inside and closed the door. Then Julia took the child and poked his head through the window while she whispered into his ear, "Sssst, sssst, sssst," to make him understand that he needed to be quiet.

The teacher below the window caught the child. To cover the sounds in the bathroom, Sophie pumped water into the bucket and flushed the toilet. Julia opened the door and grabbed an arm of each of the two children still waiting to use the CR. She pulled both in and pointed to the open window. She lifted the small boy and put his feet through the window. She lowered him by his arms, and the teacher caught him when he reached the ground.

After he had watched his friend go through the window, the fourth child started to climb out without any urging. After he was lowered to the teacher, Julia put her head out and waved her hand toward the steep hill, urging the teacher to take the children up into the forest and the increasing darkness.

Sophie opened the door of the little room and pulled in the two remaining teachers. With four women in the little restroom, it was so crowded that it was difficult for the second teacher to climb out, but she finally made it, falling on her backside when she hit the ground. Sophie continued to pump rapidly to cover any noise they were making. The third teacher was a larger woman no more graceful than the others and more challenged by the task. She grunted and forced her rotund form through the window while Sophie's pumping continued. When the last woman hit the ground, she made a noticeable "Ooofff" before she stood and started up the hillside into the darkness with the other woman.

As Julia and Sophie closed the window, Abdul pulled the restroom door open and yelled, "What are you doing in here?"

Sophie quickly stepped up to him and said, "What are you doing in the CR with women?"

"Where are the teachers and the children?" he angrily demanded.

Julia stepped up next to Sophie and said, "How would we know? You're the one who's supposed to be watching them."

Abdul went to the window and found that it opened fairly easily. He looked at Sophie. "I would shoot you, but you are going to be my wife, and then I will do with you what I please," he said with a clenched jaw. He grabbed both women by the wrists and pulled them back to the second classroom where he threw each of them down on the broken glass in front of Hamal.

"They helped the teachers and the children escape out the window in the CR."

Hamal looked at both women with narrowed eyes and spoke to Abdul in Cebuano. The women did not understand what was said, but after they had talked for a minute or two, Hamal spoke to Sophie with a hiss, "I have given you to him. You will not be his wife; you will be his property. Starting tomorrow, he will have the right to tell you what to do, and you will do it."

Sophie's heart almost froze. In the shadows, Julia could sense Sophie's panic more than she could see it.

Hamal rose to his feet and grabbed Julia's arm like a vise. He put his face almost against hers. "If you were not worth a great ransom, I would give you to one of my men." He struck her, sending her reeling across the room. Then he called out, "Mobiling, mobiling," and the other men began to gather up their packs and weapons in the darkness. Abdul and Benito tied the hostages together by the wrists again, so tightly it hurt, and the group left the little school in single file. It was nearly in shambles.

Sophie asked Benito, who was following her and pushing her with the barrel of his gun, "Why are we leaving the school? Won't the AFP be waiting in the forest?"

"AFP soldiers never fight at night. They like to sleep." Benito snorted with contempt, and they started through the forest by the light of the half moon.

In the morning, Hussein pointed his gun barrel at Julia where she lay beneath an empty hammock and simply said, "You come with me." She rose and followed him across the camp area to where Hamal was sitting. She stood silently, waiting for him to tell her what he wanted.

"Sit, woman," he finally said.

She sat on the ground, keeping the torn and dirty caftan over her legs to hide the western clothing underneath. She had tried to wipe the blood off her face where her lip had bled after the blow in the school. "Who are you, woman?" When she did not immediately answer, he added, "You wear a marriage ring. Is your husband rich? Will he ransom you?"

With her fears tumbling about in her mind, she tried to determine the wisest answer. Carefully choosing her words, she replied, "Yes, I will be ransomed."

"How rich is he?"

"I am only a woman. I know nothing of such things."

"You are American, not Muslim or Filipino. You know more than you are saying. Would he pay a million pesos for you? Are you worth that much to him?"

"That is maybe more than he can pay." She dropped her head as if embarrassed. She did not want him to think he could extort an enormous sum for her but still knew it needed to be large enough in his eyes to keep him from giving her to one of his men.

"How much would he pay for you?"

"Maybe half that much. If he doesn't have that much, he might get some money from his uncle."

"You will make a tape recording to ask for the ransom, and one of the men will take it to *Radyo Agong*." He thrust the battery-operated tape recorder toward her face. "Speak. Tell us the name of your husband and how we contact him. Tell him after he has the money for the ransom, he will call *Radyo Agong* for instructions."

Steadying her voice, she started, "This message is for Mike Legaspi of Manila." Pressing her memory for the telephone number of the Manila chapter of the foundation, she repeated it and added, "Mike, this is your wife, Julia." She stressed the word *wife* and then continued, "I'm a hostage of *Abu Sayyaf*. They want a ransom of a half million pesos to let me go. I know you don't have that much, but you can contact Uncle Mallon. He will help. Ask him for the money. When you have it, call

Radyo Agong, and they will give you instructions on how to exchange it for me. Please hurry. I am sure Uncle Mallon will help."

When she had finished the message, Hamal popped the cassette out of the recorder and called Yusuf over. "Take this to *Radyo Agong.* Call me and tell me when they play it, and then call me when they get an answer."

After Yusuf left, the group "mobilized" again, this time up a hillside so steep they had to hold onto the small trees and vegetation to avoid slipping and losing their footing. By the time they had reached the top of the ridge, they had all scraped and cut their hands, elbows, and knees on the volcanic outcroppings. Carlita was crying and shaking with weakness. When they reached the logging road near the top, the group stopped and very carefully, two at a time, ran across the road, each hostage accompanied by a captor. That evening as the Abu finally stopped for prayers, the women knelt and prayed.

Julia prayed aloud as she held Sophie and Carlita's hands, "Dear Father, we need Thy help and strength to withstand our trials. We know that Thy Son taught us to love our enemies and pray for those who despitefully use us, but, Father, we are tired and angry with those who have taken our freedom and threaten our lives. Please give us the strength to . . . to just hang in and hold on—and please send help."

Benito watched them with suspicion, as if he didn't know how to react. As Julia tried to go to sleep on the hard ground, she remembered her words to Monty. *I can handle just about anything that might get thrown at me in these islands.* She wondered if she had been tempting some cruel fate when she said that.

Terrified that at any time she might feel Abdul grab her to drag her to his bed, Sophie whispered to herself, "He was probably just trying to scare me into converting." But she didn't drift off to sleep until after midnight.

20

WITHIN FIFTEEN MINUTES, MATSON HAD reached the administrative aid to President Arroyo, and in another ten minutes, General Del Roasario had been contacted. Five minutes later the cease-fire call to the AFP troops had been made. Matson called back to tell Monty that the firefight had been called off.

"Thanks," Monty responded with relief. After he put the satphone back into the backpack, he sat with his head in his hands for a full minute. Under his breath he muttered, "Let's hope that none of the hostages were hurt." But it was Julia's face he saw in his mind. He stood and picked up his backpack. "We've got to find them and get them out of there soon. If the *Abu Sayyaf* doesn't kill them, the military might."

Instead of resting, the four men moved through the forest throughout the night. Each time they stopped to catch their breath, the sight of Julia's potentially bullet-riddled body slipped into his consciousness. He limited the rest stops to ten minutes. After each one, he stood abruptly, pulled on the night-vision goggles, and signaled for the others to follow him.

As the sun began to lighten the sky above the mountain peaks, Monty finally stopped at a small stream. "Let's get a couple of hours of rest here."

The four of them stretched out on a layer of palm fronds, each separating his resting place by at least three yards from each of the others and an equal distance off the path so in case one of them was sighted, the others might not be exposed.

They had been asleep about two hours when the voices woke Monty. He rolled onto his hands and knees. As he did so, Rick whispered, "Monty, do you hear that?"

Monty responded, "Sssst, sssst, sssst!" As the voices neared, it became evident that they were speaking Tagalog, the language of the AFP. He stealthily made his way over to Bolly, who was still sleeping and put his hand over his mouth. Bolly's eyes opened in alarm, and Monty leaned over and whispered in his ear, "AFP." Bolly remained still and Monty moved stealthily on all fours to where he could see Bing, who had heard the voices and was sitting up. He spread his hands palms down to signal that none of them were to move.

They remained unmoving for three or four minutes before eight Army Scout Rangers came along the path, about ten feet from where they were hidden by the tree trunks, vines, and shadows. They remained unmoving until the sound of the voices faded.

As the four men stood, Monty whispered, "This complicates things. We've got to get to the hostages before they do. If we keep moving day and night, we can outdistance them because they'll halt when it gets dark."

He pulled out the satphone and dialed Matson again. "We need the most recent distance and direction. Have you got it?"

"You're about ten miles to the southwest of the most recent satphone signal. There's some tough terrain between you and them. They appear to be at about six hundred feet elevation, up in the rain forest."

"The situation has been complicated by a squad of AFP Scout Rangers in the area. Do you know anything about them?"

"No. They didn't get any information from us—repeat, they did not get info from us."

"Thanks. Out."

As they turned to follow the old path again, they heard the sound of automatic weapons. They froze where they stood.

"What the devil . . ." Monty whispered. The gunfire continued in erratic and uneven bursts.

Lifting his right hand and bringing it down in a forward motion, Monty motioned for them to move in behind him on the double, and they moved toward the sound with long strides. The gunfire continued for nearly two more minutes. When it stopped, Monty put up his hand to signal a halt. They waited and listened for a few seconds and then continued single file again, slowly and quietly. In a few minutes, they could hear the excited voices of several men.

Dropping and crawling on their stomachs, using their forearms for traction, the four men pulled themselves to a position where each was able to peer from a hiding place in the shadowed undergrowth. They could see the AFP Scout Rangers as they ransacked a small cluster of huts, the size of an extended family grouping. One old man, two younger men, and a boy of about twelve lay in the dirt where a few minutes earlier chickens and pigs had been scratching and rooting. As the four men watched, one of the uniformed men pulled a terrified woman from one of the huts, dragged her down the log stairs, and pushed her down on the ground. She huddled there with her hands over her ears while he aimed an M16 at her head.

The sound of a short burst of fire from Monty's weapon brought a look of surprise to the man's face. He looked up and then crumpled in a heap. Years of training had taken over, and Monty had flipped the selector switch on his M16 to automatic and dropped the soldier without a conscious thought. Several other soldiers looked toward the sound of Monty's weapon and began to rake the undergrowth and trees with gunfire. Following Monty's lead, Rick fired a short burst, dropping a second man. The other soldiers continued to fire into the trees. Bing and Bolly lay in the shadows and returned fire. When seven uniformed men lay in the dust with the bodies of the farmers, the eighth called out from inside one of the huts. He stood in the doorway using a woman for a shield.

It was impossible to understand what he was yelling above the screams of the terrified woman. Monty yelled at her, "Down, get down." The woman apparently heard him. She folded her knees, slid out of the soldier's grasp, and dropped the five feet to the ground in a heap below the hut. As the soldier took aim at her, Monty squeezed off a burst from his M16. The man dropped like a rag doll.

When the brief firefight ended, all of the soldiers were down. Bing and Bolly each held the Berettas they had been using in the two-handed, ready position pointed at the ground as they cautiously came out of the trees.

Monty went quickly from one body to another. He found a soldier who was still alive and rolled his body over, looking into his face. With unveiled rage, he shouted, "Why did you shoot them?" The man did not answer so he took him by the hair and lifted his face nearer his own. "Why did you shoot them?"

"We thought they were Abu . . . " The man's voice shook with the recognition that an unavoidable judgment was upon him.

As Monty demanded answers from the wounded soldier, several children carefully made their way out of the forest where they had hidden. They made their way to the family members who lay dead in the dust, and wept loudly.

"You lie!" Monty spoke through clenched teeth, a look of dark intensity on his face. "There are no women with *Abu Sayyaf* except hostages, and no children. You thought you would take whatever these poor farmers had that was of value and then violate their daughters. What you did was evil." He spat out the words and let go of the man's hair.

The soldier tried to whisper something, but his head dropped to the ground where his eyes opened in a death stare. Monty wiped the sweat from his face with his bent arm.

Rick checked each of the bodies of the farmers. "Two of the three farmers are dead. The other one, the old man, won't live very long. The boy will probably be okay. He isn't hurt bad, just a crease in his scalp."

Bing and Bolly moved among the frightened survivors, speaking with the women and each of the older children who had cautiously returned to the little cluster of huts.

The woman Monty had saved was telling the twins in short, frightened bursts that the soldiers had come out of the forest, and when she had seen them she had told the children to run and hide. She didn't know why they had begun to shoot. "We have nothing of value, but they sometimes take and spoil our daughters and leave them dead in the forest. We would have given them food, but they did not ask." She could not longer fight the tears so she pulled away from the two men who looked so much alike and knelt by the body of the old farmer and cradled his head in her lap.

The four men gathered to talk. Rick voiced what they were all thinking. "We can't take the time to dig the graves. We'll lose a full day, and there may be another squad of AFP behind this one. What can we tell these people?"

By this time a few others who had fled into the forest had made their way back to the cluster of huts and stood silently watching. The woman that had been used as a shield approached the men and stood silently until Monty turned to her and gently asked, "What is it you want to say?"

She looked down at the ground. "We will care for our dead. The boys will find a way to bury the soldiers. Go on your way." She was twisting a rag nervously in her hands. "If someone comes to find the soldiers, we will tell them they were killed by *Abu Sayyaf.* Now you must go."

Monty unbuttoned his hip pocket and took several one-thousand peso bills and put them in her hand. "These husbands and fathers cannot be replaced, but please take this money and share it with the others to help buy the food your husbands would have provided for your children." The woman bowed her head toward Monty and then toward the other three before she hurried away toward the other women.

Before leaving the little cluster of huts, the four men gathered the weapons and ammunition from the bodies of the soldiers, putting the additional M16s over their shoulders and the ammunition into their backpacks. Now they suddenly had eight more M16s between them. It would be a heavy load, but they knew they couldn't leave the weapons for the *Abu Sayyaf.*

They returned to the time-worn path that led northeast and put the village of grieving women and children behind them. When they paused to drink and rest at a stream, Bing asked Monty, "Did we do the right thing—I mean back there in the village?"

"We had no choice. We couldn't let the entire village be murdered. I only regret that we didn't get there sooner."

As it grew dark, they each found a boulder or a tree to lean against and tried to get an hour's sleep. When Rick awoke and stretched his stiff legs and arms, he slipped his night goggles on and looked around. Bing and Bolly were still asleep, but Monty was missing. He carefully walked in a ten-foot circle around the sleeping twins, and he soon saw Monty kneeling with his back toward him and his head down. Thinking he was ill, Rick stepped toward him at the same time his friend stood.

When Monty turned and saw Rick, he said without embarrassment, "I thought we could benefit from a prayer—and so could those villagers we saved today."

Rick said nothing. He had known since their special forces days that Monty was a religious man. He had never asked him about it, even though he found it unusual that a man of strong religious beliefs would find a place in a military special forces unit. "Well, I hope He heard you."

"He did. If we do our part, He will do His." Monty gave the signal that it was time for the men to renew their search.

21

As the sun rose, the sound of a UAV drew the camp's attention. Hamal commanded, "Hide, hide! Don't let it see you." Wildly, the men ran for the thickest of the trees where they stood immobile. Even Benito hurried into the trees, technically leaving the hostages in the hut unguarded.

The hostages and Daud had been forced to stay in the hot and crowded hut, and Sophie and Julia had tried to ease the fevers of the other three. Dangwa was very ill, and Carlita was only slightly better.

When the drone appeared, Julia quickly pulled off her white silk hijab and peered around the doorway of the hut. She tossed it outside, hoping a breeze would carry it a few feet out into the sunlight. It did. As it floated to the ground, Hamal yelled at her, "Woman, you will pay for that!" His voice was full of rage.

The drone began to circle about six hundred feet above the camp, and Hamal yelled orders. At his command, the two men who had carried the missile launcher into camp hurried out of the trees and into the clearing. It took them a full minute to get the launcher onto the shoulder of one and loaded with a Stinger missile. Hamal continued to yell at them throughout the process. As the drone straightened out its flight pattern, they fired the missile. A small ejection motor propelled the missile several feet from the launcher before the motor on it ignited. In a burst of flame, it shot out of sight. Almost immediately they heard a great explosion above and to the west of the camp. The Abu men came out of their hiding places and began yelling in excitement and dancing around the camp.

The commotion roused Carlita. "What is going on?" she asked weakly.

"They just shot down the drone," Julia answered.

"Was anyone hurt?" the sick young woman weakly asked.

"No, the drone had no pilot. I hope it transmitted our location before it was destroyed."

At that point, they heard Hamal's angry voice. He had picked up the hijab and called, "You, the American woman! Come out of the hut!"

Julia took a deep breath and stepped out of the hut onto the notched log. "Come here and get your hijab." He held it up with two fingers as it fluttered in the light breeze.

As she made her way down the stairs cut in the log, she said, "I was so hot that I had loosened it," which was true. "I don't know how it was carried into the yard. Perhaps the breeze took it." That was not entirely true. When she reached Hamal and put out her hand to take the scarf back, he struck her jaw with his fist, knocking her down. She lay stunned, hearing what sounded like the buzz of an electrical charge surging through her head and feeling as if all the electrical lines in her internal fuse box had shorted out. He stepped closer to her and kicked her hard in the ribs. She cried out in pain as she felt at least two ribs pop. The world spun around where she lay in the dirt. For a few moments, she was aware of nothing but the pain and the sudden difficulty of breathing.

Sophie hurried down the makeshift stairs and rushed to her friend. As she knelt to help her sit up, Hamal yelled, "You will leave her there in the dirt. She will stay there." Seeing that Sophie did not move, he yelled again, "Go back to the hut. Leave the woman there." Only after he brought his gun to bear on her with a grim expression did Sophie stand and return slowly to the hut.

Julia was forced to lie in the dirt with her left wrist tied by a hemp rope to a nearby tree trunk and her right ankle tied to a stand of bamboo. She had no choice but to lie on her back, looking up at the sky, filled with a mix of emotions that ranged from anger toward her captors to grief at the thought that she might never see the grandchildren she hoped would bless her life one day. Shielding her eyes with her bent right arm she lay in the sun, kept awake by pain, insects, and heat until evening. Throughout the night, she was aware of the buzz of mosquitoes and the whine of night insects. An occasional rat or dragonlike lizard ran over or near her. At one point, she felt the soft, investigative touch of a tarantula. She twisted her head and identified it in the moonlight. Even though it sent a stab of pain through her when she lifted her arm, she took a handful of dirt with her right hand and threw it on the large, hairy brown spider that skittered away.

She controlled her tears until it was dark and the camp had grown quiet. As the moon rose, she finally got past the pain. She silently prayed with an intensity she had never known before. *God, where are you? Do you know what's happening to us? When are You going to help us?*

Finally, her heart slowed and her emotions subsided as a simple scripture filled her mind. *"Be still and know that I am God."*

What had her mother taught her? She could hear her mother's voice clearly, as if she were there beside her. "Faith pushes out fear. Your heart cannot hold both at once. Take hold of your faith, Julia." Despite the night breeze that had begun to chill her, she was filled with a quiet warmth for a few minutes.

As the hours passed, she tried to overlook the pain to study the dark world around her. A large night bird tore the fabric of the black sky with the vibrato of its cry. The darkness above her held only a half-moon that sat on its back like a bright bowl that had spilled its contents. She found a great fascination in the black velvet sky where a million stars were scattered in a great arc above her.

The words of an ancient scripture flowed into her mind: *Worlds without number have I created.* She whispered, "Worlds without number . . . Dear Eternal Father, as the One who created this great universe, our situation is known to You. Please help us endure." The pain forced her to control her sobs.

As she studied the sky, she thought of each family member: Paul, who had tried to become the surrogate father after Jack's death, and Allison, who seemed so much younger without her father. Then the sight of Aaron, lying in the hospital bed connected to the respirator and heart monitor took shape in her mind. For a moment, she wondered, *Is his situation any different from mine? Is he any less a captive than I am?* Toward morning the ocean breeze moved through the palms until they sighed and whispered among themselves.

As the large, nocturnal fruit bats returned from their nighttime forays to take their places in the highest branches of the trees, she began to drift off to sleep. Shortly thereafter the sky brightened, and she was prodded awake by the barrel of Benito's gun. "Get up, go into the hut. Now!"

After he untied the ropes, she arose stiffly, dizzy with pain, her joints feeling as if they had rusted into immobility. She unsteadily made her way up the notched log. Breathing hurt so much she could only take shallow, half breaths. When she entered the hut, Sophie rose from where she had been sitting on the floor and gave her a great hug, which made Julia cry out in pain. "I'm sorry, Julia. I didn't mean to hurt you, but Hamal has lost face. He is so angry that he may do something . . . well, something to make our lives hard."

Julia gave an attempt at a cynical little chuckle that she had to stop because of pain. "Hard? Hasn't he done that already?" she whispered.

"I mean harder."

"Why?"

"Because you disobeyed him by trying to signal the drone. You know as well as I do that it's part of their culture to extract retribution from anyone who makes them lose face." Both women remained quiet as they thought about the possibilities.

As the Abu men completed their morning ritual washing and began their prayers, Sophie knelt, and Julia, stiff and hurting, put her hand on her friend's shoulder and struggled to kneel with her. First, Sophie offered a prayer aloud, and Julia followed. Carlita sat silently in the corner, hardly noting the actions of the other two women. Benito watched with a scowl.

After the men finished their morning prayers, Hamal came to the hut. "You will not eat today, none of you will eat." He turned away, his anger and frustration evident.

It was apparent now what retribution he had chosen.

When the rice was brought to the hut for Daud, Benito kept his gun pointed at them in case they should try to eat a few of the rice grains meant for the boy. Despite her hunger, Julia told Benito in an even tone, "In my religion, we know how to fast. Hamal will not starve us into submission."

Daud asked weakly between bites, "You have nothing to eat?"

Julia smiled and said quietly, "Your father is angry with me so he will give us no rice, not even Carlita and Mr. Dangwa, who are so sick."

"You are kind to me. You should be treated with kindness. The Qur'an says that slaves and servants should be fed and treated kindly."

Sophie responded, "We are only *sabaya*; we are less than slaves."

After the rice bowl was empty, the boy sat up and said to anyone listening, "I am going to walk around. I am feeling not so weak. Benito, help me."

The guard helped him down the notched log where he walked around in front of the hut for a few minutes and then made his way to where his father sat on the trunk of a fallen coconut palm.

His father looked up at him in surprise. "So you are better today?" Without waiting for an answer, he added, "That is good. We will be mobiling today."

"The women should be given some rice to eat."

The look of surprise on his father's face changed to irritation. "The American woman with the light hair tried to signal the small plane when it flew over. They will all be punished. They are only *sabaya*."

Breathing deeply, exhausted as well as intimidated, the boy responded, "The one called Sophie, the one with the reddish hair, is not *sabaya*. She has been a good servant. I would be dead if she had not taken care of me. She is a servant, and the Qur'an says we must not be harsh with our servants, and we should feed them."

His father looked at him through narrowed eyes. "Not today."

22

AFTER THE SUN HAD PASSED the highest point in the sky, Monty called Matson. "Anything new?"

"Yes, the Abu took out the UAV. Apparently they've acquired a Stinger, but before we lost the signal we got some footage of the small camp that we think is being used by Hamal and his men. We saw three men run into the trees, but interestingly there was something that looked like a white scarf tossed out of the hut as the drone went over. Does that mean anything to you?"

"Julia was given a white hijab to wear with the caftan." He paused and added, "I think it means a lot." Matson heard the tension in his voice unwind slightly.

"We took your location from the satphone last night, and at that time, you were about eight miles southwest of the most recent signal from the Abu satphone. That camp is on the slope of one of the tallest peaks in that area."

Monty pulled the map out of his pocket and smoothed it out on his knee. "Give me their coordinates so I can calculate time and distance." After he made a note, he started to thank him, but Matson added, "Don't hang up yet; I have more. There was a tape played this morning by *Radyo Agong* of a woman who identified herself as Julia, asking her husband, Mike Legaspi, for a ransom of half a million pesos. She gave a telephone number that was answered by someone at a charitable foundation office in Manila when I tried it. I was told that he was the head of the foundation chapter but that he was out of the office. In the recording, she made a reference that might be of importance. She asked him to contact 'Uncle Mallon' if he did not have that much money. Does that mean anything to you?"

"It confirms that they've got Julia. If you check your notes of our first meeting, you will remember that 'Uncle Mallon' is her employer, the man who asked her to hire a rescue team to find his granddaughter. Get a hold of Legaspi and tell him to reach Mallon, prepare the ransom, and respond to *Radyo Agong*."

"Will do."

The men pressed on toward the heavily wooded mountain peaks in the distance.

***

While the *Abu Sayyaf* men prepared rice for breakfast, Hamal made a cell phone call to Yusuf. Julia and Sophie both thought they heard the word *quinine* as he talked.

"If he's ordering Yusuf to bring quinine back with him, I don't think it's because he cares about Dangwa or Carlita. He's knows that if Daud ends up with malaria, in his condition, he might not survive," Sophie stated bitterly.

Hamal began to yell. His words were unintelligible to the women, but his rage was evident. He was pointing to the bundle wrapped in green plastic sheeting that had been kept under his hammock. From where the women stood, it was apparent that it had been damaged. A bit of white powder spilled out of a small tear in the top.

Hamal continued to rage, and soon every Abu man in the camp was lined up before him. He walked down the ragged line, looking in the face of every man and asking one or two short questions. When he reached one of the men that had taken Chang and his daughter to be ransomed, he stopped. He looked closely at the eyes of the man. He asked him something, and the man began to visibly tremble. With a shaking head, he stuttered some kind of a denial. Hamal pointed to him, and Ali and Hussein each took him by the arm and held him tightly. He looked around at every face in the camp, including the hostages, his face filled with dread.

Hamal pointed to the other man who had brought back the ransom. The man shook his head, as if unwilling to obey Hamal's order. Hamal yelled at him and then gave orders to Ali and Hussein. They pulled the frightened man into the forest, and Hamal again yelled at the other man, who slowly and unwillingly followed the others into the trees, tears streaming down his face.

Five minutes later three of them returned. Julia turned to Benito. "Where is the other man? What did they do to him?"

"Hamal ordered them to cut off his head," Benito stated in a matter-of-fact manner.

Without further concern for the man whose body lay somewhere in the dirt of the forest, Hamal ordered that the day's hiking begin.

Changing forestation gradually reflected the lower altitude. At about ten o'clock that evening, they reached their destination, a deserted and overgrown plantation. What had once been a cleared field had been nearly overtaken by thorny shrubs and cogon grass. The man in the lead with the flashlight moved the beam around so they could all see a few banana, mango, and guavas trees. The captors hurried to the trees and, with their bolo knives, harvested a supper of the various fruits.

But Hamal did not relent. The exhausted, hungry, and thirsty hostages were ordered to lie down on the ground under their captors' hammocks with nothing to eat or drink. Before she crawled under the hammock Benito had suspended between two trees, Sophie asked him, "Why did Hamal have that man beheaded?"

"Because he took some of cocaine from the package and used it."

"How did he know it was him?"

"He looked into his eyes. The eyes will tell when a man has used cocaine."

"The other man was unwilling to behead him. Why?"

"He was his brother."

"What would have happened if he had refused to execute his brother?"

"Then there would have been two beheadings."

After a few minutes, Julia asked, "Where is Hamal going to take the cocaine? How can he sell it in the forest?"

"That is not for you to know, woman."

The execution of the man had not only made the point to the hostages that their lives had no value to their captors, but additionally it made it clear that regardless of his fluent use of the English language, the western veneer Hamal assumed was as thin and as easily scratched as a cheap enamel, and, underneath it, he was a barbarian like the others.

***

In the morning the women were awakened by the usual morning prayers. When she sat up, Sophie could see that Phillip Dangwa lay very still, completely unmoving. She crawled over to him and touched his cold throat, feeling for a pulse. He was dead. She put her face in her hands. As soon as the prayers of the Abu ended, she struggled to her feet and announced loud enough for all to hear, "Mr. Dangwa is dead."

Irritated that his abuse of the hostages had cost him Dangwa's potential ransom money, Hamal narrowed his lips and scowled at Sophie. With as much fire in her voice as she could muster in her weakened condition, she took several steps toward Hamal and said, "He didn't have to die. All he needed was some food and water . . . and quinine. He didn't have to die!" The intensity of her anger left her light-headed.

"It was the will of Allah."

"It was not the will of Allah. Your own Qur'an says that Allah is merciful; it says that many, many times. Why can't you show mercy?"

Hamal snorted at her ignorance. "Allah is merciful but only to believers. There is no mercy for unbelievers."

Sophie's anger spilled out of her like water boiling too hard. "But you killed the driver of the jeepney, and he was a believer. Your men beheaded him!"

"He will go to heaven. He died in jihad."

"He was not on jihad. He was just a jeepney driver, and now his wife and children have lost their father and husband. That was not the will of Allah!"

Instead of continuing to debate the matter with the angry young woman, he took two steps toward her and struck her so hard she flew backward several feet before she hit the ground. She was too stunned to rise for a full minute. He went to the stream and washed because he had again touched an unbeliever.

Julia knelt by her. She put her hand on the young woman's arm. "Are you hurt?"

After a few seconds, Sophie answered, "Just stunned, I think."

"It serves no purpose to try to reason with them. Apparently, it's a waste of energy and words." She helped Sophie to her feet. "Let's say a few words for Mr. Dangwa and for his family."

They both knelt and Julia quietly repeated the familiar words, "'The Lord is my shepherd, I shall not want . . .'" Benito raised his gun as if to force them to stop. Hamal had returned from the stream and put up his hand. Everyone in the camp stood still until the psalm was ended. Benito looked at Hamal with a belligerent challenge in his eyes.

"The words of The Book do not give offense," Hamal said simply.

Dangwa's body was buried in a grave about three feet deep and lined with banana leaves that Julia and Sophie gathered despite their weakness. After the dirt had covered the body, Hamal said to the women, "Go get some fruit. We will stay here for the day." The other men stayed back while Julia and Sophie harvested as much of the tropical fruit for themselves and Carlita as was left on the trees. Julia asked Benito for the use of his army knife so they could peel the fruit. Within an hour of eating, all three of them felt stronger, though Carlita's fever and chills continued.

By midday Carlita had drawn her knees up to her chin with her arms around her legs and sat unmoving with her eyes closed, propped against a tree and soaked in perspiration. She remained that way most of the day.

"I don't know how to help her. Her depression is sapping her strength," Sophie told Julia.

Julia leaned toward the young woman. "Carlita, someone will rescue us. Don't give up. There are men looking for us right now."

"I think we would need a miracle for someone to find us," she replied quietly.

"Miracles can happen. Please don't give up."

"I don't believe in miracles anymore." Carlita's voice was flat with discouragement.

***

On the evening of the third day in that camp, Yusuf arrived, perspiring heavily and carrying a bundle that included a supply of quinine and twenty pounds of rice. "*Sundalo* on the trail a few kilometers back. I had to hide."

Hamal asked, "Are they coming this way?"

Yusuf shook his head. "No, they were going the other way."

Sophie examined the bottle of quinine that was labeled Qualaquin. She gave Carlita two of the tablets. As Julia and Sophie lay down by her that night, Sophie said quietly, "Carlita, see, there are still miracles. The quinine is a little miracle. It will help you feel better." Carlita made no response.

***

After prayers the next morning, Hamal called out, "Mobiling, mobiling."

Sophie mumbled under her breath, "I hate that word. I am absolutely sick of it!" As they hiked, Julia and Sophie would arrange their pace until one or the other was at the side of Carlita whenever the path was wide enough to permit it so she could lean on one of them for strength.

Carlita whispered to Sophie as they walked together, "Why are they doing this? Why can't they live in peace and let us go home?"

"Because they believe that bad guys must die in jihad or there is no other way they can get into heaven, and I think Hamal and some of the others have been really bad, even by their own rules."

As it did every night, the darkness came swiftly, as though it had been pulled over their heads like a blanket. As Sophie handed two more quinine tablets to Carlita, Daud carefully made his way over to the women where they sat together on the ground leaning against the trunk of a fallen palm. He offered them each a mango he had hidden under his shirt. "I saved these for you," he said shyly before he made his way back to where his father was talking with the other men. The three women were deeply touched by his kindness. They did not dare ask to borrow Benito's knife lest they get Daud in trouble, so they pulled off the tough skin with their teeth and gratefully ate the soft, sweet flesh of the fruit from around the large pit.

Benito had looped one end of the rope that tied the wrists of the three women together around a small tree trunk and had joined the other men as they talked. Sophie looked at the knot in the rope. "If we had the strength, it wouldn't be difficult to undo that rope, but we're so weak that I don't think we could get more than ten feet into the trees before they caught us," she told Julia.

"Let's hope the Lord has something else in mind for us."

When Benito came back to resume his task of guarding the women, Julia asked in as casual a manner as she could manage, "Have the arrangements for my ransom been made?"

He looked at Julia and ignored her question. "You will give me your marriage ring and wristwatch."

Startled, she simply responded, "Why?"

"Because I tell you to give them to me," he snapped.

Julia pulled the watch off without regret and handed it to him. It had no sentimental meaning for her. It was different with her wedding band. She took her time, insisting that it would not come off. "It is too tight to take off," she said quietly as she twisted it.

"Give me your hand. I will take it off."

"You would touch me, an infidel?" she asked in surprise.

In a firm, businesslike manner he stated, "I will have the ring. Then I can wash in the river."

Knowing that he would think nothing of hurting her to get the ring, she twisted it off and handed it to him, quietly enraged that he would take something so precious. She tried to keep her voice controlled. "Why do you and the other men live in the forest away from your families and spend your lives fighting the AFP?"

He pocketed the watch and examined the ring. "Because we fight the jihad." Almost visibly swelling with pride, he added, "I have fought the jihad against the Soviets in Afghanistan. There I fought with the *Mujaheddin,* and we defeated the great, godless Soviets. We drove them from Afghanistan and brought down their government."

Carefully, Julia asked, "But you had much help from other nations, including America, didn't you?"

"It was the blood of the Islamic brotherhood that was spilled to drive out the Soviets! There was no American blood spilled in their defeat." He paused and smiled grimly. "They sent guns and Stinger missiles, but they spilled no blood for Islam. They are not our brothers; they only hated the Soviets."

As he continued to speak, he pulled the small book from his shirt pocket and said, "Osama Bin Laden has said that 'hostility toward America is a religious duty.'" He grew silent for a minute, and Julia thought that perhaps he had stopped speaking, but he paged through the little book until he found what he was looking for. He read with enthusiasm, "'The walls of oppression and humiliation cannot be demolished except in a rain of bullets.' Bin Laden wrote that in his first declaration of jihad."

"Has Osama Bin Laden declared a holy war on America?"

"Yes, and on Britain." He spoke with finality and satisfaction.

"But to declare a holy war—to issue a fatwa—the leader must be an Islamic scholar or teacher or an imam with recognized religious authority. What authority does Bin Laden have to declare a holy war?"

"You, woman, cannot understand. Women can only feel. Their minds cannot be trusted." He put the book back into his pocket and continued, always glad to have an audience for his thoughts. "In Afghanistan I learned to make bombs and use many weapons. I learned military tactics and killed many Soviets. I should be doing more than guarding women."

"Why does Hamal make you guard hostages? Why aren't you the leader of this group? You're much older—and you have greater experience," she added, playing to his ego to keep him talking.

"Because I am a Sunni, and these Filipino Moros are Shi'ia." He spat out the last word.

No wonder Benito seems isolated from the other Abu and is so willing to talk with us, she thought. "I understand that there is an old hostility between the Sunni and the Shi'ia. Has that changed?"

The guard stood silent for a few seconds and then finally responded, "While we fight the jihad, we must sometimes work together. When the jihad is done, then the Sunni will force the Shi'ia to convert." He spoke with a fierceness that revealed a deep well of anger.

"But what is the purpose of your jihad?" Julia prodded.

"Someday we will take back this island for Muslims and rid it of the religion brought by the Spanish who came with their swords and forced the Muslims that lived here to kneel before their crosses."

"If that day comes . . ."

Julia was startled by the flash of rage from Benito. "It will come!"

She restated her question. "When that day comes, what will you do?"

"Then we will make jihad against the other islands until they are converted to Allah, and then we will make jihad against all the Jews and Christians and other nonbelievers until they are converted to Islam."

"So you intend to convert the world to Islam?"

"Yes. The Qur'an says that we must 'fight against them till strife be at an end, and the religion of all be Allah's.'"

"Does Allah want converts to Islam who kneel and say the words but their hearts are not changed?"

"Allah does not care how they are converted. Millions have been converted by the sword. What is important is that when the world worships Allah, all men will live Shariah Law and all men will be happy. Then Allah will bless us."

"Please tell me how living Shariah Law will make men happy." Julia's innocent voice was almost like a child asking why the sky was blue. Sophie had been sitting very quietly, observing the exchange.

Benito answered as if he were explaining something very obvious to someone who was not very bright. "When all men live Shariah Law, no one will break the law. No one will steal. No woman will use her eyes to make a man look at her. No one will take another man's cattle or property. All will be happy."

"What will keep everyone from breaking the law?"

"The punishment!" He nearly shouted his response. It was evident that he thought Julia was stupid beyond belief. "If a man steals, his hand will be cut off. If his wife looks with warm eyes at another man, she will be stoned. We will live with the law of an eye for an eye, and a tooth for a tooth, and all men will obey it."

Then Julia said with total simplicity, "But you have just stolen my watch and my marriage ring. Is there no punishment for that?"

The man did not even recognize the barb that had been aimed at him. He responded, "You are an unbeliever. If you have it and I need it, it isn't stealing."

Julia simply looked at Sophie as if she had again met her match. *Why do I keep trying?* She leaned back against a tree trunk, took a deep breath, and closed her eyes. It was a better choice than shouting at him in anger, and her injured ribs hurt too much to shout at him anyway.

That evening, as the rice was passed around and she took a handful, Julia could not help but note a lighter stripe on the finger that had worn the wedding band for twenty-five years. Her tears dropped into her rice. Soon tears of disappointment and anger coursed steadily down her cheeks.

Sophie lifted her head. "I've been sitting here crying for the last ten minutes, Julia. We both can't let ourselves get down at the same time. You can cry tomorrow. Tonight it's my turn."

Julia looked at her, and they tried to smile at one another through teary eyes. "What has you so upset tonight?"

"If Hamal really gave me to Abdul, like he said, then he can come for me at any time. I can't sleep for fear that I will feel his hands on me in the night. I have been praying that Hamal only told me that to try to frighten me into converting."

Julia took Sophie's hand in hers to offer some comfort. "Just stay strong, Sophie. Monty and his men are out there somewhere looking for us."

23

THE PATH THEY FOLLOWED THE next day continued to decline, and by midafternoon, they could see an occasional Kalawa, a large sea bird with a bright red bill that lived near the coast. Finally, they came within sight of a costal mangrove forest. The great tree trunks rose from the water and were supported by stilt roots that merged with the trunks just above the high-tide level.

Despite her pain and exhaustion, Julia whispered, "It's beautiful. I've never seen anything like this." She couldn't ignore the beauty of the trunks and roots where they threw shadows on the water in a multitude of patterns. "They're mangrove trees, aren't they? This is a beautiful place. Where are we?"

Benito simply shrugged his shoulders as if there were no beauty there that he could see. "Near Panganuran. In this mangrove forest, there are many snakes—bad snakes here."

Julia started to ask just where Panganuran was when Benito flashed his irritation. "You ask too many questions, woman. Hamal will do business here. Then we will go back to the old forest."

Some of the Abu men stretched out and closed their eyes to rest in the humid, warm, almost fetid air, which was heavy with the smell of rotting leaves. As tired as she was, Julia could not sleep for the pain in her ribs and the mosquitoes and other insects that sought sweaty, human skin like a sweet dessert. She sat up and studied the place.

She had been watching the play of shadows and sunlight on the water for nearly an hour, swatting at insects, when she heard a small outboard motor. Within a few minutes, a small fisherman's *banca* moved slowly between the tree trunks and roots and glided onto the firmer ground. The man jumped out and pulled the bow of the canoe onto the water-saturated soil.

Hamal rose and spoke with the man for a few minutes before the man gave him a small packet that had been tucked in his waistband at the small of his back. It was wrapped in brown paper. Hamal opened the packet, and Julia could see that he appeared to be counting money. He motioned to Hussein and pointed at the bundle wrapped in the green plastic sheeting.

Hussein picked up the bundle and carried it to the visitor who examined the small tear in the plastic. A few more words were exchanged. The man was not entirely happy, but he put it into the small *banca*, climbed in, and started the little outboard motor again. He was soon out of sight in the Sulu Sea.

Hamal called out, "Mobiling, mobiling," and for an hour the group moved through the undergrowth until they found what looked like a well-used clearing where the cogon grass had been cut and the remains of an old fire were apparent. There they made camp.

The women sat quietly, leaning against three sides of the same coconut palm with their eyes shut. After a few minutes, Julia asked, "Sophie, you're very quiet. What are you thinking about?"

"A bubble bath. Right now, that is the most luxurious thing I can think of."

"And after the bubble bath, a great big chocolate, ice cream sundae," Julia responded with a little smile.

"I would like a big bowl of pancit noodles . . . and to see my mother," Carlita said weakly. "Will I ever see my mother again?"

Both of the other women reassured her that she would, but she remained unconvinced.

***

The next morning several of the Abu men disappeared into the undergrowth, only to reappear a few hours later, trickling into camp carrying rice, candy, and cans of soda. As the women sat in the shade, too tired and hungry to move, Ali carried a sack of hard candy over to them and, in a token act of generosity, dropped a piece at the feet of each one of them. Then he stood still, waiting for their thanks.

When Julia realized why he was standing there watching them, she said, "Thank you, Ali."

Sophie added, "Oh, yes, thank you, Ali."

Carlita paid no attention to the candy that lay by her foot in the dirt. Ali looked at her, shrugged his shoulders, picked up the candy, and, without brushing it off, popped it into his mouth. Then he returned to the others where the balance of the candy was shared among the men. As they enjoyed the sweetness of the rare treat, their laughter trickled toward the hostages like leaking water.

***

Monty and the other three men continued for the next two days, eventually coming across an abandoned *nipa* hut where the trash left by the Abu group still littered the camp.

After they had slept for three hours, Monty called Matson, who gave him the most recent GPS location of the Abu camp and added, "The altitude on the signal was at sea level, about a mile south of the costal village of Panganuran."

"Thanks. Out." Monty marked the new location on the map and, after tucking it into his pocket again, dialed the number for Estilita Roque. When she picked up, he asked without identifying himself, "Do you have anything new from your contact at *Radyo Agong*?"

Recognizing his voice, she said, "The exchange for the woman is supposed to take place in the fishing village of Panganuran the day after tomorrow at dusk. Same deal as the one for Chang and his daughter. The ransom is supposed to be in a suitcase left in a jeepney near the fish market at about dark."

"Anything else?"

"Expect some intervention from the AFP."

"Are you saying that the same source you use is also being used by the AFP?"

"Correct."

"Thanks." Monty told the others what he had learned from Estilita.

"I wonder how badly the AFP can screw up this exchange," Rick said cynically.

"Probably badly enough to get someone killed." He put the satphone into his backpack. "Let's get moving and cover as much ground in the daylight as possible. We're almost out of batteries for the goggles."

24

THE NEXT MORNING ABDUL AND Ali went to the river to bring back enough water for the day. In less than a half hour, they returned at a stooped run and hurried to Hamal. The women could hear the word *sundalo* repeated several times with Abdul pointing agitatedly toward the river.

"Why are they so excited? Did they see soldiers?" Julia asked Benito.

"There are soldiers down the river, swimming and eating."

The excited men were given instructions to return to the river with Abdul. They put their bolo knives in their belts and carried their other weapons, moving into the trees toward the river. Only Hamal, Benito, and Daud remained in the camp with the hostages. Benito's expression clearly stated that he was angry at having to remain behind.

All was quiet for about twenty-five tense minutes, and then the sound of assault rifles broke the stillness, followed by the sound of machine guns. Men's voices rose in panicked screams. Intermittent bursts of gunfire continued for nearly twenty minutes. After nearly another half hour, some of the men returned, each carrying an olive green backpack and belts of ammunition over their shoulders. Behind them were two more carrying SACO M60 machine guns taken from the soldiers. Others brought back two duffle bags containing a medical kit and food items. As they retold their story to Hamal with loud voices, excited gestures, and laughter, they proudly removed from one of the bags a small, softbound notebook, maps, and their greatest prize—a shortwave radio. As Hamal looked through the notebook, he laughed and read portions of it aloud to the men gathered around him.

"What is he reading to the men, Benito," Julia asked.

"The AFP plans to capture all the *Abu Sayyaf* and the MNLF on Mindanao. They have sent many soldiers into the mountains and forest to find us."

"Will they find us?"

"No, the *sundalo* quit when it gets dark. They think they are only paid to work in the daylight, so they stop when the sun goes down, and they won't fight when it rains. We always get away."

The excitement in camp continued until they saw Abdul through the trees assisting an injured Yusuf back into camp. His lower leg was soaked with blood.

Sophie hurried over as the injured man was lowered to the ground with his back against a tree trunk. She knelt by him. "Benito, I need your knife to cut off his pant leg." Benito stood still as if weighing the request for several seconds before he pulled the knife from its sheath and handed it to her.

"Julia, please help me. Pull the pant leg tight so I can cut it. Carlita, get some water and put it on the fire to boil."

Sophie examined the bullet wound on Yusuf's right shin. The bullet had broken the tibia. Determined not to show weakness in the face of an infidel woman, he gritted his teeth as she examined it. Looking up at Benito, she said, "I need the bandages and duct tape—and the hydrogen peroxide, if there's any left. And I need two pieces of bamboo about this long." She held her hands about two feet apart.

Benito narrowed his eyes at her for her demanding manner but finally gave orders to one of the other men to get her the things she wanted. The water had just reached a boil when Carlita brought the pot over to Sophie and set it down near her. "Stir it until it cools enough to put your hand in it."

"What shall I use to stir it?" she asked timidly.

Julia handed her the knife that had been used to cut the leg of the pants. "Use this."

Sophie looked at Benito. "I need a clean rag to wash his leg." Benito didn't move. Sophie tried to keep her voice reasonable as she added, "I will give it back, and it can be washed in the river."

Benito yelled at one of the men, who pulled off his shirt and handed it to her. Looking at the sweaty T-shirt, Sophie simply shook her head in frustration, but there was nothing else to use. She dipped it into the pot of water and began to carefully wash the blood off Yusuf's swollen leg. The wound was still oozing blood.

"The bullet must be taken out." She carefully felt around the wound and finally found a hard lump near the break in the bone. She looked at Yusuf. "I need to get the bullet out. It will hurt. Can you stand the pain?" Yusuf nodded, still not unclenching his teeth. "Hold tightly to Julia's hand. That will help."

"She is an unbeliever. I will not touch her," he responded through clenched teeth, his words filled with pain and anger.

"It's your choice." With the point of the knife blade that had been used to stir the pot of hot water, she made an incision in the flesh above the hard lump.

Unable to tolerate the pain in addition to what he was already experiencing, he lashed out at Sophie. She ducked to avoid his fist. "Leave it! It will be no problem. Leave the bullet there," he roared.

"It needs to come out. It will infect," she said.

"You will give me the medicine you gave Daud. It will get better."

Julia turned to appeal to Hamal, where he stood watching. "It must come out, or his leg will not heal."

Hamal spoke harshly to Yusuf, who lay back against a log with a scowl on his face. "You will take it out. He will allow it."

Pressing her thumb and finger on either side of the lump, Julia finished the incision and gently squeezed; the bloody bullet slid out into her hand. Then she washed his leg with the hydrogen peroxide and bandaged the leg with the gauze strips from the soldiers' medical kit. Then she put a bamboo splint on each side of the leg from knee to ankle and wrapped the splints to the leg in two places with duct tape. While she was doing that, the other men crowded around to see the bullet.

Hamal turned on the shortwave radio stolen from the soldiers and turned the dial until he located a station broadcasting the Voice of America. The other men gathered around him to listen, sometimes shaking their heads in anger and other times ridiculing the broadcaster. After about a half hour, he began to turn the dial again and finally found the BBC news broadcast. They listened to that closely for another half hour.

When the men lost interest in the broadcasts, they turned off the radio. Ali approached the women to tell them that Hamal wanted to see them. The women hesitantly made their way across the camp. Carlita stood with rounded shoulders, looking at the ground, frightened, sick, and exhausted. After several minutes, Hamal looked at Sophie. "I have waited long enough for you to convert to Islam. Because Abdul is a good Muslim, he said he does not want to take you until you are his wife, but

I have given you to him. If you will convert, you will be his wife. If you still refuse, you will be *sabayaed*. He can do anything with a woman who is *sabayaed* to him. You will be less than a slave. You have brought this on yourself."

Looking at one another, each woman took a deep breath to steady her individual courage. Sophie answered, "Regardless of what you threaten, I have told you that I will not convert. I will not deny my faith." Carlita watched the discussion with wide, frightened eyes.

He continued to look threateningly from Sophie to Carlita with narrowed eyes. "I will give you only a little more time to think about it, but remember Abdul and Ali are tired of waiting. You will convert and marry tomorrow, or you will be *sabayed*. You, woman," he said pointing at Julia, "will go with Hussein tomorrow to get the ransom." Finally, they were dismissed.

As the three women knelt to pray, they took one another's hands. Julia whispered, "This is hard for me, but I have been thinking about it for several days, and tonight I will pray for those who have despitefully used us, as the Savior taught us to do. I am a long way from being able to love my enemies, but I know we need to remember the Savior's words and try to live by them." She prayed for the strength to grant forgiveness to those who had taken them hostage and ended by seeking strength to endure.

Carlita cried quietly until the end of the prayer. "Tomorrow I will convert and marry Ali."

Julia held her hand tightly and tried to comfort her. "We understand. We really do understand. You must do what you feel is best for you." She paused and added in a forceful whisper, "But don't forget that there are still miracles in this day. Please, please, don't give up yet." She put her arms around the young woman who leaned on her shoulder and sobbed.

As Carlita wept, she asked between her quiet sobs, "Why did God let this to happen to us? Why won't He help us? Did we do something wrong?"

"Sometimes God allows bad things to happen to good people," Julia answered, not knowing what else to say.

Carlita raised her head and almost wailed, "But why?"

Julia looked at Sophie with a plea for help in her eyes. Sophie answered quietly, "God gives everyone their freedom to choose right or wrong. But they will have to answer for their choices before the judgment bar of God someday."

"I don't care about the judgment bar," Carlita responded weakly. "I just want someone to make them pay for what they are doing to us right now." Neither Julia nor Sophie had any answer for her, but Sophie insisted that she take two more quinine tablets.

After the weeping young woman swallowed the pills, she looked at Julia. "Why aren't you afraid? Aren't you afraid to die?"

"I'm afraid most of the time, Carlita, but not so much as I would be if I didn't know that if I die I'll go home to a loving God."

"But you would not see your children again. That makes me afraid—that I will not see my mother and my boyfriend again. I miss them both so much. I think you are very brave."

"Bravery is doing what you must do, even when you're afraid." Julia patted the discouraged girl. "You are very brave, and your mother will be proud of you when you see her and tell her what you have been through."

The supper of rice that evening was improved by the addition of small pieces of the canned Spam taken from the soldiers' backpacks after the gunfight. "I feel guilty eating the food those soldiers had planned to eat this evening," Sophie said quietly. "I'm so sorry for their families."

Sophie had been assigned to sleep under Yusuf's hammock should he need her during the night. As the women lay on the ground under the hammocks, brushing away the mosquitoes, she asked him, "Did they kill all the soldiers?"

"Yes, they shot them and then beheaded them."

Horrified at the brutality he spoke of so easily, she asked, "Why did they behead them?"

"So they can never enter heaven. Now be silent so I can sleep." He added, "If I am thirsty in the night, you will get me a drink."

"Then you must see that I am not tied to the others."

Yusuf called to one of the other men, and he came over and untied the rope from the three women. Sophie was sure the man had misunderstood Yusuf's orders when he untied all of them, rather than just her, but she was not about to draw his attention to the mistake.

25

MONTY ESTIMATED THE DISTANCE TO the GPS coordinates of the *Abu Sayyaf* men and their hostages to be less than four miles over rough, downhill terrain. They moved at increased speed toward that location, not halting to eat or rest. The three-quarter moon gave enough light for them to continue down and up the ancient paths, as they made their way over the weathered lava outcroppings held together by the roots of the ancient forest hardwoods. Sometimes one or another of them stumbled in the black, leaden shadows. Monty had begun to limp, though he paid no attention to it.

As soon as the sun rose, they took a few minutes to rest. Then they picked up their packs and moved down the rugged and sloping path again, refusing to allow exhaustion to slacken their pace. They had gone about two hundred yards farther when Monty raised his hand and said, "Sssst, sssst, sssst."

They halted, breathing heavily. They could hear the sporadic sound of automatic weapons farther down the mountainside. "Sounds like SACO M60s used by some of the AFP. What d'you think, Rick?"

"I can hear a couple of AK-47s, as well," Rick replied. Ducking to avoid low hanging vines and branches, they hurried toward the sound. After a few minutes, the sound stopped, as did the four men.

They could just barely make out the sound of men's voices. Some were laughing. As they paused and listened, they could make out some of the words, including *sundalo*.

"It sounds like the problem of interference from the AFP may have been taken care of," Rick whispered grimly.

They made their way farther down the path as silently as possible, and soon they could understand the voices. As the four gathered where

Monty had stopped on the path, he whispered, "We're almost on top of the camp. I want one of us on each of the four sides of the group. I'll take the south. Bing, you'll take the north. Rick, west; Bolly, east." As he gave instructions, he pointed in each of the directions. "Find a spot where you can see what's going on but can't be seen. When you're in place, I want a signal from each of you.

"Rick, time for you to imitate a zebra dove." Rick proceeded to give a close imitation of the throaty, almost gurgling cooing sound of the bird that was common in the islands. "Bing, find a couple of pieces of bamboo and put them together so you can imitate a woodpecker. Bolly, here's your chance to prove to me that you can make every female warbler on Mindanao come your way." Bolly warbled quietly with his hands on either side of this mouth to muffle the sound. Then Monty added, "I'm going to try to attract a few female bitterns." He demonstrated with an imitation of the deep "click-toom" sound of the bitterns that were common in the marshier areas of the peninsula.

"After we get the hostages, Rick, we'll head west, past your location," Monty whispered as the four men squatted in a tight group. "The obvious point of this exercise is to get the hostages out of camp tonight without getting any one of them or any of us shot. When you're settled in a good observation place, give your signal and get out your fireworks shell, launching tube, and the grenade. Keep them close and ready. For the best effect, get the launching tube pointed into the sky, not the treetops. Keep your backpacks on.

"When you hear my bittern call three times, I'll be getting ready to light my fuse. You will do the same. Then we'll toss the grenades. Rick, your assignment is to engage and reduce the enemy, covering our movements as we get the hostages out of the camp. Take out any Abu that are a threat to the hostages first. Bing, Bolly, and I will grab the hostages and head past you down the mountain." He turned and looked at Rick with genuine seriousness. "I am anticipating that you will not shoot any of us."

Rick grinned despite the tension. "Don't worry, Monty, I've got your back."

Monty gave him a thumbs-up and looked at the Jackson brothers. "Be prepared to improvise, if necessary. Now, let's move out."

Rick nodded and under his breath said, "Just like old times."

The men moved stealthily toward the sound of the voices in the Abu camp. They watched where they placed each foot to avoid an unexpected sound. After close to an hour, Monty could hear the sound of a dove from the other side of the camp. The rat-a-tat-tat sound of a woodpecker was followed a few minutes later by the call of a warbler. Then Monty gave a single bittern call.

The Abu men in the camp were oblivious to the sounds as they gathered around a wounded man who lay with his back against a log. It was difficult to determine what was drawing the attention of every man in the camp until Monty caught sight of an auburn-haired woman kneeling next to the wounded man. She was wrapping his leg in a bandage. Under his breath, he murmured a heartfelt, "There's Sophie. We've found her." His eyes searched for Julia.

The evening wore on with the wounded man receiving attention from two other women. When he saw the one in a black caftan with blond hair sticking out from under a torn and soiled white hijab, he whispered another brief prayer. "There's Julia. Thank heaven." A lump of gratitude rose in his throat.

The third woman was a young Filipina wearing a torn and filthy student nurse's uniform, which had once been white. Nowhere was there any sign of other hostages, but that didn't mean there weren't more.

From where the four rescuers were hidden in the undergrowth, they could see the leader of the group tuning a shortwave radio, and for nearly an hour, most of the men huddled around it.

The four rescuers watched as the men lost interest in the radio. The women were summoned by the leader, who had moved to a fallen tree trunk about twenty-five feet in front of where Monty crouched. Monty watched as the women stood for several minutes before the man recognized their presence. The man finally looked directly at Sophie and told her he had waited long enough for her to agree to convert and threatened to give her to someone named Abdul if she continued to refuse.

Then he raised his voice and Monty heard clearly, "If you will convert . . ." The words were lost briefly. Then the man ended his remarks to Sophie. "You will be less than a slave."

He watched as the women looked at each other and Sophie shook her head. He missed her answer. He couldn't catch the balance of the man's remarks to the other two women. From where he crouched, he could see the Filipina girl's wide and frightened eyes. He wrapped his hand around the hilt of his bolo. *Patience,* he thought. *None of his threats will be carried out.* Eventually, the women were permitted to return to the other side of the camp.

The men knelt on their prayer rugs with their weapons next to their knees, and while the Abu prayed, the guard paced near the three women, sometimes screened by large trees. Monty thought impatiently, *If he would just stand still, we could take the whole camp while they are in prayer, but I can't take the chance that he could shoot the hostages if we don't take him out first.*

Monty finally dismissed the idea of sending up the signal while the Abu were kneeling in prayer. *Their weapons are within reach, and they'll miss the full impact of the fireworks bowed like that, with their eyes closed. We'll be better off waiting until they're asleep.*

As the Abu prepared and shared the supper of boiled rice with the hostages, the smell of Spam filled the air. Bing and Bolly tried to ignore their growling stomachs. Ignoring a hungry stomach was not something they were accustomed to doing.

The camp grew quiet about nine o'clock, and the Abu men motioned for the three women to lie under the hammocks. Monty almost held his breath as he watched to see if the women were going to be tied to a tree or to each other for the night. After the wounded man had been helped into a hammock, the others seemed to forget about the hostages. One man removed the rope from the wrists of the three women. Monty watched with a grim satisfaction.

The four rescuers waited, watching the camp in the moonlight. About nine-thirty, the snores of some of the men drifted across the camp.

Monty saw Sophie crawl out from under the hammock of the wounded man at about ten o'clock and make her way across the camp. Julia rose and followed her. He watched as she located a large, plastic, water jug, and Julia held a canteen as she tried to fill it.

Now, light it now. As the water spilled over Julia's hand, Monty gave the click-toom call of the bittern three times and lit the fuse. It gave a low sizzle, and then the sound of a "whomp" preceded the explosion just above the trees. An umbrella of sparkling stars exploded and arched over the camp, falling like sizzling rain. The shortness of the launching tube kept the glimmering sparks near the treetop level. In quick succession, the other three explosions of fireworks filled the sky. Then the flash-bang grenades flew into the camp. The women dropped the canteen and the water jug and put their hands over their ears. The four rescuers closed their eyes and covered their ears as protection from the flashes and concussion of sound.

The sound of frightened monkeys and awakened bats in the trees added to the confusion. As Monty had hoped, the Abu men tipped out of their hammocks and stood looking in dumbfounded amazement at the fireworks display. The explosions from the grenades drove them to a squat position as they closed their eyes tightly and put their hands over their ears.

While they were briefly blind and deaf in the darkness, Monty and Bing ran across the open camp. Monty grabbed Julia and Sophie by an arm and yelled, "Come with me."

He pulled them into the trees on the far side of the camp, near Rick's hiding place. Bing had followed Monty, and as soon as they entered the trees, he took Sophie's arm. As he did so, he yelled at Monty, "Follow me."

After he pulled his night goggles over his eyes and turned them on, Bolly located Carlita, where she was lying under a hammock in terror. He grabbed her arm and tried to pull her out. She began to fight him, hitting him with both fists and screaming, terrified of this man who was pulling her into the forest. He lifted her to her feet, knelt, and leaned hard into her stomach with his shoulder like a football linebacker. She folded over his shoulder in a fireman's carry. After she caught her breath, she continued to scream in fear and pounded him on the back.

As the three men made it into the forest with the women, Hamal began to yell orders, and the Abu men each fumbled for their guns in the darkness. When they found them, they began to spray the trees with their assault rifles, aiming toward the sound of Carlita's screams.

Rick began to fire intermittent bursts from his M16 where he knelt in the undergrowth, dropping three of the Abu men. The other Abu turned toward the suppressed gunfire and began to spray the undergrowth with bursts from their guns. Rick dropped and belly crawled about ten feet before rising on one knee and firing again. He saw one more man go down. He dropped again, hearing the zing and thud of the bullets as they hit the tree trunks above his head. He squatted and moved toward the sound of Carlita's screams. He paused and fired toward the sounds of the men who followed. He heard one man grunt in pain, and the sound of their steps halted briefly.

Rick did a fast mental calculation and thought, *At least five wounded, and counting the one wounded earlier, that puts six out of commission—hopefully.*

He stood and pulled on his night-vision goggles, dashed down the path, and paused after about a hundred feet to turn and spray his M16 back into the darkness. The goggles were beginning to fade, so he switched them off and depended on the moonlight. At the moment, all he could hear behind him was the enraged voice of the leader. "Find them! Kill the men. Kill the men. Bring the women back!"

***

Carlita continued to scream until Bolly slid her off his shoulder, and as she stood up, he grabbed her by the shoulders and shook her. Then he put his mouth near her ear and said loudly, "Woman, we are here to save you. Shut up, or they will find us."

She stopped screaming and began to sniffle. "Who are you?" she asked in a trembling voice.

"We will talk about that later."

The three men continued to hurry the women down the path, trusting Rick to hold off the Abu. Bing and Bolly led the way. They moved steadily down the slope. Julia had been forced to hike the caftan up above her knees to allow her to run. With every hurried step, the branches and vines caught at it as if they were trying to hold her back.

"If we get separated, head for the beach. We'll locate each other from there," Monty said loud enough for Bing and Bolly to hear him.

The sound of the gunfire grew closer, so Monty urged Julia into a shallow gully near the path. "Stay down." He moved to a fallen tree trunk and watched the path. Within a few minutes, he could see Rick loping toward him, pausing and turning to fire back up the path as a few bullets zinged past him.

As he turned, Monty whispered to him loud enough to be heard, "Rick, find a place and take a position. We can stop them on the path. Julia, get farther back into the undergrowth if you can. Hurry!" Julia moved out of the gully and about ten feet farther from the path. There she located a thick palm tree and crouched behind it. Bing and Bolly continued down the path a hundred feet ahead, hurrying Sophie and Carlita along.

The three of them waited for the Abu men to come down the path, but after nearly four long minutes, the path remained empty. Occasionally they heard the pop of a twig or the swish of a palm frond. Monty whispered again, "They aren't using the path. Eyes open!"

Monty moved into the undergrowth to locate Julia. When he knelt down near her, he heard her sharp intake of breath. He looked up. Standing before the two of them was a young man holding an AK-47. As Monty moved to bring his gun up, Julia put her hand out to stop him. "Daud won't shoot us. Will you, Daud? Sophie and Carlita saved your life." She continued in her soothing voice, "We only want our freedom. Let us go, Daud, and Allah will reward you for your mercy."

The boy did not move for a moment. His eyes narrowed. Julia held her breath. He moved the muzzle of the weapon from Monty to Julia and back to Monty. Then he gradually lowered his gun. His face was filled with uncertainty. Julia took hold of Monty's arm. "Let's go. Daud won't hurt us."

The two of them slowly stood to their full height and moved toward the path, looking back at the boy intermittently as they did so. When they reached the path, they started to run, trying to put distance between themselves and the boy in case he changed his mind. They increased the speed of their flight, and after putting more than a thousand feet behind them, they made their way into the undergrowth where they located a place to hide behind a clump of palms. They sat down and tried to catch their breath. Monty began to rub the muscles of his thigh. "Are you all right?" he asked.

Julia looked at him. In the moonlight, he could see that she had both arms wrapped around her rib cage and was breathing hard. She shook her head. "The running hurts. I think I have a couple of broken ribs, but I don't want to slow us down."

He reached out and took one of her hands. "I'm so sorry if you're hurting. I'll try to be more careful." He gave her several minutes to catch her breath before they started down the sloping path again.

He started walking in consideration of her injuries, but she insisted, "I can go faster. We need to hurry." He picked up the pace.

***

From where he was hidden on the other side of the path, Rick heard Julia's voice. He watched as Julia and Monty moved out of the trees and rushed down the path. He stayed hidden with his gun ready and soon heard at least two men hurrying down the path. As the Abu men moved down the mountainside, Rick sat quietly where he was and waited for them to pass him. Then he started to follow, carefully and quietly.

At one point, he stepped on a stick that cracked, and everything became quiet as every man stopped in his tracks. After several minutes, Rick could hear them moving again—just by the sound of palm fronds and branches rubbing on fabric, almost covered by the whine of the night insects.

He stalked the sounds that were nearest him. He heard a man grunt, as if in pain. The moon slid behind a thick bank of clouds, and Rick stopped until his eyes adjusted better to the dark. On an impulse, he pulled his night-vision goggles down over his eyes. When he turned them on, he discovered that the batteries were not entirely expended. They gave him a slight advantage. As he moved through the trees, he could see what looked like a figure moving about thirty feet ahead of him. He followed the figure, noting that the man carried an AK-47 in his right hand.

Keeping his gun in his right hand, Rick paused and looked down to pull the bolo knife out of his belt with his left. When he looked up, the figure in the trees had disappeared. He set his jaw with disgust. He made his way stealthily through the trees. As he neared the position where he had lost sight of the figure, the man stepped out from behind a tree directly in front of him. In one swift motion, Rick rotated the butt of his M16, striking the man on the jaw. He dropped with hardly a sound.

Another one down, Rick noted with satisfaction.

***

Bing and Bolly continued to pull Sophie and Carlita toward the coast. Carlita was crying with exhaustion. Sophie insisted, "We've got to rest and get something to drink. We're too tired and thirsty to keep going."

Bing looked at Bolly, and both nodded. "Okay, we'll find a place." After a few minutes, they located several clumps of bamboo clustered together. Bolly pointed, and the four of them located a place to sit where they were almost encircled by the sturdy clumps and where they could lean against some of the bamboo trunks. The men handed the women their canteens.

As the women drank, Bing looked at his watch in the moonlight. "It'll be getting light in about two hours. Bolly, do you have another MRE?" Bolly nodded. "I think I have another one too. The women need something to eat." Each of the men dug around in their packs and pulled out a packaged meal. Opening it with a knife, Bolly handed his to Carlita. Bing did the same for Sophie. Even cold, the beef stew tasted good to the women.

"Who are you? Why did you rescue us?" Carlita asked between bites.

"Keep your voice low," Bing said. "You can thank Sophie's grandfather for hiring us. When Sophie disappeared, and there was no ransom demanded, he sent Julia to hire a team to find her. We're part of that team."

The two young women looked at each other in stunned silence. Then Sophie smiled and laughed quietly. "Julia said that my grandfather had sent a team to find us." She fought sudden tears of gratitude that caught her off guard. "I don't know how to thank you enough for risking your lives for us. You're really incredible men."

"Don't thank us yet. We still have to get you out of here and back home."

26

As they moved through the undergrowth, Monty and Julia paused to listen for any sounds behind them while Julia caught her breath. After nearly two hours, she whispered, "Can we find a place to rest for a few minutes. I'm so shaky—and thirsty."

Monty looked around. "Camouflage is good here. We'll rest here for a few minutes." He took her arm and pulled her into the palms far enough from the path that they would be hidden. Without saying anything, he cut several fronds, laid them down, and pointed to them. Julia sat without a second invitation. He handed his canteen to her. After a long drink, she handed it back. "Thanks."

Monty took a drink. "Get some rest. You can sleep for a little while. I'll keep watch." Without argument, she lay down and, despite the pain, was immediately asleep. Monty allowed himself to doze a little, but as the sun rose, he watched Julia where she slept as he listened for any sounds that didn't belong in the forest. He smiled at her disheveled and dirty condition, remembering her attractive appearance at the Manila Hotel. *This is a woman of courage—and character—and for this brief time, our separate worlds have merged. I wonder if our worlds could . . .* He pushed the rest of the thought out of his mind.

The birds began to communicate as the sky brightened—some trilling and others cawing. The sun appeared over the mountains before Julia stirred. Monty checked the satphone battery, noting that it had some life left in it. He called Rick's cell phone.

"Yeah, it's me."

"What's your situation?"

"I'm on the beach, waiting for everyone else to join me. Beautiful white sand with a river nearby that empties into the Sulu Sea. All I need is a cabana and some cool drinks to make it complete." Then his voice changed. "I saw five Abu fall, three in the camp, another one on the trail as they followed us, and I brought one down in the trees. Have no idea if they're in condition to join the hunt or if they're nursing their wounds somewhere. Counting the one that had the injured leg in camp—that accounts for six of them."

"There were at least ten in the video taken by the UAV. And there was at least one more that took Julia from the *banca* in Sibuco to the camp. It looks like we have at least five to worry about."

"I've got my coordinates. Can you jot them down?"

"Just give me a sec." Monty pulled out the map, located the pencil stub in the pocket of his sweaty T-shirt, and wrote the coordinates down. "How's your cell battery?"

"Getting low."

"Just stay where you are. After I call the twins and Matson, I'll get back to you." He punched in Bing's number. "Where are you?"

"Give me a minute, and I'll check my GPS." Within a second, he came back with his coordinates.

"It looks like you're about a mile northeast of Rick. Are the women all right?"

"Yes, they're still sleeping."

"I'll get back to you as soon as I contact Matson." When Matson answered, Monty said simply, "We have three female hostages. Were there any others?"

"There was a man we thought was being held by that Abu group by the name of Dangwa, but no ransom demand was ever made for him."

"We didn't see any sign of him. We're down out of the big trees and into the lowland undergrowth. Rick's made it to the beach. The rest of us are going to meet with him ASAP."

"Good to hear. What are your plans to get away from there? Do you want us to send in a helicopter to lift you out?"

"That would be better than Santa at Christmas."

"I'll contact the military base in Zamboanga City and get right back to you."

Julia had awakened while Monty was talking with Matson. She sat up and moved her arm carefully and stiffly, clumsily retying the hijab around her disheveled hair. "Who were you talking to?" she asked curiously.

"Matson. He'll be getting back to us." He cut open his last MRE and handed it to Julia.

She took it gratefully. "I'm famished." She ate half the cold spaghetti before she handed it back to him. "My stomach doesn't seem to be able to hold any more right now."

Monty finished the meal and stuffed the outer wrap back into his pack. As he did so, the satphone vibrated. He picked it up. "It's me." He pulled out the pencil and map and wrote something down. Then he said, "We think there are probably five of them."

Julia put up her hand to get his attention. "There are at least five more. Another group merged with Hamal's several days ago. They were the ones that brought the Stinger that took down the drone."

"Our problems have increased. Julia says that there are at least another five Abu to deal with. They joined Hamal's group several days ago." He paused. "Yes, apparently they're all carrying AK-47s and have a couple of SACO M60s with them." He was silent for a minute and then added, "We'll meet you there."

He called Bing again. "Here are the coordinates for the meeting point. We've got to be there by five o'clock. Matson wants to get us out by helicopter before dark. Can you make it?"

"You better believe it."

"Can you call Rick and tell him where the pickup point is?"

"Will do."

He ended the call and put the satphone back into his pack. He stood and offered his hand to help Julia up from the ground. "We need to be on our way." She rose stiffly. He did not let go of her hand as they started to move carefully through the undergrowth. "Was there another hostage with you? A man by the name of Dangwa?"

"Yes, Phillip Dangwa. He was a quiet man. Sophie said he liked to talk about his two little girls and his wife. He didn't complain, even when things were very difficult." She wiped away a tear with dirty fingers. "They never asked for a ransom for him. He died needlessly of malaria, exhaustion, hunger—" She paused and spit out the last words. "—and cruelty."

He said no more but continued to hold her hand as he led her down the slope that gradually grew more level. The feel of his strong hand was comforting. *Monty, thank God you're here.* She held on tightly.

***

After he called Rick with the location of the pickup point, Bing shook Bolly awake. As he sat up, he combed his hair out of his face with his fingers. "What's up?"

"Wake the women. We need to be moving. Monty called with the meeting location, and we've to get there before five o'clock if we want to meet the helicopter that's going to take us out of here."

Sophie had heard him and sat up. She shook Carlita awake and then stood up. "How far do we have to go?"

"It looks like it's about a mile and a half as the crow flies, maybe more, but there may be some rough terrain, so it is hard to know how long it will take. It's nearly noon now."

Carlita stood wearily. "I'm so thirsty. When can we get a drink?"

Bolly responded, "The canteens are empty, but we'll probably find a stream or a river between here and there."

Bing led the foursome, cutting the way when necessary with his bolo. They reached a fast flowing stream that churned over rocks and rushed toward the sea. They paused long enough to get a drink and fill the canteens.

After another hour Carlita begged to rest, and Bing agreed. "If you give us a few minutes, we can probably get something to eat from the stream." While Bolly caught some prawns and an eel, Bing made a little fire.

After the small meal, Bolly stood and poured water on the fire. As he stepped on the embers, the sound of an AK-47 rattled briefly and the thud of bullets hitting the trees around them threw Carlita into a panic. The four of them dropped to the ground. "They found us," she whimpered in panic. She began to sob and repeated, "They found us."

"Sssst, sssst, sssst," Bing whispered to quiet her. Looking at his brother from where he lay on the ground, he whispered, "Did you see where the shots came from?"

Bolly shook his head but pointed at the broken palm fronds that hung toward the water. "I would guess that they came from over there." He pointed in the opposite direction.

"That puts them uphill from us. That's not good." Bing took a minute to evaluate their situation. "Give me some of your ammunition magazines. I don't want to run out."

"What're you going to do?" Bolly asked suspiciously.

"I'm going to hold them off while you get the women out of here." Bolly didn't argue; he just sorted through the items left in his pack and handed his brother four magazines for the M16s they had acquired from the AFP soldiers in the village. Bing smiled grimly. "Thanks. Now get out of here."

Bolly directed his conversation at the women. "We're going to move down the river bank, staying in the shadows, until we can find a safe place to cross. Keep your heads down. Follow me, and stay close." They stooped and moved down the river. To give them cover, Bing lay on his stomach, aimed one of the M16s he had been carrying, and fired toward the hillside opposite the river. An assault rifle answered him, spurring the other three to hurry into the undergrowth.

Under his breath he muttered, "Now I have a line on you." Aiming toward the location of the gunfire, he emptied the clip, released the magazine, and quickly inserted another.

***

Monty and Julia stopped short when they heard the fire from the AK-47 answered by the sound of an M16. "That's got to be Bing or Bolly returning fire. The Abu have found them." He let go of Julia's hand and swung the bolo with increased urgency. After another several minutes of pushing through the undergrowth, the sound of the gunfire grew louder.

Monty signaled a stop. "Get behind a palm, and stay there." Julia did as she was told. Monty made his way closer to the sound in a stooped posture and raised his M16. As the other weapon rattled again, he fired a short burst. That brought the attention of the shooter around to them. The other gun fired a burst in their direction, with a series of hard thuds and ripping sounds as the bullets tore through the palms.

Monty crawled on his stomach for about twenty feet. There, he rose to his knees and fired again. There was no response. He waited for another two or three minutes and then rose to his feet. "Hopefully, that one won't be a problem anymore. Let's get going. Where there's one Abu, there may be more." They started through the undergrowth again, with his bolo swinging hard and fast.

***

Hearing the second weapon, Bing sat quietly as he recognized the sound of the M16. *That's got to be Monty.* After a few minutes with no more gunfire, he turned and made his way into the shadows along the river.

***

By the time Bolly and the women had reached the coast, the women were weak and unsteady. When they could see the azure of the ocean through the palms, Bolly had to stop both of them from running for the beach. "You'll be seen on the beach. You'll make easy targets if you're exposed like that. According to my coordinates, we're within a half mile of Rick. We've got to find him without drawing the attention of any of the Abu." He looked around. "Stay here. I'm going to climb one of these coconut palms and see if I can get us some buko juice and maybe locate Rick while I'm up there." He pulled off his tattered shoes, dropped his backpack, and put his bolo knife between his teeth. Then he took off his belt and looped it around the tree trunk, starting the process of snaking his way to the top. Once up there, he freed five coconuts, and as they dropped with heavy thuds, he paused to look around.

Hanging the bolo on a belt loop and putting his hands to his cheeks to direct the sound, he cooed like a zebra dove. He paused for a moment and repeated it, aiming the sound in the opposite direction. Within a few seconds, he heard a similar sound. He repeated the gurgling, cooing call, and waited. Again the sound was repeated, this time a little closer. He could make out Rick's figure moving toward them through the trees and shadows. He climbed down and, with the bolo, hacked the great husk off one of the coconuts and pierced it with the point of his knife. As Rick arrived, he bent at the waist and offered it to him as if he were the *maitre'd* at a fine hotel.

Rick took the offered coconut, responding with a grin. "The view is great, but the table leaves something to be desired. I'd like to be nearer the band." Then he grew serious. "Where are the others?"

"On their way, we hope." Bolly continued to cut the husks from another coconut, which he pierced with his knife and then offered to Sophie.

"I heard gunfire."

"One of the Abu spotted us, and Bing stayed back to take care of him." Looking at his watch, Bolly added, "It's near four o'clock. Hope the rest of them get here soon."

Rick suddenly held up his hand for silence. They could hear the sound of someone cutting his way through the undergrowth. As the two men rose and reached for their weapons, Bing appeared through the undergrowth.

"Do you know where Monty and the other woman are?" Bolly asked his brother.

"Behind me somewhere. It must have been Monty that used his M16 on the Abu that ambushed us."

"They still have an hour. They'll get here in time, won't they?" Sophie asked worriedly.

Rick looked at his watch. "More like half an hour. The chopper will make too big a target to hang around waiting for them."

For the next twenty minutes, they sat in the shade unconsciously swatting at insects, the men regularly checking their watches. The rapid thump-thump-thump of the double rotor blades of the Huey brought all of them to their feet. It bore the representation of the Philippine flag painted on the fuselage. It was divided almost equally into three parts of red, white, and blue with a stylized sun centered in the white triangle.

Rick shouted above the sound of the blades, "I've never seen a more beautiful sight in all my life." The five stood in the shadows of the palms and watched as it descended toward the beach. As it hovered about four feet above the sand, the wide door on the bulkhead slid aft, and two Filipino airmen in khaki waved them on board.

Sophie looked around and cried out, trying to be heard over the noise of the rotating blades, "We can't leave without the others."

The men pulled both of the women at a run toward the helicopter as it gently settled in the sand. One of the uniformed men had leaped out with his M16 at the ready, while Bing and Bolly lifted Carlita into the open door. Bing and Bolly lifted her high enough for four outstretched hands to grab her. As they lifted her inside, they heard the sound of an AK-47 and the hard thuds of the impact of bullets against the armored portions of the fuselage. Carlita screamed. As Sophie was pulled into the aircraft, she heard Bolly cry out and felt him fall away from her.

Rick and Bing each took one arm and pulled him to his feet. They pushed him into the doorway, where one of the crew grabbed him and pulled him inside. He had been hit in the lower back, and his shirt was growing bright red at his waist. As the bullets continued to fly around them, sometimes piercing the bulkhead of the Huey, a Filipino airman serving as door gunner fired one of the mounted machine guns into the undergrowth with a broad sweeping action. Bing tossed the backpack and the rifles they had been carrying into the helicopter, and then he and Rick pulled themselves through the open door. As the Huey rose rapidly into the sky, the gunner continued firing into the undergrowth. The noise was almost deafening and made the women cover their ears and duck their heads. For Rick, it was an all too familiar sound.

27

MONTY HAD BEEN PULLING JULIA through the undergrowth by the hand when he suddenly stopped. A steep, weathered gully opened in front of them. Looking at his watch, Monty took a breath. "I don't think we're going to get there by five o'clock." Julia could see the sweat dripping from his chin and arms. Suddenly, he cocked his head. "Chopper blades."

Julia looked at him in disappointment and whispered with a catch in her voice, "You're right. We won't make it." The dismay in her voice was written on her face.

He shook his head. "They hadn't better wait for us." To offer her some comfort, he added confidently, "Don't be too disappointed. We'll find a way out of here."

The sound of the helicopter increased, and soon they could see it as it descended above the beach, about half a mile from where they were standing.

"A Vietnam-era Huey. I thought most of them had been retired," Monty said under his breath, talking to himself. He shook his head in frustration. "They should've sent a cobra. This one's a slick—no weapons pods, just a couple of door gunners." They watched as the others were pulled into the open door. From where Monty and Julia were watching, they could hear the sound of an assault rifle above the sound of the rotor blades. When Bolly fell, Monty cringed. "He's been hit."

"How badly?"

"Can't tell." Monty turned to search for the location of the gunman who had shot Bolly. "There! I see something." He yanked his back pack open and pulled out his binoculars. "What the devil . . . it looks like one end of a missile launcher poking out from that clump of bamboo."

Julia shaded her eyes. "Yes, they had at least two missiles. They used one on the drone."

"There it is! It's a launcher." His voice was urgent. "I can see one end of it. We've got to stop them, or they'll bring down the Huey."

Monty handed her the binoculars. "I'm going to fire at it. You watch through the glasses and tell me how close I am." As Julia put the binoculars to her eyes, he fired a short burst.

"You're too low. Come up about ten feet." Monty fired again.

"Better, but now the launcher has disappeared."

As the Huey started to climb, Julia continued to watch through the binoculars. "There it is. I see the launcher again. It's moved about ten feet farther up the hill. Now it's near that grouping of three palm trees. Can you see it?"

It took Monty a second to identify it. "He's got it aimed again." He fired two long bursts.

Julia watched through the glasses as the man with the launcher pulled back into the palm trees. "He's moved back into the shadows, but I think the launcher is still aimed toward the helicopter."

Monty fired a long burst, moving the barrel of the M16 just a fraction of an inch as he held down the trigger.

***

The pilot banked the Huey and headed southwest for what was to be a flight of about twenty-five minutes. The speed of the ascent made the women feel as if their stomachs had been left behind. Carlita sat limply against the bulkhead, shaking with exhaustion and a renewed attack of malaria.

Controlling her disappointment at leaving Julia and Monty behind, Sophie turned to where Bolly was lying. She lifted his shirt to look at the wound. As one of the AFP airmen pulled a first-aid kit from a compartment, she yelled above the sound of the rotor blades, "Are you a medic?" He shook his head. "Give it to me. I've done this before." The man gave her the kit.

Bolly was lying on his stomach with his head turned to the side. She disinfected the wound and put her mouth nearer his ear. "You're very lucky. I don't think the bullet hit any vital organs. It's not bleeding very badly." She taped a heavy bandage over the wound.

Rick raised his voice and asked one of the soldiers, "Where are we going?"

Before he got an answer, the copilot yelled, "Someone just launched a missile. Where'd they get that thing?"

***

As she watched through the binoculars, Julia heard the low explosion of a launched missile and then the louder explosion as the solid fuel ignited. It lifted above the trees.

"It's too high." Her voice rose in exultation. "It's too high."

Monty took the glasses from her and followed the missile as it rose into the air. "I must have hit him before he locked it onto the Huey." He continued to watch as the missile spiraled out over the water. "Thank God for small blessings."

They both turned to watch as the helicopter rose rapidly. The door gunner in the helicopter raked the undergrowth as it rose. For a few moments, the satisfaction that they had prevented the helicopter from being hit by the Stinger overcame Julia's disappointment at missing the pickup. The Huey rose rapidly and headed south at a hundred miles per hour, leaving Julia and Monty behind.

28

THE HUEY CONTINUED TO RISE, and Rick yelled again, "Where're we going?"

One of the crewmen yelled back, "Camp Navarro General Hospital in Zamboanga City. It serves the U.S. military advisors in the area." After the short ride of about twenty minutes, the helicopter landed at the airport, where two ambulances were waiting with red lights flashing.

Bolly and Carlita were lifted out on the stretchers, which were laid on gurneys. The stretchers were slid into the back of the first ambulance, and with the siren wailing, it pulled away from the helipad.

As they climbed out of the Huey, Sophie and her rescuers took notice of a contingent of armed U.S. Marines standing at attention. Sophie, Rick, and Bing were directed to the second ambulance.

When the first ambulance arrived at the hospital and its two passengers were lifted out, Bolly noted from his place on the stretcher that a second contingent of armed U.S. Marines guarded the area. Carlita was too weak to take note of her surroundings.

The second ambulance arrived about five minutes behind the first. As men helped Sophie out, she also noted the second contingent of marines. "Wow, I wish I were better dressed for the occasion. What's this all about?"

A female marine with a name tag that read Lieutenant Billings pushed a wheelchair up to her. "This is an effort by the U.S. military to extend to you some special protection."

Rick laughed. "Perhaps some would describe it as 'closing the barn door after the horse is out.'" His tone became more serious, and he added, "But the U.S. military really does work in these islands with their hands tied. If the U.S. military had been permitted to go in to get you out, you would have never needed us."

She looked up him and said sincerely, "But they couldn't have done a better job than you guys did."

As they entered the hospital, Brigadier General Wilson Finchley, commander of the U.S. forces in the islands, met them. At his side was General Del Rosario, the general who commanded the AFP Southern Command Headquarters.

General Finchley greeted them. "Welcome to Camp Navarro General Hospital. We're glad to see you here, free of the threats and dangers of the *Abu Sayyaf*. Captain Matson at the U.S. Embassy has told us that you may have useful information for us regarding the Abu, but first you'll want to eat and rest."

"And shower," Rick added.

Finchley shook hands with each of the three, and spoke directly to Sophie. "It's not our intention to keep you here listening to a lengthy greeting, but we want you to know that we will be of service in any way possible. Lieutenant Billings will be at your service, Miss Adamson, for as long as you need or want her."

Sophie looked up at the young woman, who was attractive despite her severe hairstyle and military uniform. "Thank you."

"You will let me know how my brother is doing?" Bing asked with unusual seriousness.

"Of course. After you've been examined by our medical staff, my aid will show you to your rooms where you can shower and rest for a while. We'll have a meal ready for you in about an hour. You'll be directed to the mess hall at that time."

Lieutenant Billings whisked Sophie away. She took her to a hospital examination room where the lieutenant remained to assist the doctor. Sophie's head hurt, and she wanted to lie down, but in the exam room, Major Steve Whittingham, M.D., took her vital signs, and the lieutenant, who was evidently a nurse, drew blood. Sophie was given a paper gown to wear for the continued examination. "Lieutenant, can you help me get out of my clothes while the doctor steps out of the room?" Sophie said with a tired grin. Lieutenant Billings withheld her grin until the doctor had exited the room.

After Sophie had wrapped herself in the paper gown and stepped up to sit on the exam table, she called out "okay" and the doctor reentered. "I appreciate everyone's concern, but I'm not really sick. I'm just very tired—and I'm very, very hungry."

The doctor looked into her eyes. "Well, from what I've been told, you've been living in the rain forest as a hostage of the *Abu Sayyaf.* Those dark circles under your eyes are a clue. We can be sure that you have at least two or three kinds of intestinal parasites. Have you been bothered by fever, loss of weight, nervousness, and irritability?"

She nodded sharply. "And if you were being forced to walk through the rain forest day after day at the point of a gun, tied to several other hostages, nearly starved to death, and sleeping on the ground at night, I think you'd have those symptoms too."

The doctor laughed. "See, there's that irritability I mentioned."

She flushed to the roots of her hair and quickly apologized. "I'm sorry. I suppose you're right."

He reached for a small packet of pills on the counter near the examining table. "Here is a three-day treatment of Combantrin. It will clear up your problems and get rid of your many unwanted internal friends. When the blood tests are done, we may need to add some medications to your treatment, depending on what parasites may have made it into your bloodstream. Do you have any other symptoms or problems that we need to treat?"

She was sitting on the examination table wrapped in a poor excuse of a modesty cover, but to make sure he had seen the welts from the leaches, she pointed at her left leg. Using cotton pads soaked with disinfectant, he washed the welts on her left leg, while the lieutenant washed the ones on her right. All were in different stages of healing or infection. If her head hadn't been throbbing, she would have enjoyed this attention from the handsome, youthful man.

"I'm going to give you some antibiotic cream to help clear up the infection in some of the leech bites." He handed her a tube of the cream and then pointed to a bathrobe on the back of the door. "You can put that on, and Lieutenant Billings will push you to your room in the officers' wing where you can shower and lie down until they have a meal prepared for you." He grinned at her and left the room.

Carlita was dosed with Qualaquin, Combantrin, an antibiotic, and a sedative and was put to bed. She slept fitfully for the next twelve hours.

Lieutenant Billings pushed Sophie in the wheelchair to a private room where Sophie refused any further assistance from the lieutenant, who had quietly told her it was all right to call her Liz. Finally alone for the first time since the kidnapping, Sophie luxuriated in a long, hot shower, using the available bar of Palmolive soap to shampoo her hair. She was thrilled to find a toothbrush and a tube of Colgate toothpaste, which at that moment meant more to her than a pair of two-carat diamond earrings. She put on a clean set of scrubs, a pair of hospital slippers, and the robe she had worn from the examination room.

As she finished dressing, Liz knocked on her door. "Your dinner is ready, and your ride is here." When Sophie opened the door, Liz grinned. "The doctor insists that you use the wheelchair for a day or two. Before I take you to the mess hall, can I get you anything?"

"Yes, an elastic band." The lieutenant just looked at her. "I need an elastic band so I can put my hair in a ponytail." On the way to the mess hall, they stopped at an office and Liz handed her a handful of elastic bands. Rick and Bing had showered and donned clean military uniforms without rank insignia and were waiting in the mess hall. Sophie got the first word in. "Have you heard how Bolly is doing?"

Bing grinned. "The surgeon said he's doing great. Right now he is still out of it, but as soon as he's fully awake, he will be planning on how to impress his wife with his bravery and his wound."

General Finchley entered the mess hall, which was empty except for the former hostages and the Filipino cooks and stewards who were preparing what they hoped would be a meal to remember for their guests. He took Sophie's wheelchair from the lieutenant and pushed her to the table usually reserved for officers. He motioned for the rest of them to be seated. The stewards took that as a cue to deliver the meal. They brought out plates piled high with rice, fried mackerel, fried milkfish, fried pork, fried chicken, and a big bowl of *sinigang*, a soup of fish heads in a green, milky broth.

While the others ate, the general sat near Sophie and spoke quietly, leaning with his elbows on his knees so she would hear him but the others would not. "We're so glad that you have been rescued, Miss Adamson. I wanted to tell you how much we regret that the U.S. forces were not permitted to get involved actively in your rescue. But it appears that you were rescued by some very capable men, each of whom I understand was trained by the U.S. military, so perhaps we were able to assist in an indirect manner." She nodded. He continued, "You'll be given every courtesy and protection that we can offer from this point on, until you return to the states."

"Thank you, General Finchley. I don't know what else to say except thank you." The general again shook hands with the men before he took his leave.

After the meal, Rick, Bing, and Sophie were taken into a waiting room, and one at a time, they were interviewed by the base AFP intelligence officer. Liz remained near Sophie, even through the interview.

While Sophie was being interviewed, Rick called Matson. "Good to hear from you. General Finchley told me that Monty and Julia didn't get out. How's everyone else?"

"Bolly took a bullet, but he's going to be okay. One of the hostages, Carlita, is ill with malaria, and all of us are undoubtedly carrying numerous little guests in our digestive systems that we will have to discourage, but, generally, we're doing as well as could be hoped. I'm sorry that I can't give you a report on Monty and Julia."

"There'll be a couple of U.S. intelligence officers there in the morning to debrief all of you. I'll be flying down with them."

"I'm sure Sophie will want to contact her grandfather as soon as possible. Do you see any problem with that?"

"The embassy will be contacting her grandparents within the hour. The ambassador was simply waiting until she had a report on Sophie's condition before letting them know that she's been rescued. If I hear from Monty, I'll let you know. In the meantime, get some rest."

29

"The Abu are going to know that we didn't make the pickup. I think we'd better get out of here. They'll come looking for us."

"Where will we go?" Her excitement had waned, and her voice had a thin, weary quality.

"We'll work our way up the coast toward Anugan. There may be some small fishing villages between here and there where we can get something to eat and maybe hire a *banca*."

"How far is Anugan?" Julia was hoping it was close.

"It's about five miles, I think." Monty looked at her and was suddenly aware of the exhaustion, pain, and stress in her face as she stood holding her side. "Panganuran is much closer, probably only two or three miles the other direction, but that's where the exchange for you was to take place. We can't go there." Monty took her hand again and tried to be encouraging. "Hold on to me if you need to. We can make it as long as we stay out of sight."

"Can't you call Matson and get another helicopter?" Her voice was hopeful.

"I checked the satphone right after we got caught up in that firefight. The battery's dead. At least for the present, we're on our own." Monty led her through the undergrowth as fast as she could follow, at times putting his arm around her to help her over fallen trees and gullies eroded by the seasonal rains.

After another hour, she asked breathlessly, "How much farther do we have to go before we can rest?"

"I'm sorry if I'm pushing you harder than you can go. We can rest here for a few minutes. Sit down, and I'll climb that palm and get you some buko juice." He dropped the backpack and set the M16 against a tree trunk. Without taking off his battered leather boots with the thick textured soles, he pulled off his belt and put it around the trunk, leaned back to tighten it, and made his way up the palm that leaned out slightly over the beach. He cut four green coconuts.

She took a drink of the lukewarm, green coconut milk and bit her lower lip to help regain her self-control. She closed her eyes as if to shut out her present circumstances and leaned back against the trunk of a palm, trying to find a position that would give her some relief from the pain in her side.

After giving her a few more minutes to rest, Monty patted her hand to urge her along. "It's important for us to get moving again." He offered his hand to help her up, and they started moving through the undergrowth again, so close to the beach that as dusk came and the moon rose, the white sand, the dark sky, and the nearly black swells on the sea looked like the negative of a photograph.

By nine-thirty, Julia was so exhausted that she could hardly put one foot in front of the other. Even Monty was moving slower than usual, whether from consideration for her or from fatigue, she couldn't guess, but his limp had become pronounced. "Can we rest, or do we need to keep moving?" Julia asked.

"We can rest for a little while. The Abu seldom travel at night because they know the lights they use will give them away, but we'll need to be moving as soon as you feel you can."

While Julia rested, Monty planned to keep watch—or at least awaken intermittently to check their surroundings over the next hour or two. She lay down with her head on her bent arm. She fell asleep immediately. He found a place to sit, with his back against the trunk of a palm, but despite his determination to stay on watch, he drifted off to sleep as well.

About midnight, he awoke with a start. The waxing, three-quarter moon spread its light over the beach, and the gentle swells of the incoming tide reflected it back to the sky, like the reflection in an unsteady mirror, doubling the light that pierced through the trees, brightening the white beach almost as if it were day. He sat quietly, listening to the whirring sounds of the night insects, listening for any sound that shouldn't be there. All he heard was the whisk of palm fronds jostled by the breath of the night and the regular sound of the waves. *Perhaps that's all I heard. It's unlikely that the Abu would be moving around in the forest looking for us after dark.* Then he looked around again. *Except that the moonlight is brighter tonight than I've ever seen it . . .* He didn't finish the thought. The sound of a stick snapping as if someone had put too much weight on it made his head turn. *No, I'm hearing more than the breeze in the palms. We can't get caught in a firefight here!*

He leaned over, put his hand on Julia's mouth, and whispered in her ear, "We've got company. We've got to get away from here. Do you understand?" She nodded, and he removed his hand.

She struggled to her feet with his help. He took her hand and pulled her behind him through the undergrowth until they were standing in the shadows cast by the palms where the undergrowth met the beach sand. "We'll wait until the moon goes behind those clouds; then we're going to make a run for it to the water's edge. Can you do that? The surf will hide our footprints. Okay?" She nodded hesitantly.

After three more minutes, a thick bank of clouds slid over the moon, darkening the night as if someone had extinguished everything but the stars. Monty pulled her across the beach for at least forty feet to the point where the waves curled and broke against the sand. Lifting her caftan above her knees with one hand, she lengthened her stride to keep up with Monty.

Running in the sand and the waves as they broke over her feet and ankles made her legs tired, and her broken ribs silently screamed with pain. Soon her calf muscles began to ache and tighten, but Monty wouldn't let her stop to rest until the face of the moon was almost ready to peek out from behind the long bank of clouds. *When will we stop? I don't think I can go much farther.*

They had run for nearly thirty minutes. He pointed to the tree cover, signaling her to move up the beach toward it. As she staggered tiredly across the sand, he turned and made his way backward toward the tree line to sweep the sand to hide their footprints with a palm frond he had picked up. They paused to breathe in the shadows as the clouds uncovered the moon.

"That should put some distance between us and them," he panted.

Julia collapsed on the ground where she struggled to hold back the sobs the pain in her side tried to force from her. She could not speak for several minutes. After she had sufficiently caught her breath, she whispered, "How far do you think we came?"

"About a mile and a half—maybe a little more," he responded.

"It felt like ten miles. Do you think we're safe here?" She was holding her side to ease the pain as she continued to breathe heavily.

"We need to keep going until the sun comes up, if you have the strength."

She just nodded and put up her hand so he could help her struggle to her feet. For the rest of the night, they moved through the trees and the undergrowth, treading on the dead palm fronds and other detritus deposited by the high tide where the undergrowth met the beach. The shadows the palms cast on the lighter beach sand were like ink stains on a beige carpet.

As the sun began to rise and the mountain peaks became silhouettes against the light, Monty stopped. "You can rest now." Julia dropped.

As the sun reached its zenith, she awakened in a fit of shaking chills and aching joints that felt as if someone had beaten her with a club. Monty was nowhere to be seen. His backpack, M16, and handgun were lying near her.

Had there been anything in her stomach, she would have given it up. The sudden nausea was nearly overwhelming. She rocked back and forth, holding her arms against her chest with her teeth chattering. "Monty, where are you?" she whispered. Within the hour the chills had turned into a fever, and her torn and dirty clothing grew wet with perspiration that made her blond curls turn dark where they stuck to her forehead.

Dragging herself into a patch of darker shade, she lay and wondered if she would die before he got back. *Oh, dear God, please help me. Send Monty back . . .* She slid into unconsciousness.

Nearly an hour later, Monty found her that way, unconscious and quietly moaning. He carried a small pouch of boiled rice, two mangos, a small bunch of bananas, and a papaya. He was soaked with perspiration and was breathing heavily. He put down the rice and the fruit. Using his bolo, he cut the hem of her caftan and then tore off a long swath from the bottom of it. He soaked it with water from his canteen and began to wipe her arms and face. As he did so, he talked to her gently. "Julia, Julia, can you hear me? Nod your head if you can hear me." Her head nodded slightly, but her eyes did not open.

"Can you drink some water?" She gave another hardly measurable nod. He lifted her head and shoulders with his left arm and held the canteen to her lips with his right hand. The water flowed almost unheeded over her lips and chin. "Swallow, Julia, swallow. You're dehydrated." She swallowed a few times, and her eyes flickered open.

"Where were you?" she whispered.

"I went up the coast a mile or two until I found a fishing village. I got some rice and fruit. I rushed back here to find you sick with malaria. I'm afraid they won't have any quinine in that village. It's too small."

"Malaria? Why do I have it if you don't?" she asked weakly.

"Because I have some immunity to it. I had it years ago, but it comes back on me now and then. You've been bitten by a malaria-carrying mosquito, probably not long after you got here. Malaria takes about two weeks to incubate."

As foggy as her thinking was, she realized that she was probably bitten on the day she and Mike had visited the foundation clients in the lower, mosquito-plagued metropolitan areas.

He wiped her forehead again. "Can you eat something?"

She shook her head weakly. "Not now. Maybe in a little while."

He laid her back down. "We'll need to keep moving northward to get to Anugan. It's a fishing village that's large enough to have more than one sari-sari shop. Maybe I can get some batteries to recharge the satphone there—and maybe even some quinine. I'm not sure what I'll use for money, but I can probably barter my watch for what we need."

Julia opened her eyes and tried to smile, despite the headache that felt as though a blacksmith were at work in her head. "I have money in my money belt. I've been wearing it around my waist all this time."

Monty grinned and patted her hands gently in approval. "Then we're going to be okay, despite the fact that right now you're feeling miserable."

"That's an understatement."

"I've got some boiled rice, and I'll cut up a mango for you. You need something to eat if you're going to be strong enough to keep going. You'll have these fevers and sweats fairly regularly until we can get you some quinine. They'll last about four or five hours—or more—and the headache and joint pain will be with you most of the time. You're generally in better health than most Pinoy, so I don't think that you're in danger of dying like Dangwa. You'll just wish you could die when it gets bad."

"If you're trying to make me feel better, it isn't working," she whispered.

As the fever began to abate, she ate a little fruit. Then Monty let her sleep. About five o'clock, she woke, shivering and aching so badly that as hard as she tried, she couldn't keep from crying as she rocked back and forth. He took his extra T-shirt from his backpack and wrapped it around her. Then he pulled her against his chest, put his arms around her to warm her, and held her against the shivering that racked her body.

"I wish there were more I could do for you, Julia," he whispered, as he laid his cheek against her hair. He remembered clearly the fierce chill and burning fevers of his own malarial sieges of earlier years. After a half hour, in exhaustion, she fell asleep again.

When she woke at about ten o'clock, the moon was lighting the night like a halogen bulb hanging in the sky. Monty was leaning against a tree trunk asleep and still had one of his arms loosely around her. She lay very quietly for another fifteen minutes, drifting in and out of sleep. She felt safe for the first time since she had been kidnapped from Bolong, but somewhere in the back of her mind, she was nudged toward the awareness that things could change quickly. When she felt the shift of his weight and knew he had awakened, she sat up, pulling away from him.

He straightened. "You're awake."

"Yes."

"How are you feeling?"

"Better. I'm a little hungry. Is that good?"

"Yes, that's good." He reached for the papaya and another mango and swiftly peeled them, cut them in slices, and handed each slice to her.

As she ate the last of the mango, she was suddenly filled with guilt. "You didn't have any. I'm sorry, but it tasted so good."

He chuckled. "I'm fine. I've had a couple of bananas. It's important that you eat whenever you can." He began to stuff the T-shirt into the backpack. "How strong do you feel?"

"I feel a little better, but if I had gotten any worse, I think I'd be dead. I don't feel like running a marathon, but I can walk. How far do we need to go?"

"We need to make our way up to that little fishing village where I'll try to buy some more food and hire us a ride to Anugan. I need you to get some pesos out of your money belt. Can you stand up?" He took her hands and almost lifted her into a standing position. He grinned as he turned his back to her. "I won't look while you get the money."

Her hands shook as she pulled up the caftan and untied the money belt that had been under her blouse for the many days she had been a captive. It was terribly painful to lift her right arm.

She took out a bundle of ten-thousand pesos and handed it to him. The bills were damp with perspiration. She could hardly tie the belt around her waist again.

He took the money and put half of it in each front pocket. "You let me know when you need to rest. Don't push yourself beyond your limits, or the next siege of fever or chills will be much worse." He took her hand, and they started through the undergrowth, walking just inside the tree line and making their way by moonlight.

Exhaustion made Julia feel as though her feet were stuck in the thick mud of a lahar that resisted every step. After four hours of slow progress and increasing periods of rest, they finally came within sight of the fishing village where Monty had bought the fruit. While still hidden by the trees and undergrowth, he made a place for her to lie down on a bed of palm fronds. He sat and leaned against the trunk of a palm, and they both slept until the sun rose.

When he woke, she was still sleeping. He took off the holster and put it and the Beretta into the backpack. He strolled into the little village where the men were pushing their *bancas* out into the sea to begin a day of fishing.

The little nameless village of about two hundred natives was made up of perhaps ten or twelve families. He approached a woman with a tray of fruit on her head and asked her if she knew of anyone who would take him to Anugan in a *banca*. She pointed to one of the fishermen who sat under the shade of a palm mending his net.

He walked casually up to the man, who was probably no more than forty but whose sun-darkened, leathery skin made him look seventy. In a friendly manner, Monty asked if he would be willing to take two people to Anugan in his *banca* for a hundred pesos. The man raised three fingers and Monty agreed to the price of three hundred pesos. The man brightened and, in his enthusiasm, started immediately for the canoe. Monty told him he would need to go and get his wife, who was resting in the forest after a long walk. The man nodded vigorously and said he would wait. He returned to mending his net.

After he had gone a few steps, Monty turned and asked the man if there were somewhere in the village where he could get a caftan or burqa for his wife, as hers was soiled and torn. The man thought for a moment and then hurried to his hut. He came out of it a few minutes later with one of his wife's caftans. She was following, scolding him, like an agitated hen pursuing a bandy rooster.

He hurried to Monty and offered him the well-worn, dark blue caftan. Monty held it up and could see that it would be too short for Julia by six inches but thanked the man and offered him five hundred pesos, which the man took and handed to his wife. It silenced her complaints, and she smiled and bobbed her head in thanks.

He located the small sari-sari shop and asked the woman operating it if she could feed two people. She nodded proudly as she pointed to each item. "*Opo,* I have boiled rice, *pancit* noodles, fish, and fruit."

He hurried back to the spot where he had left Julia. He gently tried to wake her. She was feverish and soaked with perspiration but was aware of what he was saying. "Julia, I need you to get up. Can you stand?"

"If you help me," she whispered.

"I need you to change into this caftan."

She didn't ask why. She tried to pull the one she was wearing off over her head. She was too weak. Monty had to help her take it off. Then he helped her put on the one he had obtained from the fisherman. He quickly wrapped the M16 in the old caftan. He retied her tattered hijab over her hair, tucking the ends under the scarf to hide its light color. With her leaning heavily on him, they started back to the village.

When they reached the sari-sari shop, Monty set the backpack and the gun wrapped in the caftan on the dirt floor by a battered table. The little shop was about six by six feet and open to the weather, with a *tolda* of striped fabric for an awning and a counter made of a long board on two tall sawhorses.

Monty helped Julia into the chair near the old table that faced the back of the shop. He took the one that faced out into the village where he could see everything going on around them. After he spoke to the shop owner, she brought them some *bibingka*, a Filipino dessert of boiled, sweet rice covered with a brown-sugar coating. She cut up a papaya and put it before them.

As they sat in the shade inside the little shop, Monty watched three men carrying AK-47 assault rifles as they came out of the forest. "Don't turn around. Just keep eating. There are three Abu who have come into the village. If they don't see your white face, they may not bother us."

Julia involuntarily shuddered. Sensing her alarm, Monty smiled at her. "Take a deep breath. Don't faint on me." He reached out and put his hand over hers. She grasped it like someone trying to keep from drowning.

The shop owner had stepped over to the little makeshift counter and began to nervously straighten the narrow-waisted Coke bottles and packages of stale Fritos and potato chips that were always a part of the stock of a sari-sari shop. She seemed to have forgotten her customers. Much of the normal conversation that had been ongoing in the marketplace had grown quiet as villagers watched the men with wary eyes.

Monty let go of Julia's hand and returned to eating the rice. She whispered, "What if they see you?"

"They don't know what I look like, and you're wearing a different caftan than you were wearing in the camp. Sit still, and they may overlook us."

Monty appeared to be unconcerned about the arrival of the men, but he reached out with his left foot and scooted the wrapped gun closer to his chair.

"What do they look like?" Julia whispered.

"One is a tall man, very dark skinned with a crooked nose," he said quietly.

"That's Hussein. Sophie said he was one of the two men who kidnapped her and Lily."

"The other man is wearing a red T-shirt and a necklace of wooden beads."

"Ali."

"The other man is short, maybe five feet, five inches, and has a scar on his scalp."

"One of the men that joined Hamal's group a few days ago. He was one of the men who brought the rocket launcher."

"Keep eating. They're walking this way. Keep your feet under the table so they can't see your white ankles."

Julia extended her legs and feet, partially hiding them at the side of Monty's extended legs. She put a piece of papaya in her mouth but was so nervous that she could hardly swallow it. She pulled her arms and shoulders further into the caftan so the sleeves nearly hid her hands.

Monty watched the three men out of the corner of his eye. They walked through the market, making their way past the row of fish vendors, another sari-sari shop, and a shop where a family of five was sewing nipa fronds into hut shingles. They steadily neared the shop where Monty and Julia were eating.

They looked at Monty but evidently saw no reason to suspect the man in the ragged, black T-shirt. They did not see the backpack or the wrapped weapon in the shadows behind his chair. Nervously, as Julia looked down at the table, she checked around her face to see if any of her hair was poking out from beneath the hijab. The men saw little reason to pay attention to the woman in the blue caftan.

They continued past the sari-sari shop, looking closely at the owner of the fish stall next to it and the man buying fish. They moved throughout the village, looking over every man and woman they saw and eventually stopped to talk among themselves. All eyes in the market were on them.

"The one called Hussein is making a cell phone call," Monty said quietly. After a conversation of about two minutes, the three men returned to the path and disappeared into the forest. The silence in the village was quickly replaced by the nervous, relieved chatter of the merchants and fishermen.

The woman had quit straightening her limited merchandise; her relief at the departure of the three men was evident. Monty thanked her and handed her two one-hundred peso bills. She smiled and nodded. He offered her another hundred peso bill and pointed to several mangos. She nodded and put them in a cloth. She tied the four corners together and offered it to him.

He handed the bundle to Julia and asked the shopkeeper, "Do you know who those men are?"

"*Abu Sayyaf.*"

"Do they come into your village often?"

She shook her head. "Most in this village are Christian. We do not like *Abu Sayyaf.* They killed our priest two years ago."

Monty signaled to Julia with a nod of his head that it was time for them to go. She stood unsteadily, so he reached out and laid his hand on her shoulder. It was reassuring and calming. After he swung the backpack over his left shoulder and picked up the caftan-wrapped M16 gun with his right, he put out his left arm for her to hang on to. He nodded in respect to the woman and thanked her. *"Maraming salamat, Lola."* She beamed at the term of respect.

The fisherman hurried to them, all smiles. "We go to Anugan now?"

Monty nodded and thanked the man for being patient. The boatman continued to chatter in Cebuano, and Monty whispered in Julia's ear, "He is asking if you are ill."

Julia smiled weakly at the fisherman and responded, *"Opo, sakit ako."* The fisherman understood the Tagalog, which translated to, "Yes, I'm sick."

The fisherman made sympathetic clicking noises with his tongue as Monty helped her into the small *banca* and had her sit in the bottom where she could lean against one of the thwarts. He tried to make her comfortable by putting the backpack behind her. He and the fisherman pushed the canoe out into the water. After they climbed in, the fisherman started the little ten-horsepower engine.

While Julia ate one of the mangos, Monty carefully took apart the M16 and put the parts into his backpack so the gun would not draw attention in Anugan. The fisherman did not seem particularly surprised at the sight of the weapon. In an area at times almost overrun by *Abu Sayyaf,* he had seen many similar weapons.

***

The clock on his nightstand read four o'clock when the telephone rang in the Mallon home. When Mallon picked it up, there was a woman on the line. "I have the United States ambassador to the Philippines on the telephone. She would like to speak to Mr. Mallon."

"Yes, that's me." His voice was tense with alarm.

"Mr. Mallon, this is Ambassador Zina Whitesides in Manila." Her voice was well modulated and controlled. "We have good news for you. Your granddaughter, Sophie, has been successfully rescued and is presently recuperating in the hospital at the Southern Command Center in Zamboanga City on Mindanao. She is well, considering the experience she has been through."

"Thank you, Ambassador Whitesides, thank you for your call." He hurriedly added, "What do you know of the other woman, Julia Wentworth?"

"She and a man, Diego Montalbon, did not make the helicopter pickup. We'll be in contact as soon as we have any more information. In the meantime, we can arrange for you to see your granddaughter if you choose to come to Mindanao. Otherwise, we will make arrangements to get her home to you as soon as she feels well enough to travel."

"I'll come there, immediately."

"If you will keep us posted as to your travel arrangements, we'll see that you have ground transportation once you get to Mindanao. Here's my private telephone number. Do not hesitate to call me at anytime." He picked up a pen and wrote down the number.

"Thank you, Ambassador Whitesides. This is such good—such good news." His voice caught as he spoke. "I will notify you as soon as I know of my arrival time there."

After the call ended, Mallon sat on the edge of the bed with his head in his hands and did not move for a full minute. His wife had been listening, and she rose to sit by him on his side of the bed and put her arms around him.

He returned her embrace. "You need to lie back down. I have some arrangements to make." He picked up the telephone and called his secretary. "Shirley, I'm sorry to wake you, but Sophie has been found . . ."

"That's wonderful!"

He continued. "I need you to contact Executive Air at the airport as soon as the office is open. See how fast I can get a charter jet for a flight to Los Angeles."

"For one?"

"Yes, for one. Then see if there are any first-class seats on any major airlines from Los Angeles that will get me to Manila as soon as possible."

"Yes, sir."

The man who had been growing older before everyone's eyes for the last few weeks was vital again. His wife noted that the color had returned to his face. He rose from the bed and moved around the room with purpose, still holding the telephone.

"Also, cancel all my appointments for the next week. I'm not sure when I'll get back from Manila."

Mallon was on a Citation Bravo private jet headed for LAX at 450 miles per hour by ten o'clock that morning.

***

The next morning at the hospital was one of eating and continued debriefing for Rick, Bing, and Sophie. Sophie thanked Lieutenant Billings and insisted that she didn't need her assistance any longer but gave her a hug as a thank you. Carlita remained too ill to leave her hospital bed, and her marine nurse sat quietly in her room.

At the doctor's insistence, Bolly unwillingly remained in bed, but by midafternoon he had ignored the doctor's advice and joined the others in the doctor's lounge. He was quick to lift the top of the scrubs he was wearing to show his bandages with pride. He thoroughly enjoyed being pushed around in a wheelchair.

Throughout the balance of the day, on an individual basis, each of the four spent another hour with AFP intelligence officers and two more hours with the CIA. Matson had arrived to sit in on the CIA debriefing, where he quietly listened.

That night Sophie tossed in bed and occasionally rose to pace before the window, peering out at the dark sky, wondering and worrying about Julia.

Late in the afternoon of the next day Sophie and Matson sat in the nearly empty mess hall, where the cooks in the kitchen were making their usual music with pots and pans, preparing the dinner that was to be served in an hour. Matson smiled broadly. "I asked to meet with you alone because I have some good news for you."

"You've found Julia and Monty?" Her face brightened.

His smile disappeared. "No, but I'm sure I'll hear from them in the next twenty-four hours. The good news is that the U.S. Embassy has notified us that your grandfather is on a plane and will be here to personally take you home."

"That's great—but I won't leave until I know Julia is safe."

"Regardless of when you decide to return to the states, your grandfather wants to see you and make sure that you're all right. Also, we have a couple of State Department counselors flying in tomorrow who specialize in hostage situations. They may be able to help you unwind."

Sophie looked right at him. "When I see that Julia is safe and whole, I won't need much more unwinding."

He returned her look. "You may feel that way now, but you should take advantage of their experience and advice. It will make a great difference to your peace of mind a few weeks or months from now."

30

THE TEN-HORSEPOWER MOTOR ON the little *banca* putted unsteadily for three miles up the coast to Anugan. After the fisherman beached it, he located an empty gas can in the stern and climbed out. "I get more gas here. You want to go back to my village?"

Monty thanked him but responded, "*Salamat po, Lolo.* No, we won't be going back with you." He helped a very weak Julia climb out of the canoe. The fisherman chattered as they walked toward the market, which was no more than a hundred feet from the beach. Julia leaned heavily on Monty's arm as they walked up the beach, feeling as if she were trying to climb Everest.

They stopped at the first sari-sari shop they found to purchase six D batteries and a roll of duct tape. Monty asked the woman in the sari-sari shop if she could point the way to a medical clinic where he could purchase quinine. She nodded and pointed toward a Quonset hut on the east edge of the village.

As they waited for the clerk in the little *pharmacia* to locate some quinine, Monty sat down on one of the two chairs in the tiny waiting area and taped the six batteries together in a series. Then he taped the terminal of the first one tightly to the battery of the satphone before he put it all back into the backpack. He looked at Julia who was sitting white-faced and feverish on the other chair. "I've heard that this can recharge the satphone battery, but I've no idea how long it may take." She did not respond. As he looked more closely at her, she seemed to melt as she slowly slid off the chair into Monty's arms, just before hitting the floor.

As he laid her down, he called out to the young man behind the counter who had finally found the quinine, "Get a doctor. The lady is sick." The alarmed young man ran down the hall and in a moment came back, followed by a short, rotund man in a white coat, who was wiping his mouth with a paper napkin. The doctor knelt and felt Julia's feverish forehead. He gave orders for her to be put in a bed and given two quinine pills when she was conscious. Having done all he felt he could do, he returned to his office and his bowl of rice and fish.

Two orderlies brought a gurney, and they stood by while Monty lifted Julia onto it. He quickly grabbed his backpack and put it over his shoulder. They pushed Julia to the ward at the end of the hall where there were four beds, one occupied by an unconscious old woman and another by a boy of about fourteen with a broken arm, a bandaged leg, and a bruised face. Monty placed Julia on one of the two empty beds and took off her tattered running shoes.

One of the orderlies, evidently the senior of the two, spoke. "You tell us when she wakes up." They turned to leave the ward to return to unseen duties elsewhere.

Knowing that the orderlies might be hard to find when Julia awoke, Monty called out, "Wait a minute. Get me some drinking water and the quinine pills. I'll give them to her when she wakes up." Both of the young men hurried out of the room, and one returned a few minutes later with a bottle of water and a packet of pills.

Monty set down his backpack and pushed it under Julia's bed. Then he sat wearily in the metal straight-backed chair next to the bed. After a few minutes, he noticed a basin filled with water on a battered chest of drawers. He crossed the room and opened one of the drawers. He took a small towel from the drawer, dipped it in the water, and rung it out. He returned to the chair and pulled the hijab off Julia's hair. When the boy in the second bed saw her blond hair, his eyes widened. Monty gently washed her face and neck. Then he pushed up the sleeves of the caftan and washed her arms.

In response to the cool water, she opened her eyes and looked around. "Where are we?"

"In a small clinic in Anugan. Here, take these two pills. They're supposed to be quinine." He lifted her head and held the bottle of water to her lips. She could not help but grimace at the bitterness of the medication. "Now try to get some rest," he urged her.

She had been resting for an hour, with Monty dozing in the chair near her, when the sound of raised voices awakened them both, voices of men shouting demands. Listening for only a moment, Monty sprang up and pulled the chair he had been sitting in to the door of the ward and jammed it under the doorknob. He flipped the one empty bed onto its side and pushed it crosswise in front of the bed where the comatose old woman lay.

"Get down on the floor. There may be shooting," he called to Julia.

She weakly slid out of the bed onto the floor, and he quickly flipped her bed onto its side and added her mattress to the first one where it leaned against the bed frame. "Grab my backpack and get behind the mattresses."

He called to the boy, telling him to get down on the floor. The boy rolled out of bed and crawled over to sit next to Julia. Monty flipped the third bed over, pushed it against the door, and added the third mattress to the other two. Then he pushed the chest of drawers in front of the mattresses.

Leaping over the bed frame and joining Julia and the boy, he opened the backpack and began to deftly assemble the M16. The boy watched the process with wide eyes. He had it finished by the time the clinic invaders had searched the other rooms and began pounding on the door.

Julia asked from where she sat on the floor, weak and shaking with her arms around her knees, "What are they saying? Who are they?"

"I think they're some of our Abu friends. Do you recognize any of their voices?"

The boy spoke to Monty in a frightened voice for a moment. Monty explained, "The boy is sure they're Abu. He was beaten when his father, the doctor here, refused to go with them a few weeks ago when they came recruiting." Above the din of the men pounding on the door, he asked, "Can you recognize any of their voices?"

Julia listened for a few seconds. "One of them sounds like Abdul." She paused and listened again. "I can't tell who else is there."

From the other side, the Abu men penetrated the door with a burst of automatic gunfire at a height that would have hit anyone standing in the room. Monty returned it, and a man's voice cried out. Another burst of gunfire exploded into the room, shattering some of the windows and piercing the thin walls. One of the bullets ricocheted off the concrete floor, and Monty crumpled where he had been kneeling.

Julia cried out, "Monty! Monty!" His head was bleeding profusely. She shook his shoulder. He did not respond. After a half second of hesitation, she picked up the M16 he had dropped.

One of the men in the hallway reached in through the shattered door and moved the chair and bed frame that had been braced against it. Two men carrying assault rifles burst into the room. They hesitated a fraction of a second as they looked around.

In a combination of anger and panic, Julia squeezed the trigger of the M16, hitting both as the gun sprayed wildly in that direction. The muzzle drifted upward and a few bullets stitched into the ceiling.

The boy knelt by Monty's unconscious body. He looked into the open backpack and pulled out the Beretta. Another man came through the doorway, and Julia put her hand out as a signal to the boy not to fire. It was Daud. As he raised his gun, Julia called out, "Daud, don't shoot. Don't become a murderer. You're a good boy. Don't do something you will regret."

He looked into her eyes for a full three seconds. "I must not dishonor my father." He raised the weapon toward her and the boy, who held the Beretta in both hands. From his place behind the mattresses, he pulled the trigger three times, hitting Daud twice. He fell, the martyr his father had demanded.

For a moment, Julia looked sadly at the young man on the floor. She wanted to weep for him, but her concern for Monty was greater. The boy chattered excitedly in Cebuano and patted her shoulder in excitement. She wiped the blood from Monty's face with the sleeve of the caftan. *He's got to be alive! Please, God, he's got to be alive.* He moaned. "Monty, can you hear me?" Grabbing the closest thing she could find, she pulled the sheet partially off the elderly woman, who had not stirred during the conflict, and used one corner, carefully wiping more blood from the wound and trying to measure its seriousness.

He moaned and opened his eyes. "Hey, take it easy." He smiled weakly. "Help me sit up."

After a few seconds he moved unsteadily to his knees and looked over the mattresses, wiping the blood out of his eyes. He could see the three bodies where they lay in the doorway, with blood spattered on the floor and the wall. Taking the .45 from the boy, who was standing proudly behind the mattresses, Monty patted him on the shoulder and then made his way over to the bodies.

"Julia, can you identify these men?"

She followed him across the room. "The boy is Daud, Hamal's son. The other two are Abdul and one of the men who kidnapped me. Their leader, Hamal, isn't here."

"He wouldn't be. He's probably waiting for his men, and when they don't come back, he'll disappear into the rain forest," Monty responded contemptuously.

He looked down the hallway. "You and the boy stay here behind the mattresses while I check out the rest of the building." He picked up the M16 and carefully moved from room to room. From the deserted rooms, he gathered that the staff had fled, with the exception of the doctor, who was lying dead in his little office. It looked like he had been struck on the back of his head with the butt of a gun.

He made his way to the door, which the fleeing staff had left open, and peered out. He could see no movement in the nearby huts or in the trees beyond them. It was apparent that the villagers had hidden themselves in the forest when the shooting began.

Monty searched for the stock of Qualaquin that was somewhere on the shelves behind the counter in the waiting room. Finding a small supply, he slipped it into one of his pockets and, without thinking, removed three one-hundred peso bills from his other pocket and pushed the bills into the cash drawer to cover the cost.

He called out as he made his way back down the hallway, "It looks like the staff has disappeared into the forest along with the villagers. We need to get out of here quickly. They may blame us for this whole mess."

When he reached the ward, the boy asked where his father was. Monty took the boy's shoulders in his hands and looked him in the eyes. He explained that the Abu men had killed his father. The boy tried to pull away from him, but Monty held on. "It's better that you don't see him." In his grief, the boy tore away from Monty's strong grip and ran to the office. His wails pierced the deserted village.

Julia was standing unsteadily. "The old woman is dead. One of the bullets hit her in the neck, but she didn't bleed. She's probably been dead for some time, well before the Abu men broke in." She pulled the sheet over the old woman's face and gently smoothed it. Turning to Monty, she noted that he was holding his forehead in his right hand. "Are you all right?" She stepped over to him and put a hand tenderly on his arm.

"I'm okay—just a heck of a headache."

She raised her voice as the boy's wails filled the little building, "What will we do with the boy?"

"The word'll get out. A boy his age will never be able to keep a secret like this. The Abu will come after him, and the villagers won't hesitate to give him up—for their own safety."

Julia leaned against the side of one of the upturned beds while she tried to think. The boy's cries had quieted. "We've got to take him with us."

Monty put his arm around her to steady her wobbly stance. He pulled the chair over and set it upright. "Sit down while I talk to him." Her knees buckled as she sat.

When he returned, he explained, "The boy's mother is dead. That was why he was staying here in the hospital near his father. He has no other close relatives here. I've explained that he will need to come with us because the *Abu Sayyaf* will come after him. He's thinking it over."

The boy entered the ward, wiping away the tears he had shed for his father. His father's blood stained his shirt and pants. Monty turned to him. "Are you coming with us?" The boy nodded. "What's your name?"

"Sammy."

"Sammy, we need to get you and the lady some clean clothes. Where's the closet where the uniforms are kept?" The boy led him down the hall to a small storage room where Monty located a pair of green scrubs for both of them. He gave a pair to Julia. "Your caftan is bloody and will draw attention. You'll need to change." He handed a set of scrubs to the boy and told him the same thing.

She nodded. "Just give me a little help." He helped her pull the caftan off over her head, leaving her dressed in the sweat-stained cargo pants and blouse. She took the scrubs. "Give me a few minutes."

Monty paced in the clinic waiting room while she changed. She took her Blackberry with its dead battery from the pocket in her cargo pants and put it in the little pocket on the scrubs. By the time she had finished changing, she was limp and shaking. He returned to the ward to find her sitting slumped on the chair with the hijab on her hair.

While the boy changed, Monty put the .45 into the backpack. He swung the pack over his shoulder and moved quickly around the room, carrying the M16 and gathering the pillows that had been thrown on the floor. When Sammy came back into the room, Monty gave the pillows to him to carry. Holding Julia's hand, he led them down the hall.

"Are you going to be all right?" Monty asked, and Julia nodded, but her white face belied her words. "Sammy, stay close to the lady and me, and we'll get you out of here." They made their way carefully from one hut to another, moving toward the beach and watching for movement that might mean trouble from anywhere in the village or in the trees. When they reached the deserted marketplace, Monty asked him if he knew which of the fishermen's *bancas* was the fastest. The boy nodded and led them to a twenty-five-foot canoe that had a ramshackle cabin built over the control panel and steering wheel.

"We take the boat?" Sammy asked with wide eyes. "Mr. Rivera will be very angry. He is mayor and very important man."

"We will pay Mr. Rivera for the use of his *banca*, and we will get him a new one if we need to," Monty promised the boy.

Monty helped a chilled and shaking Julia into the cabin, and taking the pillows from Sammy, he arranged them in the corner of the cabin. "Sit here. Try to make yourself comfortable." He motioned for the boy to help him push the craft off the beach. As it slid out into the water, they both clambered into it. Monty located the gas tank and unscrewed the cap to check the fuel. It was nearly full. There were several five-gallon plastic gas cans in the bow of the boat. He shook each one. Three of them were full. The key was still in the ignition, left there by the trusting owner who must have been sure no citizen of the village would steal the boat of such an important man. *Thank you, thank you, thank you,* Monty thought as he smiled with satisfaction. The big engine roared to life. He turned the boat to the southwest, and when he opened the throttle, it seemed to fly across the water.

Julia settled herself on a pile of fishnets in one corner of the cabin, sitting on one pillow and leaning against the others. She closed her eyes. After a few minutes, Monty motioned for Sammy to take the wheel while he pulled the satphone out of the backpack. *It's working. The charge is increasing. It should be strong enough for a short call soon,* he noted with satisfaction. Making sure the flashlight batteries were still tightly taped to it, he returned it to the pack. After more than two hours of moving in a southwesterly direction, always keeping the shoreline in sight on their left, Monty put the engine into neutral so they could talk above the rumble. He made his way to the stern of the boat and removed the cap from the gas tank to check the level of fuel. It was still more than half full. He filled it and returned to sit on the center thwart of the canoe where he calculated the distance they had to go in the *banca*. Because the big canoe had a broken compass, they needed to hug the coast to keep them from straying out into the Sulu Sea. He estimated it to be about a hundred kilometers, roughly about sixty-five miles, from Anugan to Zamboanga City. He would try to keep the throttle wide open and the speedometer at about twelve kilometers an hour unless the wind increased and the water became rough. With the gas in the cans stored in the bow, he hoped they could make it to Zamboanga in seven more hours, sometime after dark.

After another hour, he put the engine into neutral again, took the satphone from the backpack, and checked the charge. It was strong enough to support a short call. He hit the speed dial for Matson, who answered on the first ring. "Monty, are you okay? Where are you? How is Julia?"

"I borrowed a *banca* with a big engine, and I think we're somewhere near Sibuco. Julia's with me but ill with malaria. I've got enough fuel to take us to Zamboanga City, unless we run into problems. Rather than have you try to pick us up by helicopter, I think we'll stay on the water. Right now we're making good time. I don't want to inadvertently beach the boat in an area of Abu sympathizers."

"Call when you get closer to the base. We're ready to trace your signal."

"Will do." Monty rose and put the big engine into gear and let Sammy drive again. The boy seemed to be enjoying it, and he needed something to take his mind off the death of his father.

While Sammy held the wheel, Monty peeled a mango for Julia. After eating some of the fruit, she pointed to the boy as if to tell Monty that he was probably hungry too. Monty offered him one of the mangos. The boy gratefully ate it with one hand while he held on to the wheel with the other. After she had swallowed two more of the bitter pills, she lay back against the wall of the little cabin and closed her eyes again.

The big canoe continued in a southerly direction for the next four hours. Monty occasionally pulled his binoculars from the backpack and searched the shoreline, looking for landmarks that would tell him where they were. As dusk slid over them from the east, wrapping the scenery in dark, he watched for the lights of some of the costal fishing villages.

Julia roused herself. "How far have we come?" She had to repeat herself to be heard above the engine. It took all her strength.

"I'm guessing that we're well over halfway. I think we can make it to the Southern Command Headquarters in Zamboanga City in about three or four hours." Looking more closely at her, "How are you feeling?"

"I think the quinine is helping. I feel a little better."

He continued to search the coastline with the binoculars, making sure that in the dark they did not lose sight of the coast.

31

Sophie and Matson were talking in the quiet mess hall when the satphone rang. He answered quickly and looked at Sophie excitedly. "It's Monty." He listened for a few seconds. "We'll send in a helicopter for you. You just name the location point." There was a pause. "Yes, yes, everyone is okay, more or less." He was quiet a minute. "You're sure you want to do it that way? Call when you get closer to the base. We're ready to trace your signal." After he ended the call, he took a deep breath and answered the question in Sophie's eyes. "Julia is ill with malaria." Sophie's eyes widened with worry. "The two of them have commandeered—for lack of a better word—a large *banca* and are making their way down the coast. Monty will contact us again when he's closer, sometime after dark."

***

Monty had taken the wheel from Sammy, and as the *banca* continued to move in a southwesterly direction, parallel to the coast, one particular village appeared to be much larger than most and well lit by electricity, rare on the peninsula. Monty aimed the boat toward the lights, slowing as he brought the boat nearer the beach in the hope that they could buy something to eat there. "This place has electricity." He paused only briefly before he yelled, "And that looks like it has a guard tower!"

He turned the boat so sharply that the boy tipped off the thwart where he had been sitting and Julia had to put out her hands to steady herself against the bulkhead. He opened the throttle as wide as possible, and the boat roared back out into the sea and the cover of darkness. After nearly ten minutes of moving as fast as the *banca's* engine could push it, bouncing and pounding over the waves, Julia cried out, "Monty, what's wrong? Can you slow down? The bouncing is too much to tolerate." As he slowed the unwieldy craft, they could hear above the sound of the engine the unmistakable sound of bullets hitting and splintering wood.

"Get down, and hold on!" Monty yelled. He steered the boat from starboard to port as quickly as the bulky craft would allow. Bullets ripped into the *banca* again, showering wood splinters throughout the small cabin.

Julia cried out and grabbed her upper arm. Above the noise of the engine she called out, "What's going on? Who's shooting at us?" She looked down at her arm where blood oozed between her fingers. A knot of panic formed in her stomach.

"That's the San Ramon Penal Colony. They probably think we're trying to help someone escape," Monty yelled.

Monty put the binoculars to his eyes with his left hand as he held the wheel with the right and turned and looked behind the *banca*. He could see a boat that looked like an older converted U.S. Coast Guard motor lifeboat pursuing them out into the darkness. In its spotlights, several of which were aimed at the *banca*, Monty could see the Philippine naval flag flying above the wheelhouse. The vessel was about forty-five feet in length and painted a haze gray with a bow-mounted, .50-caliber machine gun. He watched as the distance between the two vessels began to close. He motioned for Sammy to take the wheel and signaled for him to continue their flight out into the Sulu Sea. He picked up the backpack, pulled out the satphone, and pressed the speed-dial button that would connect him with Matson.

He squatted down near Julia and put one finger in his other ear. "Matson, we're near the penal colony, and we're being chased by the AFP Navy. Call them off. They're shooting at us." He could not hear Matson at all. He wondered if Matson could even hear him above the sound of the engine of the *banca*. He stood and shifted the engine into neutral and then shut it off. Sammy looked at him, thoroughly scared.

"Matson, can you hear me now?" He was quiet for a moment as Matson replied. "We're going to be boarded by the AFP Navy. Get hold of the U.S. ambassador, and have her call Malacañang Palace. She's got to reach President Arroyo. Get us out of here! I'll leave the satphone on so you can hear what's going on. Get a fix on our position, and come and get us!"

Sitting in the darkness of the little cabin, he told Julia, "We can't outrun them." By this time the naval vessel had neared the *banca* where it was rising and falling on the chop created by the larger boat. Monty pulled the flashlight batteries off the satphone and, keeping the connection with Matson, slid it into his shirt pocket. Then he took the M16 and pushed it into a corner and piled some fishnets on it.

The spotlights from the larger vessel spilled into the little cabin. In their glare, Monty could see Julia's bloody hand where she was clutching her right upper arm. His eyes widened. "Julia, you're hit." He moved over to her to look at her arm.

"I don't think it's very bad, probably just a large splinter of wood. What will they do with us?"

He looked at the wound as he spoke. "Hold us until someone with clout makes them let us go. Let's hope that happens soon." Taking the satphone out of his pocket, he asked Matson, "Are you still there? Did you get that? Julia's hurt. Get us out of here fast." Without waiting for Matson's response, he slid the phone back into the pocket again.

A disembodied voice came over the water through a loudspeaker. In Tagalog, it ordered them to give up and come out of the cabin of the *banca* with their hands raised. Monty quickly interpreted. "Let's do what they say. I'll go first."

He helped Julia to her feet, and as she and Sammy leaned on the door frame to steady themselves, he exited into the spotlight with his hands lifted, leaving the backpack behind. Julia followed him out, raising both her hands, while her injured upper arm continued to ooze blood. A frightened Sammy exited last. They stood unsteadily in the bow of the *banca* where the larger craft, unable to come alongside because of the outriggers, nudged up against the large canoe.

Two men in naval uniforms with automatic weapons over their shoulders climbed down the ladder on the gunwale of the boat. Steadying themselves in the bow of the *banca*, they motioned for the three of them to make the climb from the *banca* to the deck of the larger vessel. They offered no assistance and prevented Monty from assisting Julia. As she pulled herself up the ladder and finally reached the top, two of the crewmen pulled her over the gunwale and onto the deck where her legs buckled underneath her and she went down. An AFP Marine poked her in the ribs with the barrel of his M16 to make her get up.

As weak as she was, she struggled to her feet, turned toward him, and in a cold and controlled voice said as forcefully as she could, "I've had enough of armed men poking me with their guns. First, the *Abu Sayyaf* and now you! Will you stop that? I am no threat to you!" The man, who understood English, stepped back, startled at her reaction and the fact that she was obviously an American.

Sammy then followed Julia, climbing onto the deck, where he slipped in the blood that had dripped from Julia's injured arm.

The senior officer on the boat, who wore the bars of a first lieutenant with a name tag reading "Lopez" stepped forward. "Who are you, and what are you doing here? We could have shot you out of the water for being in a restricted area."

Monty calculated his response, making sure he was as respectful as possible. "We are trying to get away from the *Abu Sayyaf,* who have been holding this woman hostage. We regret that we entered the restricted area around the penal colony, but we've been navigating simply by keeping the shore in sight. The compass on the boat is broken. We're trying to reach the Southern Command Headquarters in Zamboanga City. You can speak with Captain Matson of the U.S. Embassy about our situation if you would like. I have him on the satphone." He took the satphone from his pocket and handed it to the officer.

Lopez put the telephone to this ear. "Who is this?" He listened for a few seconds. "There's no way to tell who that man is. You will come with us back to the prison until we straighten this out." He turned off and pocketed the satphone.

The three of them were ordered to follow the young officer along the deck and down into the larger boat where they entered a sparsely furnished room. There, he ordered two marines to guard them. Monty insisted that someone bring him a first-aid kit so he could wrap Julia's arm. After making the demand a second time, one of them left and returned with the kit.

Monty carefully wrapped her arm. "I'm sorry, Julia. I shouldn't have let this happen. It's been a long time since I've been on the peninsula, and, frankly, I'd forgotten about the penal colony. Maybe I should've had Matson send a helicopter for us when he offered, but I thought the *banca* would attract less attention."

She patted his hand. "It's not your fault, Monty. Let's face it, the AFP is a bit too quick to shoot first and ask questions later. Thank heaven they didn't hit any of the gas cans in the boat, or we'd all be dead."

The lieutenant came down the stairs into the cabin with Monty's M16 and his backpack in his hands. "What is this? One of my men found this hidden in the *banca*. Why are you armed with an automatic weapon and night-vision goggles?" he demanded.

Not intimidated, Monty looked at him tiredly. "Do you think I would try to mount a rescue effort with my bare hands? The *Abu Sayyaf* would not have simply handed their hostages over at my request. I had to be armed."

The man narrowed his eyes and looked at Monty with increased suspicion. Monty's voice changed and continued with a tone that bordered on a threat. "The M16 and the goggles are property of the U.S. government and must be returned."

To break the tension between the two men, Julia leaned back against the bulkhead and asked, "Can I have a drink of water?" She was starting to shake again.

Lopez signaled one of the guards with a nod of his head, and the man pulled open one of the cabinets and offered her a bottle of water.

She looked at Monty. "Do you have any more quinine? The chills are coming back."

As Monty pulled a packet of two quinine pills from his pocket, one of the marines leaped forward and grabbed them from him. Julia sat up with an indignation that would have been more intimidating if her voice had not been so unsteady. "I have malaria. I need the quinine. Give me the pills now!" Then she added a little more contritely, "Please." When the man hesitated and looked at Lopez, she looked at the lieutenant as well. "It would be very bad for you if I die while I'm in your custody."

The lieutenant nodded at the guard, who retuned the pills to Julia. Monty opened the water bottle and broke open the packet of pills for her. With a shaking hand, she put them in her mouth and swallowed them, grimacing at the bitter aftertaste. The officer left the three of them there with the two marine guards while the naval boat returned to the pier at the penal colony.

After leaving the vessel, they were taken to a small holding room in the main building where they were left alone. There were only three chairs and a plain, battered metal table under a single, bare lightbulb. Sammy looked at Monty with wide eyes and asked what was going to happen to them. Monty patted his shoulder. "Someone will come and get us by morning." After an hour, a guard entered the room and demanded that Monty follow him. He returned more than an hour later, his shirt sticking to him with perspiration.

Then the guard motioned Sammy to follow him. Julia threw Monty a worried glance. "What did they do?"

"They asked me about two hundred times what we were doing so near the prison. Evidently, there was a successful escape a few weeks ago, and they are unusually nervous. I explained repeatedly, but Lopez seemed unwilling to believe me. I think he is experiencing a loss of face because I explained that our group of four was able to free three hostages, while the AFP hasn't managed to do anything lately but get their own men killed. Don't worry. The truth is our best defense, and I think Matson will have some help for us soon."

"Poor Sammy. He's so frightened. I hope they're not hard on him," Julia whispered. Monty patted his own left shoulder, encouraging her to lean against him so she could get some rest. She did so and closed her eyes. He pulled off the dirty and torn hijab. Then he tenderly put his right hand in her hair and laid his cheek against her head almost like a parent comforting a child. "We'll get this worked out, Julia. I promise," he whispered. After another hour, the red-eyed boy was returned to the room, and the guard motioned Julia to follow him. Monty stood. "She's too sick. You can't question her." The guard just shrugged his shoulders as if the matter were out of his hands and motioned her out the door.

As Julia followed him down the hall, she noticed a humming in her ears that steadily increased in volume. Within a few more steps, the hallway began to glow with a red hue, then everything turned black, and she crumpled to the floor. The AFP Marine stood looking down at her as if he weren't sure what to do. Then he turned and ran down the hall to an office door that he opened and entered. After a minute, the lieutenant hurried out of the office with the guard trailing behind him. "Get the man who was captured with her," Lopez said as the men knelt beside her. The officer hurried down to the holding room and urged Monty to follow him.

Monty rushed to Julia and knelt beside her. Looking from one man to the other, he concluded that he would get more response bargaining from a position of authority. "I need a bed for her. She needs medical help."

"We have a hospital infirmary," Lopez answered.

"Are there prisoners in it?"

"Yes."

Monty's voice took on an edge. "No, that won't do. We need to put her in your room, Lieutenant, until we are released from this place. If you have a doctor, call him. Now please show me the way." He bent over, picked her up like a rag doll, and, with a slight limp, carried her toward the lieutenant's personal quarters. He noted with an internal smile that Lopez was furious, walking with stiff, fast strides. Sammy, who had followed Monty out of the holding room, walked behind him, looking around with wide eyes.

Monty looked down at Julia as her eyes opened and finally focused on his face. He grinned. "Hang in there, Julia. Just hang in, and we'll get through this." As he laid her on the bed in the lieutenant's room, he asked Lopez, "Has anyone from the Southern Command Headquarters contacted you about us?"

The man simply shook his head. He turned and exited the room, leaving one of the guards behind.

"He's evidently using us as a pawn in some battle of egos. He appears to have rank-pulling down to a fine art. He knows he had better treat us well but isn't about to turn us loose until someone of undisputable authority pushes the right button."

"Then I'm going to try to get some sleep. Wake me if the right button gets pushed," Julia responded wearily. She gave Monty a tired smile and curled up on the captain's narrow bed.

Monty lay down on the floor and invited Sammy to do the same. They slept from exhaustion.

***

As the former hostages talked in the mess hall after dinner, the satphone rang. Matson answered it and rose from the table to avoid the noise of the conversations around him. Sophie left the table and followed him.

"Monty, Monty, I can't understand you. The engine's too loud. Where are you?" After a moment he responded, "That's better. I can hear you now. Stop yelling. Where are you?"

Sophie could hear Monty's voice yelling something about a penal colony. His last words ended with, "Get us out of here!"

"We will." Matson continued to ask questions, but Monty had stopped responding. The State Department intelligence officer, the CIA men, and several of the others in the room halted their conversations and turned in their seats to watch Matson, with questions in their eyes. After several minutes of listening to what he could hear on the satphone, he said, "This is Captain Matson of the U.S. Embassy. Who are you?"

When he put the phone back into his pocket, everyone burst into questions. Matson raised his hand for silence. "Captain Montalbon and Mrs. Wentworth were captured by the AFP Navy near the San Ramon Penal Colony, where their *banca* was fired upon and boarded. They have been accused of trying to help prisoners escape and are being held there. He has asked me to have the U.S. ambassador contact President Arroyo to intervene. I don't know anything else, so please excuse me while I make the necessary phone calls."

Matson spent the next ten minutes sitting in the general's office, trying to locate the U.S. ambassador by satphone. The embassy operator told him that when she returned, she would be given the message that he was trying to reach her.

General Del Rosario attempted to call the head of the penal colony but could get no answer to his repeated telephone calls. After pacing the floor in his office for a few minutes, Del Rosario made a decision. He picked up the telephone and called Southern Command Navy Headquarters. Speaking to the telephone operator, he stated, "I have an emergency and need to reach Commodore Cantoneros. Will you put me through to his home?"

After some resistance from the operator, who was hesitant to antagonize the commodore with a late call, he finally made the connection. When the commodore answered, Del Rosario put on a cheerful voice. "Hey, Marco, I hope I haven't interrupted a cocktail party. If I have, maybe next time you will invite me." He paused as the other officer responded. "I hate to bother a man as busy as you, but I need to know the name of the officer who is in charge of the navy MLB that does guard duty over at the penal colony. It seems his wife is having a baby here at the hospital, but she's having some pretty severe complications, and we can't get any information from her. We need to contact him right away."

The line was quiet except for background noises that sounded like the party the commodore insisted he was not having, and then Cantoneros answered, "That would be Lieutenant Lopez. Frankly, I didn't know he was married. You can reach him on the radio. That boat is number 117, if memory serves me correctly, so the call letters for it are *PNMLB117*. There should be a radio operator on duty."

"Thanks, Marco, I'll be looking for an invitation to your next get-together." The general hung up. Matson, who had been taking in the conversation, just shook his head at the ingeniousness of the general's story.

Del Rosario gave a bark of a laugh. "There may be heck to pay on my end when he figures out that he was fed a—what do you Americans call it?—a cock-and-bull story? I won't get any cooperation from the navy for a good, long while." Then he gave another bark of a laugh. "But, then, they never cooperate with the army anyway."

32

AT MIDNIGHT, MATSON FINALLY REACHED the U.S. ambassador. He explained Monty and Julia's situation. "Can you contact President Arroyo and encourage her to call Commodore Cantoneros and get him to order the crew of the navy vessel to free them? We hope to get in by helicopter to pick them up in the morning, but we don't want to ruffle any diplomatic feathers and inadvertently cause an international incident."

The ambassador was quiet for a moment. "I'll try calling Malacañang Palace, but if I can't raise anyone this evening, or they won't put me through to President Arroyo this late, I'll have to wait until morning to try again. Can your friends hold on until then?"

"They really don't have much of a choice in the matter, but thank you so much for your assistance."

The base radio operator was not able to raise anyone at the radio of the navy vessel until six o'clock in the morning. In the meantime, General Del Rosario went to bed with orders to be awakened when the connection was made.

At six o'clock, Lieutenant Lopez was notified that he had a call from General Del Rosario's aide-de-camp. After speaking with the general's staffer, he chose not to act on the request to free Monty and Julia. After all, he reasoned, the army was not in a position to tell the navy what to do.

Within twenty minutes, the lieutenant received a telephone call from Commodore Cantoneros. The senior officer spoke with authority. "I have received a telephone call from President Gloria Macapagal-Arroyo, and she has informed me that you are to have the American woman and the man you captured last night ready to be picked up by helicopter at oh-eight-hundred hours. Is that understood?"

"Yes, sir," Lopez responded immediately. "Sir, what do we do with the boy?"

"I was unaware there was a boy. Who is he?"

"They said his father was killed by the *Abu Sayyaf* and he was fleeing with them."

"Then have him ready to travel as well. Oh, and congratulations on the birth of your baby. Hope your wife came through the complications in good shape." The commodore hung up.

Lopez, a bachelor, stood looking at the receiver and wondering what the commodore meant. Shaking his head, he gave instructions to have the prisoners fed and at the helipad at eight o'clock.

***

At seven forty-five, the door to the lieutenant's quarters opened, and an AFP Marine entered and ordered them to follow him. Monty helped Julia to her feet and supported her as they walked down the hallway to the door at the end. When they reached the helipad, Monty asked the marine what was going on. The marine shrugged his shoulders but didn't answer.

From where they stood, they could see the guard towers and a long portion of the high fence topped with razor wire that surrounded three sides of the penal colony, a series of square, cement-block buildings. The fourth side was open to the sea. Behind them was the long pier where the gray naval MLB was berthed.

"What will they do with us?" Sammy asked Monty nervously.

As Monty started to answer, they heard the sound of the rotor blades of a helicopter in the distance. Then they could see a large black Huey approaching from about two thousand feet. Monty turned to the marine who stood nearby. "You will tell Lieutenant Lopez that I must speak with him before we get on the helicopter." The man looked confused and unsure what to do, so Monty said with increased authority in his voice, "You will tell Lopez to come out here now."

The marine turned and set off at a brisk trot for the little building they had just left. As the helicopter drew nearer, Lopez appeared, walking at an unhurried pace toward the prisoners. When he reached them, he raised his voice enough to be heard. "What do you want?"

"I'm sure you would not want to forget to return my equipment."

Lopez stood for a fraction of a second as if he wanted to debate the matter, but the helicopter was nearing the helipad. Lopez turned and ordered the nearest marine to retrieve the requested property from his office.

Shortly after the helicopter landed, the marine returned with the equipment. Monty accepted it and gave a nod to Lopez by way of recognizing his courtesy. As the rotors began to slow, the door on the fuselage slid aft and two AFP Marines sprang out. One hurried to Julia and asked loudly, above the noise of the rotors, if she needed a stretcher. She shook her head, and he took her uninjured arm and assisted her into the helicopter. Monty gave a nod of his head to Sammy as a signal for the boy to get in the big aircraft. The marines looked at one another with raised eyebrows because no one had mentioned the boy, but they took the hands he raised and pulled him inside.

Monty followed them to the helicopter, handed up his equipment, and climbed in. The big door slid closed. The three passengers were pointed to the bench seat behind the pilot, and the rotors began to turn more rapidly. The flight took less than twenty minutes, and as the aircraft settled to the pavement on the helipad, Julia was unsuccessful in fighting back tears of relief and exhaustion. Monty put his arm around her and pulled her against him. "It's over, Julia. It's over and it's okay to cry."

The men helped her out of the helicopter, and she could see a contingent of armed U.S. Marines standing at attention. She sat in the wheelchair Lieutenant Billings offered her and closed her eyes, squeezing them shut in an attempt to stop the tears building behind them like an over-full reservoir behind a weak dam.

When they reached the ambulance, Monty helped her climb inside and Lieutenant Billings climbed in after Sammy. They sat two on each side of the vehicle for the bumpy ride to the military hospital, with Monty steadying Julia. Again, at the hospital another contingent of armed U.S. Marines marked the way from the ambulance to the hospital door.

Lieutenant Billings pushed Julia through the double doors into the hospital where Sophie swooped down on her friend to give her a hug. "Julia, you're here, and you're going to be all right. I've prayed for you over and over again, and this morning, I knew you would be all right."

Julia put her uninjured arm around the young woman's neck. "There were times when I think your prayers were all that got us through . . . your prayers and Monty's strength."

"Lieutenant Billings is going to be your den mother, just like she was for me. Just call her Liz. She'll take good care of you." Lieutenant Billings pushed Julia to an examination room, where she was examined, poked, prodded, disinfected, stitched, medicated, and bandaged.

Major Whittingham paused when he saw the bruise on her ribs. "How did you get that?"

"From the boot of an *Abu Sayyaf.*"

"I think you may have three broken ribs and a couple more that are badly bruised. Do you want me to wrap them?"

"Will that make it harder for me to breathe?"

"Yes, it will ease some of the pain, but it limits your breathing."

"I would like some relief from the pain. Go ahead and wrap them."

He gave her some pain pills, and Lieutenant Billings pushed her to her room, where the lieutenant helped her shower and dress in clean scrubs. Then they went to the mess hall, where she ate only a little of the food the cooks had prepared.

She looked for Monty but hadn't seen him by the time she was pushed back to her room. She asked Liz to find a way that she could call her children to tell them she was okay. She didn't care what time it was in Missouri.

As she spoke with her two children, Paul's yells of pleasure and Allison's tears of gratitude were all the medicine she needed. After she handed the satphone back to Liz, she crawled into the bed and slept.

***

After the doctor had examined Monty's head and put in a few stitches, Monty spent much of the day debriefing with the AFP and the CIA. While he was closeted with the intelligence officers of both nations, a Cebu Pacific Airlines jet landed at the city airport, and among the passengers were two U.S. State Department counselors and Melton Mallon. In an unmarked military sedan, they hurried to Camp Navarro General Hospital.

When the three men climbed out of the vehicle and entered the hospital, Brigadier General Finchley and General Del Rosario greeted them. Shaking Mallon's hand, Del Rosario asked the rhetorical question, "So you are the man who started this effort to rescue the hostages?" Without waiting for an answer, he added, "You selected some very capable men. I would like to recruit them into my forces." Then he laughed at his own joke.

"I can't take credit for the rescue team. Julia Wentworth recruited the men, based upon some recommendations given me by one of your Supreme Court justices, but I am grateful to hear of their success. Mrs. Wentworth has been safely rescued?"

The general nodded and beamed as if he had participated in the rescue himself. "Yes, yes. She has been receiving medical help since her arrival here at the hospital."

While the men spoke, one of the hospital staff went to notify Sophie of her grandfather's arrival. She hurried to greet him. "*Lolo!*" she called out as she ran to him. Their embrace said everything about the stress, anguish, and intense relief they had lived through during the past weeks. When they let go of each other, she asked, "How is Grandmother?"

"She's doing a little better. She wants you to come home so she can see for herself that you are unharmed. How soon can you fly back with me?"

"When Julia and Monty are okay. Then I'll go back with you just as soon as possible, but when Grandmother is better, I want to come back to *Umaga* House. I'm needed there. I don't want to let the bad guys win by frightening me into leaving this country." Sophie stopped suddenly, and then she asked, "Do you know how my friend Lily is doing? Is she alive? I'm so ashamed that I didn't think to ask someone sooner. There's just so much that has happened."

Mallon patted her hand. "I was told that she was released from the hospital a week ago. She'll be able to go back to work at *Umaga* House before very long." He changed the subject. "When can I see Julia?"

"When she wakes up. I know she'll want to see you."

33

When Julia awakened, it was nearly six. Her first sensation was one of hunger, but as she tried to turn over, pain in her side and arm stopped her breath for a moment. Carefully, she looked around the room and was startled to see Monty sitting in the chair next to her bed. The wound on his head was covered with a bandage, making him look like a rakish pirate with a white, misplaced eye patch. He put down the pocket-sized New Testament he had been reading and grinned at her. He looked tired, and the lines around his mouth were deeper than she had ever seen them, but the smile was genuine.

She smiled when she saw what he was reading. "Is that all you could find to read?"

He nodded. "A refresher course is always in order." He pointed at the bandage she was staring at. "Eight stitches. It wasn't very serious, and the pain pills the doctor gave me have finally eased the headache. When the CIA finished with me, I asked if I could sit with you. It was okay with the doc."

"How long have you been here?"

"About an hour. How are you feeling?"

"Hungry, hurting, and in need of some social contact with folks who don't carry automatic weapons."

Monty frowned and acted as though he were a little offended. "Does that include me?"

She was suddenly very serious. She impulsively reached out and took his right hand with her left. "No, of course not. I owe you my life. I will always consider you to be my very good and very dear friend—whether or not you're carrying an automatic weapon."

He smiled broadly. "You know, Sammy told me that at one point in that little clinic, you saved my life. I think that makes us even."

"No, no, that was just a small installment on the debt I owe you. I'll always owe you more than can ever be repaid."

They held onto one another's hands a moment longer than was necessary. Then Monty stood. "Let's get you into a wheelchair, and I'll push you down to the mess for some dinner. It won't be the buffet in the Manila Hotel, but if you're hungry enough, you'll be able to find something you'll like."

She sat up carefully, and after she had put her legs over the edge of the bed, she sat there for a minute to catch her breath.

"Let me help you into the chair."

"Oh, I'm sure I can do it."

Ignoring the rejection, he lifted her in his arms.

Liz rose from the chair where she had been sitting unobtrusively in the corner and stepped forward to hold the chair while Monty gently placed Julia in it. Liz smiled at her patient as Monty pushed her from the room. "It's about time you were up and around," she teased. "You know, most physicians want their patients up and walking within a few hours of major surgery. I think I would've been in trouble if you had slept any longer."

As they entered, the other hostages, rescuers, and government officials who were waiting for dinner stood and cheered. Julia beamed and weakly waved.

Mallon and Sophie hurried to her from where they had been talking with Matson. Mallon took her hand between both of his. "You're to be congratulated, but I never intended for you to compromise your own safety. We're all so glad that you're safe. All I can really say is thank you for getting my granddaughter back. I'm sorry it came at such high personal cost."

Julia smiled. "Tomorrow, when I'm not so tired, I hope we can have some time to talk." He nodded and stepped back so she could be pushed up to the table to eat.

The next day the two counselors from the State Department met with each of the other hostages who were strong enough, including Sammy. Monty translated for the boy. Sophie admitted that she had been having bad dreams of her captivity. After two hours of counseling, one of them summed up the advice they were giving. "Don't try to understand your captors. Their motives aren't important. Do what's best for you, and make every effort to get on with your life. Don't second-guess your actions. You were doing the best you could as each situation arose."

***

In the morning, Julia asked Liz to find Mallon so she could talk to him before breakfast. By the time he arrived at her room, Liz had helped Julia dress in hospital scrubs again, and she was sitting in a wheelchair. Her short blond hair curled around her face, making her look as though she felt stronger and better than she actually did. He took her hand and asked how she was feeling. "I'll feel better when I know that the four men who risked so much to rescue us have been paid." She explained the verbal agreements she had made with Monty and with Bing and Bolly. "I made no promise of payment to Rick, but his life was in just as much danger as the others."

Mallon had been taking notes. He smiled. "I'll see that our financial obligation to each one is met, including Rick, though money is poor payment for what they have accomplished."

"And there's someone else we have to reimburse—the mayor of Anugan. We stole his *banca*, and the AFP Navy shot it up."

"I don't know what the going price for a *banca* is right now, but we'll settle with him too." Putting his notepad back into his shirt pocket, he said, "Now may I push you down to breakfast?"

She nodded. After breakfast, the CIA men asked again if they could talk a little with her, and she put up her hand to still any objections from Monty or the doctor. "Yes, I think I can handle it." The "talking a little" lasted nearly two hours as Julia struggled to recall the details of the experiences that would most likely give her nightmares for the rest of her life.

When asked to sum up her impression of the overall purpose of Hamal and his men, she thought for a minute. "Their basic motivation appeared to be a desire for the money that could be raised through ransom demands. I saw only perfunctory religious customs carried out but no real plan to forward the cause of Islam or Shariah Law. They just seemed to 'wing it' from day to day. Any cooperation the villagers gave them appeared to be out of fear. Those forest paths and hills were a maze to us, but I'm sure that most of the Abu were very familiar with those paths and the locations of the empty huts they could use. That's probably how they are able to keep ahead of the AFP."

"Was there much formal structure among the group? Did it appear that Hamal was taking orders from someone?" the interrogator asked.

"I don't know. He spent time on the satphone almost daily. Often after he ended a call, he would make us move camp again."

"Did you think at any time that they might kill you?"

"Yes, I realized very quickly that if they didn't believe that they could obtain a ransom for me, they would think nothing of killing me or any of the others." She stopped suddenly. "Has Phillip Dangwa's family been notified of his death? He often spoke of his wife and two little girls."

The two interrogators looked at each other, and the senior man admitted, "I'm not sure, but we'll check on it for you."

"I would like to be put in touch with his wife, if possible. I have a message for her from him."

"A message?"

"Yes. He asked Sophie to tell her that he loved her, but since Sophie is going home, I would like to do it. He believed that he wasn't going to live through our ordeal, and she needs to know that his thoughts were always with her and his little girls."

"I'll find out where she lives so you can arrange it."

Even though Julia was very tired after the CIA had finished their questions, the AFP military men grew impatient, insisting that they could wait no longer. She spent the next two hours talking with them.

***

After breakfast the next morning, intelligence officers from both governments left the base, but the State Department counselors remained behind to spend time with Julia and Carlita.

At the end of two long therapeutic sessions, the counselors gave each woman the same advice they had given Sophie. "Don't look back. Don't condemn yourself. It never changes what was, and it can only slow the healing. They stole several weeks of your life. Don't let them steal any more."

That afternoon all of the hostages with the exception of Julia were given a clean bill of health by the doctor, including Bolly, and told they could travel again. The doctor insisted that Julia remain hospitalized for a few more days. "Mrs. Wentworth's temperature is excessively high, and she is much too weak to be released."

When Julia was told that the others could leave but she had to stay, she tried to argue—without success, unhappily accepting defeat. Before the evening meal, Monty pushed her wheelchair to the mess hall, with

Liz walking beside it. As a group, they would share one last meal before the others went their individual ways.

After they had finished the meal, Bing and Bolly approached her and each shook her hand. Bing spoke for both of them. "Now we can go home heroes to our wives. That newspaper reporter from Manila called and interviewed us, and now we're heroes to all our neighbors. Look at this." He pulled a newspaper article from his wallet. "I'm going to get this framed." Looking at his brother, he added, "We're looking forward to going home."

Julia was somber. "I want you to know that I'll always be grateful to you for your courage and help."

They each gave her a little mock salute and grinned. They were as excited about going home as they had been about beginning the adventure.

Rick took her hand. "I've come to have a great respect for American women, especially if they are all like you and Sophie." He dropped her hand and added, "I'll be riding back to Cagayan de Oro with Bing and Bolly to make sure the truck gets back to the rental lot in one piece. By the way, you had better give Carlita a hug because she's going with us. Mr. Mallon assigned me to see that she gets home to her mother—and her boyfriend."

"Rick, how will you pay the rental fee for the truck?"

Rick grinned. "Mr. Mallon has given us enough cash to cover the rental costs and the plane tickets back to Manila. My car's in the parking lot at Aquino Airport, if it hasn't been stolen." He laughed as if that would be a big joke on him. "If you ever get up to Angeles, I hope you'll come and meet my wife and family."

"I will. God bless you. I'll always be in your debt."

Rick gave her a gallant bow, turned, and signaled to Carlita that it was time to be leaving. Carlita, who had been standing quietly aside, hurried over to give Julia a hug. "I'm going home, and I will tell my boyfriend that we are getting married very soon." She paused and then added, "I will miss you. You are my special friend, and I will never forget what you taught me."

Surprised, Julia asked, "What did I teach you?"

"That miracles can still happen."

Julia returned the hug. "Oh, yes, yes, they do still happen. Never forget that."

Rick escorted Carlita out the door, hurrying to catch up with the Jackson twins.

Sophie bent over and gave Julia an apologetic hug. "My grandfather needs to be getting back to the states, and I have promised to go with him. When Grandmother is better, I'm coming back to *Umaga* House. Grandfather feels that my coming home for a little while may do my grandmother some good."

She stepped back and Mallon stepped up, taking Julia's hand. "We are going to fly to Manila this evening with the State Department people. I have arranged for tickets to Los Angeles tomorrow for the two of us." He added with genuine regret, "I wish you were coming with us, Julia, but the doctor will not release you yet, and I must be getting back to the office. I've put five thousand dollars in your personal account. It went in as salary, which means that you will have to pay taxes on it, but I hope in some way it will cover a small part of what you have endured in carrying out my request. Thank you for your part in Sophie's rescue." Putting his arm around his granddaughter, he added, "And I hope you can get back to St. Louis right away. I'm sure there is a pile of work on your desk." He grinned and waved as they followed the others out of the mess hall.

Julia looked up at Monty. They were the only two left except for Liz, who was standing a discreet distance from them. Julia could hear the cooks in the kitchen as they cleaned up after the meal. "Oh, Monty, I feel so, so—desolate. Everyone is leaving. Are you going right away too?"

"No, you can't get rid of me that easily. I made an agreement to rescue Sophie and the other hostages. As it turned out, that included you, so I'll hang around until I see you on a plane for the U.S., if that's okay with you."

She smiled and reached out to take his hand. She held on to it tightly for a moment. "That is very okay with me." She leaned back in the wheelchair and closed her eyes. "Right now, I'm very, very tired. I think it's time for me to go back to my room."

He pushed her to her room, accompanied by Liz, and when they reached the door, Julia said, "I can make it from here. I'll see you both in the morning."

"You're sure?" Liz asked.

Julia nodded. After she had closed the door, she made her way unsteadily to the bathroom where she took the pills the doctor had given her that were sitting on the sink. Then she slid wearily into bed. For the next ten hours, dreams of men with automatic weapons and bolo knives chased her through the dark forest of her sleep.

***

In the morning, Monty and the lieutenant approached her door together. Monty knocked, but there was no answer. A second knock received no response. Concerned, Liz pushed it open. They found Julia soaked with the perspiration of a malarial fever and mumbling in delirium.

Liz checked her pulse and heart rate and put her hand on Julia's forehead. "Much too hot. We need to get the doctor in a hurry. "

When Major Whittingham arrived, he shook his head. "That interrogation was too much for her. I should've put a stop to it. I'm going to increase the antibiotic dosage and the quinine." He checked her temperature with a digital thermometer against her temple. "Hundred and four. Not good."

The beeper on his waistband went off. He checked it. "There's a soldier with a viper bite in the intake area. I'm needed there." He looked at Monty. "Will you get a wet cloth and keep her head and arms cool?" Then he ordered Lieutenant Billings to bring an IV drip with a powerful antibiotic in it. "Stay with her and keep me posted on any changes." Not waiting for an answer, he turned and was out the door.

Monty soaked a washcloth in cold water and sat down next to her bed. Within a few minutes, the lieutenant had returned and had inserted the IV. Then they both sat down to watch her.

Monty wiped her forehead and arms and kept up a steady, one-sided conversation. "I've been told that you can probably hear me, so I'm going to keep talking until you answer me. If you want to get rid of me, you'll need to respond. When I was at St. Luke's, after they dug that bullet out of my leg, I remember people talking around me, thinking that I couldn't hear them. I still remember some of the things they were saying. It's always amazing what people say when they think you can't hear them."

Julia moaned and muttered something about Aaron. Monty decided to use that as a reference point. "Julia, tell me about Aaron."

She murmured again. Monty leaned over and could just barely make out the words, "Can't let him go . . ." Then she grew quiet.

He continued to wipe her forehead and arms, and she seemed to sleep. A med tech stuck his head in the door. "The doctor wants to know if she is doing any better."

Liz nodded briefly. "I think she is sleeping a little more soundly."

"He wants to know what her temperature is."

Liz checked it. "One hundred and three."

The technician left, and Monty returned to wiping Julia's forehead and talking to her. "You need to wake up, Julia. Wake up, and tell me more about your family. Don't make me do all the talking."

She began to whisper again. Leaning close, Monty caught the words, ". . . like reeds blowing in the wind." He shook his head, attributing her words to delirium. "Like reeds in the wind," she repeated.

About ten, the doctor returned and checked her vital signs again. "How's she doing?" Monty asked.

"Temp is down to a hundred and two. That's good. One of you needs to stay with her until she regains consciousness. Let me know when that happens." He left the room.

Liz checked her temperature regularly and replaced the IV bag.

By late afternoon, Julia awakened. She lay very quiet with her eyes closed, feeling the general ache in her body that seemed to be localized in her ribs, arm, head, and joints. "I'm thirsty," she said hoarsely through a parched throat. A cup of water with a straw in it appeared within range of her vision. "Is that you, Monty?" she whispered.

He spoke as he helped her hold the cup. "Yes, it's me. I told you that you're my responsibility until I can get you on a plane to the U.S."

She swallowed some of the water. "I think you've gone the extra mile."

"That's okay. I'm good on the trail. A few extra miles have never hurt me."

She relinquished the cup and smiled—a weak little smile. "Is my den mother here too?"

Liz stepped up cheerfully. "Yes, your den mother is here too."

"You're back to stay now, aren't you?" Monty asked.

"Yes, I'm back to stay—and I'm hungry. Is that good?"

"I think that's very good. Do you want breakfast, lunch, or dinner?"

"I would like a little bit of fried chicken and some fruit."

"That won't be hard to get. Just give me a minute."

The doctor arrived about the same time as Monty, who had returned carrying the tray with the chicken and fruit. Dr. Whittingham scolded her gently, "That temperature of yours gave us a scare, Mrs. Wentworth.

It's good to see that you're feeling better. I'm going to increase your oral antibiotics and continue with the quinine, and maybe in a few days you can be released." As he turned toward the door, he told Monty, "By the way, there's a reporter from Manila by the last name of Roque who has called several times and wants to speak to one or both of you. The office personnel would appreciate it if you would return her call, Mr. Montalbon, so she will cease to harass our staff." He grinned and left the room.

After Julia had eaten a little, she lay back and slept again. Liz sat quietly by the bed.

Monty found a telephone in the hospital office and called Estilita. As soon as she heard his voice, she demanded, "You owe me a story, Monty. I've had to make do with the interviews of the Jacksons, but you need to give me the whole story."

The conversation continued for nearly an hour, with Estilita taping it. When Monty insisted he had told her everything newsworthy, she said, "The story will hit the paper tomorrow morning. I expect that it will be picked up by the wire services because it involves the two American women. This is great! I owe you."

***

For the next two afternoons, while the kitchen staff fussed over and fed Sammy, Monty pushed Julia around the garden outside the hospital. They paused at the hand-carved bench near a gardenia hedge covered with fragrant blooms nestled in the foliage. Finally, he asked the question that had been in the back of his mind for many days. "Julia, how did you draw the attention of the two men that kidnapped you from Luz and Enrique's hut?"

"That was all my fault, Monty. I thought that after dark I could go out in the water without being seen, but on the second night, I saw someone in the undergrowth, and after I rushed back to the hut, they came after me."

"I'd scold you, but I think you learned your lesson the hard way." His look and voice were somber. "But if you had been kidnapped by a different group—maybe the MNLF—and had been separated from Sophie, things might not have turned out so well." His words chilled them both.

For the balance of those days, they talked, shared laughter and family stories, and thrived on each other's company. Their laughter was as healing for Julia as any of the medications had been.

34

ON THE THIRD DAY AFTER the others had left the hospital, Major Whittingham brought good news as Julia and Monty were eating breakfast. "Mrs. Wentworth, as soon as you feel strong enough, you can be discharged."

She smiled broadly. "Thank you, doctor, for all you've done and especially for this good news. I may still be a bit unsteady, but I'm ready to go right now. All I have to pack is a toothbrush. You have treated me wonderfully, but I'm looking forward to putting this place behind me."

"My patients always seem very glad to go. Perhaps I have a serious personality disorder that I need to address." He chuckled as he walked away.

Monty was sitting across the table from Julia. "I think you might need more than a pair of scrubs to travel in. This morning while you rest, I will tear Sammy away from the kitchen crew, who have been overfeeding him, and I'll borrow one of the military vehicles to drive back to Bolong. We'll get your bags."

"Give Luz and Enrique my love. Tell them I'm sorry I left the way I did. I would much rather have stayed with them." Monty smiled at the understatement. After he and Sammy left for Bolong, Julia walked slowly back to her room with Liz, who was keeping an eye on her.

Monty was back by lunchtime to present her with the handbag and suitcases. As she sat on the bed in her room, going through the items in the bags, she thanked him repeatedly. Then she added with a nearly childlike wistfulness, "How soon can we leave?"

"I've got a flight to Manila tomorrow morning for both of us. It's all arranged."

She shooed him out of the room so she could change into a pair of navy blue slacks, a white cotton blouse, and a comfortable pair of leather sandals.

As they walked to the mess hall for lunch, she felt a great sense of relief. "It feels so good to be in something other than scrubs—or a dirty caftan." As they sat at the table and the stewards began to bring out the food, Julia asked, "Where's Sammy?"

"I left him with Luz and Enrique. I suggested that the boy stay with them and help in the fish market. All three of them thought it was a great idea. Sammy is grateful to have a family and a place to stay where he is wanted. He'll be a great help. He's young and strong. I gave my uncle a thousand pesos. That will feed the boy for at least six months."

"I'm sorry that I didn't get to tell him goodbye."

"I'd have shared my plan with you, but it wasn't a plan until we were nearly in Bolong. Then it occurred to me that a home with my relatives would fit the needs of all three of them."

***

As they sat at breakfast the next morning, Monty handed her a newspaper. "You might want to read the story about the brave American women who were held hostage by the *Abu Sayyaf*."

She took the paper as if she were just a little bit anxious about what it said. The story continued on page A-4. When she finished, she laughed. "Estilita really did it up right. Do you think we can hide from our newfound celebrity status?"

"I think our fifteen minutes in the sun will fade very quickly. At least, I hope it does." An American officer drove them to the airport, and they boarded a Cebu Pacific plane for the flight to Manila.

The flight took three hours, laying over for an hour in Cebu City. From there it hopped over to Manila. Julia rode most of the way with her eyes closed but very much aware of Monty's nearness. As they collected their luggage, he said, "I made a reservation for you at the Manila Hotel for this evening. We need to talk about what you want to do tomorrow."

"Before we go to the hotel, can we go out to Cavite City. I need to talk to Phillip Dangwa's wife and children."

"You're not too tired?"

"I am, but this has to be done, and I would like you to be with me when I do it."

He nodded, and when they reached the cabs at the curb of the lower level of the large terminal, he grabbed the first one. "Will you drive us to Cavite City and back?"

"That ride *mahal, mahal.* You pay? Long ride."

Monty nodded and opened the door for Julia. "How much?"

The cab driver thought for about two seconds. "Two thousand pesos."

Monty looked at Julia, who nodded. The task of telling Mrs. Dangwa of her husband's death was not made any easier when they met her in her little apartment in Cavite. Her eyes were swollen from crying, and a small girl who looked about two was holding onto the hem of her dress. A four-year-old girl watched from the doorway.

As they talked, Julia told her, "I only knew your husband a few days. He was a good man. He suffered with us without complaining. He often spoke of you and your family. He knew somehow that he was not going to survive, and he wanted me to tell you that he loved you and his little girls."

Julia paused, and the woman put her hands over her face and began to sob. Julia impulsively put her arms around the weeping woman. "I'm so sorry. I'm so sorry" she said as she stroked her hair. The little girls watched with wide eyes.

When the woman had calmed somewhat, Julia guided her to the couch, and they both sat. Monty pulled up a chair. "How will you support your family now that your husband is gone?"

"My brother has a sari-sari shop. I will work there with his family." She began to sob again. "I miss Phillip so much. My little girls will never know their father." The woman pulled away from Julia and looked into her face. "I don't even know where he is buried. Does God know where he is?"

"It was a beautiful place. We lined the grave with banana leaves and said a prayer over it. He just went to sleep and didn't wake up. He looked very peaceful. Yes, God knows where he is, and you will see him again someday. I'm sure that he will watch over you as your girls grow up."

The young widow wiped her eyes with the sleeve of her dress and lifted the smallest child to her lap. "Thank you. I will tell the girls that they will see their father someday and that he will watch over them."

Julia stood. "I will keep you in my prayers."

"*Salamat po,*" she quietly responded. Julia and Monty made their way back to the cab. As they sat in the backseat, Julia said, "There seems so little we can do for her, and her loss is so great."

"Filipinos are survivors. She will have the support of her extended family. She and the children will be okay."

"Will you see that two of those nice young men in white shirts and ties and black name tags find her? There is so much they can teach her. " Julia smiled as she looked at him. He nodded.

They sat quietly in the backseat of the cab, and despite the traffic, Julia closed her eyes and slept part of the way back to Manila. It was getting dark when they reached the Coastal Road in Las Piñas City. When the driver resentfully stopped at a red light to let a fast-moving delivery truck through the intersection, Julia sat up and looked out of the cab window to see where they were.

Between the pools of light dropped on the pavement by the occasional streetlights, she could see a beggar with no legs sitting in the gutter, hoping for a few pesos from someone in a passing car. She had a surging desire to help. She hurriedly removed her wallet from her big handbag and pulled a thousand peso bill out of it. She quickly wrapped the bill around two twenty-five peso coins to give it weight. Then she rolled the window down and tossed the money as close to him as she could before the cab accelerated.

Monty smiled. "You have a good heart, Julia."

"I'm being selfish. I want to be able to sleep tonight, and I can only do that if I know he can eat."

As the cab moved up Roxas Boulevard, she asked, "Will you come into the hotel and get something to eat with me?"

"I'll admit, I'm hungry—and I'm feeling the miles we hiked up and down those mountainsides in the forest more tonight than I have before."

When they reached the hotel, he carried her luggage in, and after she was registered and her bags had been sent to her room, they stopped to eat in the dining room. They were both very quiet, but the silence was so much more than an absence of words; it was the mantle of a comfortable friendship. When they were nearly finished, Monty asked, "When do you want me to arrange for your return flight home?"

The fork paused above her plate, and she looked at him with a somber expression. "I need to get home as soon as possible. Paul and Allison need to see me and know that I'm okay, but . . ." She paused and then continued. "I will hate to tell you good-bye. You've been the best friend I could have." Her throat tightened, and she waited until she could speak again. "But if I can get a seat on a flight to L.A. tomorrow, I think that would be good."

"I'll see what I can do."

She reached out and put her hand over his. Knowing that their good-bye could only get more difficult the longer they were together, she added, "I can get a cab to the airport tomorrow. I've been a heavy load on you, and it's about time I let you go back to your own life."

"I told you that my job would not be finished until I saw you onto a plane to the States. Remember?" She nodded and smiled, glad that he had turned down her offer.

He called at nine that evening. "Your flight leaves tomorrow afternoon at twelve-thirty. I'll be by to pick you up at ten."

On an impulse, she asked, "Could you make it nine? I would love to take a walk in Rizal Park before I go."

***

In the morning, she checked out of the hotel and sat in the large foyer, studying the explosion of color that made up the floral display on the table near her chair. Suddenly, she knew he was there; she didn't know how she knew, but she could sense it. When she stood and turned to face him, he filled her like warm sunshine on a rainy day.

They stored her bags behind the desk and walked across the street as if they had all the time in the world. After a walk around the park, they sat on a bench beneath a great, old narra tree and watched the changing of the guard at the monument to José Rizal.

Monty turned to her and asked something that had been on his mind. "When you were delirious with malaria in the hospital, you repeated something that I have wondered about. You said, 'Like reeds in the wind.' You said it twice. Do you have any memory of what you meant?"

She rose from the bench and turned away from him. As she walked, she put her fingers over her mouth in thought. He rose and followed her. Finally, she dropped her hand and turned to him. "I vaguely remember a dream. I was standing in a marshy field of reeds and cattails, and the wind was blowing, making them bend and touch each other. When the wind stopped, they stood tall once more, each in its own place, independent of the others. Then the wind would pass over the field, and they would bend and briefly touch again."

"Do you have any idea what it means? Most dreams mean something."

She stood unmoving for a moment but finally said, "I think you and I are the reeds, and the wind has been blowing." Her smile was melancholy. "Sophie's kidnapping made the wind blow for us, and it has been bending us and making our lives touch. Now the wind has stopped, and I must go stand in my place and you will stand in yours."

Monty smiled a little sadly. "And our places are an ocean apart."

They both turned and walked without speaking toward the hotel. When they reached the steps to the entrance door, the cab was waiting. He asked the doorman to get her bags. As the bags were put into the trunk of the cab, he looked at his watch. He slid into the backseat next to her. "Traffic is heavy, and we may get hung up in it. It would be easy to miss the plane." But he was thinking, *From this point on, every moment that I spend with her will make it harder to see her leave.* They rode to the airport in silence. At one point, the alert cab driver stomped on the brake as a heavily loaded jeepney made a right turn from the lane to the left of the cab. The stop threw Julia against him. For a moment, she longed to stay there and feel the warmth and protection of his arm around her again, but she pulled away and straightened up in the seat, a little embarrassed by her feelings.

When they reached the airport, he let the cab driver leave and carried Julia's luggage inside the terminal to check the bags for her. When they reached the sign that said "Only passengers beyond this point," they stopped, and she turned to him, offering him her hand. "Good-bye, my friend. I have learned many things in the time I have been here, but first and foremost, I have learned that the world can be made a better place when certain lives touch." She looked into his eyes and added, "I think we made the world a better place. No matter how long we live, I hope you will always be my friend." There were other thoughts running through her mind—unspoken thoughts. *And how I will miss you, my friend, but I must go . . .*

"I will." He cleared his throat. "The next time you're in Manila for the foundation, call me. I'm a good tour guide." He handed her a paper with the number of his new personal cell phone on it. "I hope there are no more winds for you, but reeds in a breeze can touch now and then."

She tucked the paper into her pocket. Her voice tightened. "Saying thank you seems so inadequate . . ." Her voice trailed off, and the silence grew thick and heavy between them for several moments. All the other people pulling suitcases or carrying boxes or small children as they moved through the concourse seemed to melt away, and as she looked into his face, Julia suddenly found it hard to think. *There's so much I want to say—but it's better if my thoughts remain unspoken.*

The muscle in his jaw tightened as he reached out and wiped a tear from her cheek. She laid her hand lightly on his shoulder, raised up a little on her toes, and tenderly gave him a kiss on his cheek. Then she stepped away, took a slow, deep breath, turned, and hurried down the concourse and around a corner to the gate. She resisted the urge to wipe away another tear until she was out of sight.

Monty stood unmoving until she had disappeared. He caught a cab back to his apartment in Quezon City. There, he sat in the big, overstuffed chair and remained unmoving in the room lightened only by the weak sunlight that made its way around the sides of the window blinds. *Reeds in the wind that must stand in their own place. Like reeds in the wind . . .* He shook his head with regret. *Of course, she's right. But if things were different . . .* He pushed the thought from his mind.

He stood and walked to the bedroom where he picked up the little box wrapped in faded gift paper from Alicia. He sat on the bed and unwrapped it. Inside was a pearl tie clasp that matched the pearl cuff links he often wore.

He smiled and whispered, "Thank you, Alicia—and good-bye, until we meet again."

He reached for his cell phone and dialed the familiar number of the Metro Manila police headquarters. "Montalbon here. Tell the chief I'll be in tomorrow."

35

AFTER SHE HAD BOARDED THE plane, she asked the flight attendant for a bottle of water. Then she took one of the pain pills the doctor had given her in the hospital, and for the first time in her travels, she slept as the plane crossed the Pacific. Sleeping, she could keep at bay the awareness that she was moving farther and farther away from Monty with each minute in the air. When she disembarked at St. Louis Lambert Field it was early Saturday morning, and she had answers to questions she had previously been unwilling to face.

As she neared the luggage carousels, she could see several familiar faces. They closed around her as if pulled by a drawstring, and she embraced her son Paul and her daughter, Allison. Then Sophie pushed her way close enough to give Julia a hug as well. Everyone laughed, though if they had been asked, no one would have been able to say why. It just seemed appropriate.

When the laughter quieted, Sophie spoke first. "Julia, at Grandfather's insistence, I have arranged a couple of newspaper interviews for Monday. Hope you don't mind. He felt it would bring the foundation some good publicity—and he's very proud of you. By the way, he's planning on serving brunch at his home, so you'll be coming with us."

"Oh, Sophie, that will be too stressful for your grandmother," Julia objected.

"Grandmother is doing much better—and it's being catered, so it won't be a burden on her. She wants to see you very much."

The four of them walked out to the short-term parking lot into a softly falling snow. "Oh, I had forgotten that it's still winter here," Julia said as she turned her face up to feel the flakes on her skin. "It feels like a very long time since I have felt anything as wonderful as new falling snow."

Sophie answered with a smile. "Enjoy it while you can. March is just around the corner. This snow won't last long." When they reached the Lexus, Sophie opened the trunk so Paul could put Julia's luggage in it. Then she slid behind the wheel. "Julia, come and join me in the front seat."

Paul and Allison slid into the back. Everyone wanted to hear about Julia's adventures so it was nearly noon when, once more, Melton Mallon offered his thanks and they took their leave. Sophie drove them back out to the airport, where Paul picked up his car from the short-term parking lot and drove his mother and sister home.

"Oh, it's so good to be home. There were so many days when I didn't believe that I would ever see my family or my home again," Julia whispered as they pulled into the driveway.

Julia rested for an hour, but by midafternoon, she knew what she had to do.

"We need to go to the care center to visit Aaron," she quietly told both Paul and Allison. "I have thought about it and prayed about it, and I know now that it's time to tell him good-bye. We need to let him go home." Her voice choked in her throat for a moment. "I have no right to hold him hostage to my lack of faith." She looked from her son to her daughter, waiting for their confirmation.

Allison looked at her hands in her lap and quiet tears fell. Paul put his hand over his mother's. "Mom, you know that I was against putting him on the respirator from the beginning. He'd never have wanted to continue indefinitely in a vegetative state. You're doing the right thing. We need to let him go home to God. Don't you agree, Allison?" His sister simply nodded her head, but she couldn't speak.

They drove to the care center in silence. Julia asked if the doctor on staff was in the building, and the nurse behind the desk nodded. "I'm sure he is. He should be finishing his rounds shortly."

"Please send him to us. We'll be in Aaron Wentworth's room."

Paul brought in a third chair from one of the empty rooms. They sat near the bed, saying little, listening to the click and hiss of the respirator that steadily filled and then emptied Aaron's lungs and to the low beep of the heart monitor. After about five quiet minutes, Paul chuckled under his breath. "Do you remember our Eagle Court of Honor, Mom? Aaron had finished his merit badges and other requirements ahead of me, but he waited so we could have the presentation of our Eagle awards together."

"How could I forget it? The ceremony was so formal and went so perfectly. Then we all went to the cultural hall, and Kenny Hampton started to eat the frosting on the cake with his fingers. When his mother tried to pull him away, he grabbed the table leg, and it collapsed and the cake and punch went everywhere. Oh, what a mess!" She smiled and shook her head at the thought.

Allison brightened. "So you and Dad took everybody to get root beer floats. I liked that better than that bakery cake and punch anyway."

Paul continued, "Then there was the time Dad went with us to be tapped out for the Order of the Arrow initiation, and he said that I started walking in my sleep. He finally got me back into my sleeping bag, and then it started to rain. It rained all night. We had been assigned to sleep in the woods, and we were lying in what almost became a river. But we couldn't talk and had to stay put for the whole night or fail the test. In the morning, we made our way back to the lodge, dragging our soaked sleeping bags. On the way home, Aaron said that he had never known that having so much Scouting fun could be so miserable." The three of them laughed at the memory.

Allison took up the thread of memories. "Then there was the time my date for the junior prom broke his leg the day before the dance, and Aaron stepped in and took me. He had only been home from his mission a few days, so very few of my high school friends had ever met him. They thought I had the dreamiest date, and he kept the secret." For the next twenty minutes the reminiscing continued.

They almost forgot that they were waiting for the doctor. When he arrived, the reminiscing stopped in midsentence. "Mrs. Wentworth, you wanted to see me?"

Julia stood and rubbed her hands together, almost as if they were cold. "We have made a decision, and we think it's time to let Aaron go. His dad is waiting for him on the other side."

To confirm that he had understood her correctly, the doctor repeated what he had heard. "You feel that it's time to end it?"

Julia's composure was so fragile that she could only nod. Paul spoke for her. "Yes, it's time."

"I'll get the papers for you to sign." He disappeared for a few minutes and then returned with legal forms on a clipboard. "As his nearest of kin, I would like each of you to sign the form."

Silently, each one signed, and when the doctor took it back, he glanced at it to make sure everything was correct. "I know this is a hard decision, but it's the right one." He looked at each one of them. "I'm going to unplug the respirator now. Do you want to step out of the room?"

Paul put his arm around his mother to guide her into the hall, but she took a deep breath and lifted her head. "No, we will stay here."

The doctor stepped over to the wall and disconnected the plug to the respirator. The respirator went silent, and within thirty seconds, the heart monitor made one long beep and the line went flat. The doctor switched it off. "I'll leave you alone with him for a few minutes." He stepped out of the room.

Julia leaned over to the figure in the bed and kissed him gently on his still-warm forehead. She stood and whispered, "You're free now, son. You're free."

After a few minutes of silence, Allison's tears stopped, and she lifted her head and said in a voice full of rising inflection. "Oh Mom, I know he's happy now. I can feel it. I can feel him here in the room."

Julia put her arm around her daughter. "I can feel him here too." She put her other arm around Paul, closed her eyes, and said, "You can go home now, Aaron. Go and give your dad a hug from all of us."

***

The funeral was a joyous event. The heavy mantle of grief that had weighed on Julia for so long, the grief for both husband and son, was finally lifted. She stood by Aaron's casket as it was suspended above the open grave and whispered, "Jack, Aaron, I'm going to make it on my own. I didn't think I could there for a while, but I'm going to make it, and I'll rejoin you both eventually. Until then, there is *so much to do*." She stepped forward and laid two long-stemmed white roses on the casket.

Bibliography

Ali, Abdullah Yusuf. The Qur'an Translation. Tahrike Tarsile Qur'an. New York. 2007.

Berlow, Alan. *Dead Season: A Story of Murder and Revenge*. Vintage Books: New York. 1998.

Burnham, Gracia. *In the Presence of My Enemies*. Tyndale House Publishers: Wheaton, Illinois. 2003.

Hemley, Robin. *Invented Eden: The Elusive, Disputed History of the Tasaday*. Farrar, Straus and Giroux: New York. 2003.

Rashid, Ahmed. *Taliban*. Yale University Press: New Haven and London. 2000.

Schlegel, Stewart A. *Wisdom from a Rain Forest*. London: University of Georgia Press. 1997.

Spencer, Robert, ed. *The Myth of Islamic Tolerance: How Islamic Law Treats Non-Muslims*. Prometheus Books: Amherst, New York. 2005.

———, Central Intelligence Agency. *The World Factbook: Afghanistan*. Downloaded 8/30/09.

About the Author

Jean Holbrook Mathews has been a student of history and geography most of her life. She served as the administrative director for an international foundation headquartered in St. Louis with chapters in five countries, including the Philippines. She has traveled in Asia and Europe and lived in the Philippines for nearly two years while on a mission with her husband for the LDS Church. During that time she studied the culture, history, geography, government, and language of that nation, learning to love the people and those beautiful islands.